Also by Howard Norman

The Northern Lights (1987)

Kiss in the Hotel Joseph Conrad (1989)

The Bird Artist

THE
BIRD
ARTIST

Howard Norman

Farrar, Straus & Giroux

New York

For Jane and Emma

For George

Suddenly, with extreme violence, he felt himself seized by the desire to be, rain or no rain, at any price, in the midst of the valleys: alone.

GIORGIO BASSANI, *The Heron*

The Bird Artist

1

The Garganey

$\mathbf{M}$y name is Fabian Vas. I live in Witless Bay, Newfoundland. You would not have heard of me. Obscurity is not necessarily failure, though; I am a bird artist, and have more or less made a living at it. Yet I murdered the lighthouse keeper, Botho August, and that is an equal part of how I think of myself.

I discovered my gift for drawing and painting birds early on. I should better say that my mother saw that someone had filled in the margins of my third-form primer with the sketches of wings, talons, and heads of local birds. "I thought this primer was brand-new," she said. "But it's full of these bird drawings. Well, somebody has talent." After a night's sleep she realized that the pencil work was mine and was what I had been concentrating on during my school lessons. Actually she seemed quite pleased, and at breakfast

the following morning said, "Awfully nice to learn something so unmistakable about one's offspring." She tore out
a page full of heads of gulls and ospreys, wrote, "October 28, 1900," on it, and nailed it to the kitchen door.

Witless Bay's librarian was Mrs. Paulette Bath, a spirited
woman in her late fifties or early sixties when I was a boy.
She claimed to have read every one of the hundreds of books
in her library, which was her own living room, dining room,
and sitting room. She had not claimed that in a bragging
way but as if it had been a natural obligation. Her house
overlooked the wharf. She gave out hand-printed library
cards. "Like in the city," she said. Each card had the silhouette of a woman reading in a bathtub, which I assume
was a humorous turn on her own last name. You either
remembered your card or had to fetch it. No exceptions
were allowed. No book left her library without the date
printed in her cramped script on a piece of lined cardboard
tucked into a pocket glued to the inside back cover. She
kept scrupulous records. She had taught my childhood
friend Margaret Handle the fundamentals of bookkeeping.
She would reprimand borrowers in public about overdue
books. She featherdusted, humming, and was all but constantly alarmed about book lice. Some afternoons I would
come in and immediately be aware that she had been spray-
ing book spines with rubbing alcohol, her own remedy. On
her mantel was her framed certificate of Library Science,
earned in London, where she had been raised. She had left
there when she was thirty-four.

In her library I discovered a few books on natural history,

including *First Book of Zoology*, by Edward Morse, which was published in the United States. But it contained only technical illustrations. Whereas the volume that changed my life—I should better say gave me purchase on it—was to be found in Mrs. Bath's private collection, sequestered in a glass case that had five shelves. The book was called *Natural History of Carolina, Florida, and the Bahama Islands, 1731–1748*. It had been a gift from her Aunt Mina, a patron of libraries in London; Aunt Mina's photograph was next to Mrs. Bath's certificate on the mantel. This book was a true revelation for me. It held 220 hand-colored engravings of North American flowers, weeds, and wild animals. But what I memorized and actually dreamed about were the 109 birds. The naturalist's name was Mark Catesby. He was the first real bird artist I knew about.

I sat every afternoon, I think for two years, in Mrs. Bath's living room, the main reading area, turning the pages of Catesby's work. I can still smell her sofa. At the thick-legged oval table, with its lion's-paw feet, I would set out my scrap paper and copy. Copy, copy, copy. One morning Mrs. Bath stood next to me, looking over my shoulder. "Mr. Catesby, dead so long now," she said. "Yet his birds are so alive in these pages. To you, Fabian, I imagine this art is as important as Leonardo da Vinci's."

"Who's Leonardo da Vinci?"

"A great genius."

"Did he ever paint birds?"

"Truth be told, I don't know. He never painted them in Newfoundland."

She laughed, sharpened a pencil for me, and left me alone until she closed the library, at exactly six o'clock, by the chimes of her clock.

When I finally stopped my formal schooling after fourth grade, having learned to read and write, my mother kept after me to read books. She would make lists of words, set them out on the table after supper, and go over them with me. "I'm not as good as the real dictionary," she said, "but pretty close."

I did keep up with my reading. I struggled to write clearly, too. I took pride in my secret diaries. These were not diaries full of a boy's confessions, though a few of those might have crept in. More, I made up travels to places I had read about, and described birds, landscapes, certain dangerous encounters with the local natives, and there always seemed to be earthquakes, volcanoes, and monsoons as well. Anyway, by age eight I was practically living out in the coves, the wetlands, or at Lambert Charibon's trout camp. Lambert was a friend of my father's. He let me stay around sketching kingfishers, ospreys, and his crippled pet owl. At age eleven, I put a lot of time into a field guide to coastal species, made up of my own drawings, of course. I sewed the pages together and donated it to the library. Now and then I would check to see if anyone had taken it out. "People here know the birds already," Mrs. Bath said. "They don't need a guide. Every book is a curiosity of sorts, I suppose. Yours is a local example of that. But maybe a tourist will pass through and need it. You never can tell."

All through those years her advice, given once, but very

firmly, rang in my ears: "Just *draw*. It's a God-given gift."
Before she died, when I was seventeen, she often provided
me with money out of her own till for pens, pencils, inks,
special paper. Drawing birds was what I most loved. It had
been from the beginning.

Besides Mrs. Bath, I showed my drawings only to Margaret Handle, beginning when I was fifteen. Margaret was
four years older than I. She lived with her father, Enoch,
who piloted the mail boat, the *Aunt Ivy Barnacle*, the first
steam-engine vessel I ever saw. Her mother had died when
she was seven. She had, I was told, her mother's red hair;
colorwise, this contradicted her father's ancestry, which was
part Beothuk Indian. There were no longer any Beothuks
left in Newfoundland by the time I was born, in 1891. As
my own mother once put it, Margaret was on her own
earlier than most, because Enoch was away for such long
periods of time, collecting and delivering mail north and
south along the coast. I might have been merely two or
three years old, but I remember a night my father carried
me on his shoulders past the lighthouse and all the way into
the village to show me Margaret's house lit up by candles.
As far as I am concerned, this was my first memory. Lambert Charibon accompanied us that night. We stood about
a hundred feet away. There was a candelabrum on the
dining-room table, consisting of five candles. There was a
candle in each window as well. "She can't sleep, Enoch told
me she told him, unless the house is lit up like Christmas,"
my father said.

"If that's going to be a lifelong habit," Lambert said, "she

might want to learn to dip candles herself, to save money."
Lambert carried me back home.

One day when I was thirteen Margaret found me sketching scoter ducks at the wharf. She sat down next to me.
She had just cut her hair. It was the shortest I had ever
seen it. She looked at my drawing. "You know," she said,
"my father taught me to shoot ducks, him being away so
much. I've seen scoters close up. I've cleaned them. In my
opinion, you've caught its likeness, except for the face. Close
up, a scoter's got a more delicate face. You've got yours
looking like a decoy. A wooden face. But you're an artist,
Fabian, and I've never sat with an artist before." It was a
hot summer day. No breeze at all off the sea. She tightened
her hand around mine, the one with the pencil in it, and
drew my hand to her chest and fluttered her own on top.
She moved my hand to her breast for a moment. Then she
got up and walked home. Well, for days after, I drew only
scoters. I went too far at first, making their faces almost
human, and then, after many hours of work, came around
to something Margaret approved of. I thought she would
put my hand on her breast again, but she did not.

For several years in decent weather we took long walks
together. I brought a feeling of nervous mystery to these
walks, based mostly on one thing, really: when would Margaret provoke me out of my silence? I desired not to talk.
She would get annoyed. "Don't you have an *opinion*? If you
don't have opinions, you're the village idiot." The actual
provocation reminded me of a saying that aptly pertained
to the unpredictable and sudden shifts in Newfoundland

weather: *Every breeze may messenger a storm.* One time, for
instance, Margaret was just talking along about this or that;
then, as if interrupting herself, said, "I saw your mother
touch Botho August's collar. Well, no doubt she was flick-
ing away a moth—"

"I've seen her do that to one of our window curtains at
home," I said.

"Alaric's particularly fussy about that sort of thing, I
guess."

"I guess."

"Still, it was an intimate gesture, don't you think?"

"How far away from them were you, to see it?"

"Here's what. I was in Romeo Gillette's store, along a
wall aisle."

"Left or right of the counter?"

"Right, facing the counter."

"And—"

"And I was looking at a pair of fancy stockings."

"I know the store pretty well. I didn't know that Romeo
had lady's stockings in there."

"Have you ever seen a pair, let alone *on* anyone?"

"No."

"Anyway, you know the customer bell Romeo has. Well,
Botho and Alaric were standing at the counter. And neither
of them was tapping the bell. Romeo must've been in the
stockroom, maybe."

"My mother's so rarely in the store. Botho's rarely in the
store, too, I'm told. What a coincidence!"

"Your mother bought sewing thread."

"This was yesterday?"

"Yes."

"That's right, then, because she brought home black thread."

"Botho told Alaric he was there to pick up gramophone records, which my father had brought from Halifax."

"So, all right. My mother was there for thread. Botho for the gramophone discs."

"Nobody was ringing the bell. They were talking with each other."

"And."

"And. With somebody mid-sentence, I think it was Alaric, she reached out and touched his collar. I for one didn't see a moth, though a moth might've been there. I right away stepped out and said, 'Hello, Mrs. Vas!' and she nearly jumped out of her shoes. 'I have stockings,' I said. Botho walks right up to me, takes the stockings out of my hand, holds the pair the length of my legs, impolite as an ill-bred child. Says, 'I don't yet have anyone to buy French stockings for.' At which moment Romeo steps out from the back room. 'They're not French,' Romeo says, 'they're from Montreal, Canada, though a French seamstress might well have made them.' Botho squints and tilts his head and narrows his eyes, like he does."

"I've seen him do that."

"And *Alaric*—your mother got so flustered, she rang the customer bell! Romeo standing right there! She says, 'I'll come back for this thread,' sets it on the counter, walks to the back of the store, turns around, and pays Romeo for the thread and leaves the store."

"And Botho?"

"Says, 'Did my gramophone discs come in yet?' Yes, says Romeo. 'Well, then, I'll pick them up tomorrow,' says Botho. He leaves the store."

"Where are we walking to, anyway?"

"Guess what else? I went to the store this morning and found that Botho August had *paid* for my stockings. I have them in a dresser drawer at home."

"Wherever will you wear them?"

"Maybe only by myself, Fabian. At home. In the privacy of my house."

"We're almost to the cliff. Where are we going?"

"We can turn either left or right, or go back down the path. There's choices."

"Margaret, this conversation—Botho, my mother in the store. It feels like an insult to my father. That's my opinion."

"Probably it was just a moth."

She took my hand.

"Where are we walking to, anyway?" I said.

"We're just walking along and talking. It's enough not to be chaperoned on such a balmy night."

"I agree."

The eeriest thing about fate, it seems to me, is how you try to deny it even when it's teaching you to kiss. A few weeks after my sixteenth birthday in April, Margaret said, "I'm going to give you a lesson." Just like that. We were standing on a dock. The *Aunt Ivy Barnacle* was tied up at the end. "Fabian, you kiss like I imagine an old man does. Like you used to know how but can't quite recall. It makes me almost start laughing. And I don't want to laugh when I kiss somebody, Fabian. I want almost the opposite, whatever that is. Maybe to be on the verge of tears every second of it."

She led me from the dock onto the *Aunt Ivy Barnacle*, the wooden, two-tiered wedding cake of a boat. We climbed down into the bunkroom. Margaret said, "Lie down there. It's all right." I looked around as if there was some place other than the bed she might have meant. "The bed," she said. I got under the one blanket, fully clothed. Watching, Margaret simply shook her head back and forth. Then she took her clothes off entirely and got in next to me.

Now Margaret was at the center of my life. I did not fully recognize this fact at first, did not consider it possible while lying with her that night. Maybe I had come to believe that tenderness was the least practical part of my nature, so what could be the use of it? "It's all right," she said in the middle of the night. She may have been asleep when she said it.

I think it was about five o'clock in the morning when we heard Enoch up on deck. When he started down the stairs, Margaret wrapped her legs tightly around me and said, "Shut your eyes." We heard Enoch go back up the stairs.

"I've never been all night anywhere but my own house," I said.

"Now you have."

"I'm going to have to explain it."

"Not to me."

"My mother, I meant. My father."

"If we walk right up to your house hand in hand, stand

right in the kitchen and ask for breakfast together, I bet they'll get the hint."

"Margaret, my mother doesn't like you. You know that."

"She can't bear me. But I can keep you separate from Alaric. I don't know if she can."

"Your father's right up on deck."

"Put on your clothes, Fabian, and walk up there. Say good morning to him, because it's morning. You don't have to add anything. I'm getting more sleep."

I climbed up and said, "Good morning," to Enoch. He was mopping out the steering cabin.

He did not look up. "You know, I've let Margaret steer this boat since she was ten. Why, she could take over my job any minute, if need be! She can take apart and put together this newfangled steam engine. She just learned it with native intelligence, eh? She's always had a talent for mechanical things. That's something she might not have told you, so I thought that I would."

Roughly from 1908 to 1911, I was faithfully apprenticed to a bird artist named Isaac Sprague. I had followed up on his advertisement in the journal *Bird Lore*, which Mrs. Bath had ordered specially on my behalf. In her will, in fact, she left me all the back issues.

Sprague lived in Halifax. Above my desk I had tacked a reproduction of his painting of a red-throated loon, which I had torn from an issue of *Bird Lore*. It was so graceful and transcendent that each time I sat down in front of it to work, it made me want to give up. But then after I had stared at it, the loon became an inspiration. It was uncanny how that change overtook me. The pencil seemed to move of its own volition. The brush made a beak, feather, eye. It was as if to hesitate or think too much, to resist in any way, would impede the progress of my calling. I was convinced that birds were kinds of souls. Not the souls of people but of previous birds whose mystery and beauty were so necessary on earth that God would not allow them to be anything in their second life but birds again. This was an idea I had come up with when I was nine or ten, just after Reverend Sillet's sermon on the transformation of souls in heaven. I sometimes went to church with my mother. Witless Bay had the Anglican Church of England. I would sit antsy in the pew, or daydream. Having made my own connections between God and birds, I felt moral enough not to have to listen too closely to Sillet's sermons. Besides, I had already passed my own judgement on Sillet; I had made a few drawings of him taking potshots at a woodpecker on the church belfry.

It went like this. I would send five carefully packed drawings or watercolors to Halifax, and Sprague would comment by return mail; this might take one summer month, if the *Aunt Ivy Barnacle* was in good repair and if Enoch did not dawdle on his mail stops, and if fair weather prevailed. But when I sent drawings out just before winter, I would not get Sprague's reply until spring, because the *Aunt Ivy Barnacle* would be in dry dock. Anyway, once I did get a letter from Sprague, I would send him two dollars, a lot of money for me. For anyone in Witless Bay, for that matter. To pay my parents' room and board, which I had done since I was thirteen, I worked at the dry dock, repairing and painting schooners, trawlers, dories. I sometimes worked side by side with my father. Still and all, I was barely able to afford the inks, special paper, and brushes which I ordered through Gillette's store, especially after Mrs. Bath died.

Isaac Sprague's letters were detailed and impersonal. They kept to subjects such as the shaping of a beak, shadows, color accents. He wrote to me about consciously denying certain background landscapes the opportunity—as he put it—to dominate rather than feature a bird. In one letter he said that bird artists should *invoke* a bird, feather by feather, not merely copy what we observe in the wild. He had, for me, a difficult vocabulary and I wrote him a separate letter to say that. He sent me a dictionary for Christmas, 1909, along with a note saying, "Read each of my letters from now on with this book in hand. I'm not going backwards in my education on your behalf." The dictionary had arrived in October, Christmas greetings inscribed in advance.

Sprague offered strong opinions in each letter, not just about my work but about bird art in general. Much later, after our correspondence had ended, I realized that all of his musings, asides, complaints, all of his fervor added up to a rare education, not just in craft but in his own passionate character as well. "Birds," he wrote, "and the making of a bird on the page is the logic of my heart. And yours?" He examined life closely and described things in close-up language. "That belted kingfisher you sent me," he wrote, "is pretty good—fine. A solid effort, Mr. Vas. Yet the foot does not seem to encircle the branch but to be laid on a differently pitched surface." I looked up "pitch" in the dictionary. I drew kingfisher feet on branches for hours, days in a row.

Whatever praise he divvied out I was intoxicated with for weeks, months! When I would hear that the *Aunt Ivy Barnacle* had tied up, I would drop everything and run to the wharf. I would follow the burlap mail sacks up to Gillette's store, even haul them myself, and watch as Romeo distributed envelopes into slots. My family did not have a slot. "Anything for me from Halifax?" I would ask Romeo, a question meant only to narrow down my possible disappointments to one, since Halifax was the only place from which, and Sprague the only person from whom, I had ever received a letter.

Each of Isaac Sprague's letters began: "Dear Mr. Vas, Student #12." I learned that at any given time throughout the years I worked with him, he kept three dozen or so students through the mail, and also taught a night course, "Nature Drawing," in a small museum on Agricola Street, the stationery of which he used. The date of each letter was printed below his signature, and each letter ended in an identical way:

In hopes for improvement,
Isaac Sprague

I have kept all his letters, my own inheritance from those years. "You've got a knack," he wrote on September 7, 1909, "but you are no genius."

Out of financial necessity I maintained my other employments, yet privately I considered bird art to be my profession. In secret, a journal such as *Bird Lore* truly defined my world, or a world I wanted more and more to belong to. I wanted someday to report birds back from Catesby's Florida, or from Africa, South America, Siberia, any place really; just looking at a globe would keep me awake half the night painting. I was squirreling money away to flee. And though I was stuck in Witless Bay, or thought of it that way, I was in fact able to improve, slowly, to the point where two reputable journals, *Maritime Monthly* and the more specialized *Bird Lore*, solicited my sketches and watercolors, both as fillers and to accompany feature articles. Each request, each acceptance, made me feel more hopeful, more alive to the possibility that bird art could be my life. *Maritime Monthly*, for instance, had paid $1.50 Canadian for the first work I had ever sold, ten pencil sketches of barn swallows which it did not publish yet kept on file. Sprague, of course, had recommended me. He wrote to tell me that he had. I thought of this as a generosity and it was, yet it was also an investment in his own future. The success of his students, within the small world of bird art, reflected well on him, and he asked that I mention him in any correspondence I might have with a journal's editor. I am certain that he asked the same of all his students.

In fact, when I had sold the barn swallows, Sprague requested that I send him a 25¢ commission, that one time only. I sent it; I would happily have sent the entire amount I was paid. And I enclosed a lengthy, no doubt overwrought description of a magnolia warbler, along with a torn-out page from my daily sketchbook, as intimate a document to me as any diary. However, the audacity of a student offering "a preliminary sketch," as he called it, heartily offended him. He wrote back: "I herewith return your warbler without comment." That was comment enough. Perhaps it was his custom to give his students a cold shake early on, to slowly step back once they had entered his professional domain. I cannot say for certain. When our work together ceased with sudden abruptness, it was a mystery to me, and upsetting. Late in October 1910, I had sent him the required five drawings: a murre, a crow, a gull, a cormorant, a black duck, knowing the likelihood of not hearing from him until spring. Yet in April and May 1911, the *Aunt Ivy Barnacle* made a number of round trips, and there was no letter from Sprague.

Anyway, I had been earning money from bird art and was proud of it.

In 1911, I still had a steady hand and could set aside personal torment for the duration of a drawing or painting. I still could concentrate for hours in a row, day and night, and had not yet fallen completely into the habit of drinking twenty to thirty cups of coffee a day. That happened in earnest after I had murdered Botho August and holds true of me to this day. I had never enjoyed alcohol, though I would drink whiskey with Margaret Handle, because she hated to drink alone. And she drank alone much of the time. But coffee is a different thing. It is a peculiar addiction and few people understand it. In my case, however, it can be traced back to Alaric's, Orkney's, and my household; I had drunk coffee since I was five years old. There were the long winters, you see, and coffee was what you came in to out of the cold.

So much to tell. Though I am a bird artist, you would not have heard of me. None of my paintings resides in a museum. My sketchbooks gather dust in Enoch Handle's attic. My first wife, Cora Holly, whom I married in an unfortunate arranged marriage, may still own an ink portrait of a garganey in eclipse plumage, I do not know. It was a wedding present, actually.

The garganey is a surface-feeding duck, and even Enoch Handle, who knew every bird along the coves, inlets, the entire coastline (he delivered mail from Lamaline at the southern tip of Newfoundland, to Cook's Harbour at the top; another boat, the *Doubting Thomas*, serviced the western seaboard), found it a rare visitor. Enoch was in his sixties and told me he had identified only two garganeys with total certainty. He admitted that at a glance a garganey might easily be mistaken for a cinnamon teal or a blue-winged teal. And it was true that you could live your entire life in Witless Bay, in Newfoundland for that matter, and never see a garganey, even if you were desperately searching for one.

Yet I had drawn Cora Holly's wedding present from life. It had been as though an otherwise meandering summer day, the day I had spotted the garganey, had lured me to Shoe Cove. Just before dawn I had packed my sketchbook, pens, binoculars, and had set out from our one-story blue cottage. I had already drunk five cups of coffee. I walked

weathervane shaped like a whale, spout and all. The light-house loomed at the end of its brief peninsula with a splendid jurisdiction over the wooden structures of day-to-day village life; the older cottages, the newer two-story houses, the stilt houses on shelves of rock along the water, the ice-fishing shanties lined up off-season at the end of the sawmill road, cold storage shacks dug into hillsides, the seine gallows, trestles made of rough rails we called "starrigans," used for drying newly barked nets.

I had had my closest look at Botho August long before the close look at his murdered body, however, when my family and assorted neighbors all had Canadian Thanks-giving at the widower Romeo Gillette's house, adjacent to his general store. In part, Romeo saw his annual Thanks-giving as a protest. "This is *Canadian* Thanksgiving, mind you," he would never fail to say, beginning the prayer. "God, we ask that Newfoundland will get out from under the yoke of Great Britain. And soon. Amen." The holiday dinner I am referring to here was in 1909, and I sat directly across from Botho August. Neither of us had chosen such an arrangement; when Romeo swung the school bell to call dinner, those were the chairs we were each standing next to.

It was a rare night of socializing for my family. My mother, Alaric, who was thirty-nine that year, had a slight build, dark brown eyes, and had as usual braided her black hair up in an inventive style. She wore a flower-print dress, exotic for Witless Bay, that her sister, Madeleine, had sent from Vancouver, and over it a cotton vest of her own design.

The dress had taken the better part of ten months to arrive and was accompanied by a chatty letter full of old news pinned to the lace end of a sleeve. "Even though I'm hearing it for the first time, it seems like stale news," my mother had remarked, setting down the letter. "Still, her handwriting is lovely. And I know that overland mail takes an eternity. Besides, what are my sister's choices? To write about our childhood. To write about her present life. That's it. Or else, to try and predict the future, I suppose. Oh, that'd be definitely too risky for her. Definitely."

My father, Orkney, was forty-three. He wore a Scottish herringbone suit he had bought from a tailor in Bonavista and a freshly laundered white shirt, starched and ironed, buttoned to the collar. Most men in Witless Bay wore knitted underwear all year round. It was lined with "fleece calico," which kept it from being itchy next to the skin. My father's sentiment was, what will keep out the cold will keep out the heat. He was an accomplished carpenter, boat builder, and harvester of wild birds. He was as meticulous a person as I have yet to meet, in how he washed his face, wrung out the washcloth, squared it, hung it to dry; in how he scrubbed out his coffee mug; in how he tested the strength of each shoelace before tying it. "All things are connected in this world," he would say, showing me how to drive a nail. He would sing a philosophical song: "The nail shall not forget the forge, the plank not the darkly woods," the kind of verse hospitable to just about anything you might think of, object, animal, human being. My father despised any sign of privilege, and he had the confidence of someone self-taught in a number of hands-on occupations from a young age. In all of this I admired him. Though he was occasionally edgy, capable of saying harsh things, he generally spoke well of people, perhaps more efficient in his assessments than generous. He seemed to harbor a very private system of prejudices. He kept his thoughts mostly to himself, though. I thought of him as a quiet man. His favorite response in the face of savage gossip, claim of insult, or just plain bad news was "Well, it's no matter to die for, now, is it."

My father was of average height, I would say, solidly built, though he got on the thin side when he spent months harvesting birds, an enterprise he took part in every few years. He had thick black hair combed straight back from his forehead, salt-and-pepper sideburns. He had a handsome face, compromised by his older brother, Sebastian. My father called him Bassie. I thought of him as Uncle Bassie. My seldom-seen uncle. Bassie was a career bank robber, or that was the only steady occupation of his I knew about. He would send a letter every Christmas, often from a work camp or prison or local jail, asking for cigarettes, asking not to be forgotten.

When my father was ten, my father's story went, Bassie broke his jaw while teaching him to box, a rock in each fist. The break had gone unattended for too long; then it was improperly set, reset by a second doctor, and, when it finally mended, left my father's jaw misaligned, his lips having the effect of the wrong two jigsaw pieces forced together, never fitting tightly. This affected his breathing at night. He may have breathed oddly during the day as well, but I did not notice. Lying in my bed all the way across the house, I would picture my father settling into his own bed, propped up by pillows, which allowed him to sleep. No doubt in part to cover the considerable scar, he had grown a beard as soon as he could. By Thanksgiving, 1909, his beard was white-grey.

At social gatherings my parents were attentive listeners, but each preferred the other to do the talking. They knew that their natural reticence would be more sharply featured if they sat next to each other, so they never did. That Thanksgiving, I remember, went by with my mother saying the hellos, my father telling Romeo, "Rare as I've ever seen, for a man to cook like you can," both of them managing a few sentences during the meal, and my father saying good-bye for all three of us. They were good listeners, though, and I always got the impression that people liked them, my father in particular, and maybe even liked puzzling over their natures.

The meal was potluck. We had brought cod and sweet bread. Romeo had provided five wild turkeys. Botho August had contributed a dozen roasted puffins, those clown-faced birds the locals called sea parrots. There was a small population of them on the cliffs beneath the lighthouse, and thousands out on Witless Bay Island.

By that time I had earned a reputation in the village for painting and drawing birds. I had had work in journals and magazines. Romeo Gillette even had framed two of my drawings of kittiwakes and hung them on the wall behind his counter.

Margaret arrived late and wedged her chair between mine and my mother's.

Right after Romeo's prayer, Botho August turned a puffin over on its platter with his fork and said, "Ever drawn one of these, Fabian?"

"Not a dead one. I only draw from life. From the wild."

Botho stared at me, a hostile squint, as though I had talked down to him.

"Well," he said, producing what I thought was an involuntary hiss, "this one here's got an awfully wild look about the eyes, wouldn't you agree, eh? Would you care to make a quick sketch before we hungry folks tear away at it?"

There was tense laughter all around. "No thanks," I said. I then made certain to cut the first slice of puffin; in fact, I ate the entire bird. And from that moment until the last time I saw Botho August alive, he and I said barely a handful of words to each other.

Botho August was a tall man, over six feet, slim but wide-shouldered, in top health, I imagine. What seemed to contradict his physical stature, though, was his frail skin, which freckled up and needed protection from the sun. He often wore his sleeves cuffed to the end, even on the hottest days. He wore a British sea captain's hat, which rankled Romeo, who took anything of British make personally. "Excepting ancestry," he said. "*That* one can't help." Botho had hair perhaps a shade lighter red than Margaret's, and wore it longer than most men in Witless Bay wore theirs. He was, I would guess, a few years younger than my mother. He had a red-brown, short-cropped beard and blue-grey eyes. He had a way of coming alert, of both squinting and holding his eyebrows aloft. It was a look of impatient curiosity and resignation all at once, as though he had a predetermined notion of serious regard, and you either fit into it with your first few words or you did not. And if you did not, it was as though you had failed him in some personal and unforgivable way, and he would tilt his head at a surprising angle, squint, appeared as bored as a child in church on his birthday. It was a rudeness that provided both him and you with an immediate reason to turn and pace away as in a duel. He was a man who disagreed with the world, is how I thought of him. A man able to make judgements as easily as another man might flick a moth from a table, without afterthought or regret. I had seen him be cordial, yes, but in a way that seemed painful to him, not at all natural.

I feel obliged to say that schooner crews, lobstermen, and the like spoke highly of Botho, in terms of his operating the lighthouse. I worked with these men. I heard them talk. In Witless Bay, a lighthouse keeper held a sacred trust. Berserk gales, blanket fogs, fairy squalls, even zigzagging water spouts—weather that had for centuries drowned sailors, lovers, fishermen, and indeed battered Witless Bay countless numbers of days and nights during any given year—are what Botho had to contend with. So his profession lay at the heart of life and death to my neighbors; tuna and sea-bass fishermen out in the before-dawn or evening hours, coming home well into the night; leggie and capelin fishermen; codfish trappers, lobstermen—all of whom made up the grandfathers, fathers, and sons of most of Witless Bay's families.

"Botho August can pin a schooner in trouble to the sea with that beam," Romeo Gillette once said. "He can shade the beam just right and beckon a dory in, just like it was Jesus on the water following some holy-lit path home. He's damn good at that. We're lucky on that account to have hired him. But he'd rather be up in his crow's nest than down among common men. I'm not suggesting, mind you, that there's a judgement on his part toward us in all of that privacy. I'm saying that for Botho August, there's no card playing, no pissing off the dock after a drunk, no socializing for five minutes of obligation on the church steps, no church. He's a person with the distance in him."

Anyway, back to the day that I drew the garganey. Leaving the lighthouse, I continued on past Gillette's store. His sign read: PROVISIONS / GILLETTE'S / GROCERIES in large black letters. It had a wide porch with four chairs nailed down and a rocking chair a customer could move here or there.

A quarter mile or so farther, on the way to the codfish drying flats, was the sawmill owned and operated by Boas LaCotte, and beyond the flats and down a rocky slope across a slat bridge were the wharf, dry dock, and four adjacent peninsulas. At the end of each peninsula was a single square-up house; in that part of the village, people often visited by rowing a dinghy house to house.

Well past these peninsulas was old Helen Twombly's cold-storage shack, roofed in dirt and sod. It held her milk bottles and rectangular pats of butter. Even with dawn just breaking, I figured that Helen might be there, and she was. In 1911 she was eighty, and though her house was next to Gillette's store, since childhood I had thought of her as living more at her shack. In late spring she would plant flowers on its roof. Her garden was only a few steps away. She had had her husband, Emile, buried near the shack, forsaking the family plot in the cemetery west of the sawmill. I would often stop and watch Helen rearrange her milk bottles in her own finicky way, lifting, sorting. Bent as she was, you could almost balance a bottle on her back. No one person of course could have drunk as much milk as Helen hoarded. A lot went to waste. As children we believed that she drank only rancid milk; when we got older we learned that she drank it fresh as well as rancid, and that she considered milk as generally medicinal. "For which illnesses?" I once asked her. "For the ones I never get because I keep drinking the stuff" is what she said. When she came into the store, Romeo never hesitated or said, "Helen, come now, ten bottles!" He simply lifted the milk from its bin of ice blocks and set them on the counter, as Helen opened up her snap purse. She had enough money to get by. I think she poured milk into her parsnips and carrots—watered her garden with it, I mean. The garden had a milky air about it. The nozzle of her watering can was crusted white.

That morning, Helen wore a housedress, a knit sweater, a shawl, long underwear, and black galoshes.

"Hello, Helen," I said, just loud enough so she would hear, yet not be startled. "Good morning."

"Loathe to anyone steals my milk," she said. Her eyes were bright, with the shocking beauty of a goat's in a decrepit goat's face. "I can be a harpy if I choose to."

"I respect that, Helen. I'm just passing by. I'm going off to try and find a bird to draw for my fiancée."

"Where's the wedding?"

"Halifax. In October, most likely."

"Yes, yes. I heard that you and Margaret Handle have been practising all along. I always liked that Margaret. Ever since she was a little girl, she never came near my milk."

"I like her, too."

"Why are you two going down to Halifax for the ceremony?"

"I'm not marrying Margaret."

She put a finger to the side of her head. "I get it. Margaret's been practising for somebody else, too."

"I suppose that's true."

"Margaret's had a difficult past. I hope her future's better. I hope no man ruins it. I hope she won't let that happen. The bicycle accident, you ask me. You ask me, that was the start of Margaret's troubles on this earth."

Exactly on her thirteenth birthday, July 2, 1900, Enoch had brought Margaret a bicycle from Halifax. There were few bicycles in Witless Bay then, not a lot of good places to ride them. But Margaret learned to ride hers quickly. She would risk various horse trails as well as the path that ran behind the lighthouse, high above the water. She would careen around the wharf. She would skid sideways to the last slat of a dock, front wheel spinning over the edge. She spilled in a few times and the bicycle had to be salvaged. It got rust-pocked.

One morning in late August of that year I had just come into the store to buy groceries when I heard a loud slap. This was followed by a girl's voice crying out, "I'm sorry! I'm sorry!" At first I did not recognize the voice. I walked to the counter. My father was away visiting Bassie in Buchans. My mother was just getting over the croup and had not been in the village for a week. I had been back and forth to Lambert's trout camp. All this to say, we had not heard any news.

Boas LaCotte was in the store. "Fabian Vas," he said, "let me introduce you to the constable, Mitchell Kelb."

Mitchell Kelb stepped forward and we shook hands. "Son," he said, nodding.

"He's come down from Her Majesty's Penitentiary in St. John's—well, the magistrate court up there, to carry out a formal investigation," Boas said.

"What's that?"

"Investigation's when a British official looks into the hows and whys and wherefores of a crime," Boas said.

"Or an accident," Kelb said.

"That's Margaret Handle in the back room," Boas said. "Poor girl, she collided on that bicycle of hers with Dalton

Gillette, on the path behind the lighthouse. I have to put this plainly, Fabian. Dalton fell to his death."

Dalton was Romeo's father, who was slowly recovering from a heart attack.

"That can't be," I said.

"It could and is," Kelb said.

I looked into the storeroom, the one old Dalton Gillette had been recuperating in. Romeo stood over Margaret, who was sprawled on the bed. He had just slapped her and looked almost as shocked at what he had done as Margaret did. His face was contorted and he was trembling, staring at his hand.

Mitchell Kelb now stood next to me. "Mr. Gillette," Kelb said into the storeroom, "you just struck a witness. Don't do that again."

He said this with such severe reprimand that Romeo retreated to a corner like a schoolboy dunce. Finally, head down, Romeo walked to the front door of the store, turned, and said, "My father died in a humiliating way, after all that hard labor to be able just to take a walk again."

Mitchell Kelb was a short man, no more than five foot six, I would guess. He was in good trim, had curly brown hair, a fair complexion, and wore spectacles. There was a bookish aspect to him. He spoke with authority, though, and said to Romeo, "That's a personal matter between you and your God, and the girl there, and maybe her father. I'm just taking down the facts of this incident on paper"— he held up a leatherbound pad of paper—"to report back to the Board of Inquiry. I've been out to the exact spot it happened. It's hardly a blind corner, that I'll admit. This is tragic, Mr. Gillette. You've lost your father. I'm sorry for you, for the girl. But don't hit her again."

Romeo left the store.

Flung across Dalton Gillette's bed now, Margaret looked as though she was stretching her arms and legs as far out as possible, clawing at the bedcover, trying to get purchase. She went into a weeping jag unlike any I had heard; her shoulders quaked, great sobs welled up. She wailed, almost a howling. I could not seem to turn away.

"If you had any sense, boy, you'd bring her a glass of water," Kelb said. "She's crying for her own future, as she's got to live with what a goddamned stupid thing she's done."

Years later, I came to believe that every drink of spirits that Margaret took had, in a way, its wellspring in that incident. And that no amount of whiskey could take a complete enough vengeance on herself. But at that moment in the store, I simply carried in a glass of water and handed it to her.

Mitchell Kelb had questioned Margaret for over an hour, and had made her go out to the cliff and show him exactly where she had crashed into Dalton. Boas had gone along, too, as Kelb had requested. Later, Boas said that Margaret had collapsed in tears, and that both he and Kelb had to keep her from flinging herself over the cliff. She had actually run toward it. "She was kicking and screaming," Boas said. "Saying suicidal things nobody that young should've even had in their vocabulary."

By the time I had seen Margaret in the store that morning, Dalton Gillette had already been laid out in Henley's Funeral Parlor overnight. He had fallen onto some jagged rocks, then rolled into an inlet and was easily found. Mrs. Henley had washed all of Dalton's clothes, hung them out to dry, and, when they had dried, sewn together rips in the shirt and trousers. She had hung up his shoes by the laces to a clothesline. Romeo had provided his own suit for his father to be buried in. Now Romeo would need a new one.

I was eight, and that is about all I remember, except that at the funeral the reverend at the time, Weebe, said, "Dalton Gillette has surely established our strong and loving memory of him, and God resides therein."

I did not see Margaret for three weeks after, some feat in Witless Bay. My mother at first said that Margaret had gone to live with her aunt in Bonavista, north up the coast, because that is what my mother had been told. But rumor was mistaken. It turned out that Margaret had been home all along and simply could not be consoled. She had lost a startling amount of weight and vomited up each meal, or most of it. Enoch finally told Boas, who of course told some others, and so on. "She was under sedation," my father said one morning at breakfast, then explained what sedation meant. I would have thought that such news might draw sympathy from my mother, but I was wrong. "I don't know. I just don't know," she said. "Sometimes I swear that Margaret's got an untoward mind, just a little right or left of center. Mind you, my heart goes all the way out to Romeo and Annie Gillette, and to Enoch, of course. But I'm afraid only half as far to Margaret." I was at best puzzled. I looked at my mother, waiting for her to say something more. She only shrugged, pouring herself a cup of tea.

Helen leaned against her shack. "Well, whoever your bride is, when you bring her back here, keep her away from my milk," she said.

"If we come back, I'll do that."

"You know, this shack's my true address." Helen sighed deeply. "I only sleep in my house. I generally stay away from people. Everyone's jealous of me, because I'm old enough to have witnessed mermaids and mermen, and they aren't. Nowadays, people have to travel to get important memories. Not me. Mark my word, Fabian Vas, jealousy leads to stupid behavior, even among Christians. Where they could delight in my memory of mermaids, they hold it against me as eccentric. They think I'm lying. Memory is a pox. A *pox*, to remember all that I still can. It won't leave me alone. One night, I saw mermaids and mermen attain a shipwreck. Right out there on the rocks."

She looked out to sea. She heaved another sigh, and it made her lose her balance slightly. I reached out to help, but she pushed me away. She raised her fists in anguish to her face. "What difference, anyway—there's nobody left to talk to. I could have educated the village children."

"I'm going now. Goodbye, Helen."

She turned back to her bottles.

In Shoe Cove, between Witless Bay and Portugal Cove, I saw the garganey. It was a male, asleep in the early sun, head tucked to his breast. There were no other birds or

people in sight. It was a small, high-cliffed cove, and I made
my way down to some flat rocks near the water, where I
sat watching the garganey for a few moments. Then, moving to a more comfortable rock hollowed out almost like a
chair, I sat sketching the garganey for a good two hours. I
drew him as he slept. I drew him as he lifted his head,
preened, skitted across the surface. He mostly held to one
place, though at a certain point he flew off, circled, then lit
down on what I thought was the exact same spot, hard of
course to determine on a sun-glinted sea. It was as though
he had enacted his own dream of flying, then had returned
to his body. He fed awhile, scooping, shoveling, shaking
his head, dipping, drifting, slowly turning with the random
eddies. The sea brightened, the wind picked up, and there
were whitecaps. I drew. Those were the elements: water,
rocks, sun; the garganey, a migrant here for a short stay,
whose life I had only happened upon because of that morning's particular luck. Luck like no other I had ever had, or
have had since.

Three days later I purchased a simple wooden frame from
Gillette's store, with money I had earned from *Bird Lore*.
On the back I etched: *This is for Cora Holly, my fiancée.
Begun June 26, 1911, completed June 29, 1911.*

2

C o r a   H o l l y

My mother smuggled Cora Holly's photograph into our house. On the evening of September 17, 1910, we had cod, bread, and potatoes for supper, apple cobbler for dessert. During the cobbler, my father said, "We've been hired to repair the *Aunt Ivy Barnacle*. A crack in the hull, warped cabin planks, and the like. We need the money, eh? It's already hoisted up. Enoch, he'll be there to watch, 5 a.m. on the nose."

"Ah, Enoch's home," my mother said. "Poor Margaret, nights alone in a cold bed."

"Alaric, that's not the present subject," my father said. "Anyway, it being the mail boat, Enoch will be there but won't give advice. He just likes to see things get patched up, so he won't worry at sea. It soothes his mind about it."

"I'll get up at 4:30 to make your coffee," my mother said. "But I won't be in a civil mood."

"You'll hardly know we're here," my father said. "We'll be father and son ghosts at the table. Just set out coffee mugs, scones, you'll see bites disappearing. The table'll be cleared. The door'll open. The door'll close. You can go right back to sleep."

"It should all work out fine, then," she said. "I'm in for my bath now."

My father pointed to my sketchbook, which I'd placed on the table. "Is that your day's work?" he said.

"I was out at Lambert's camp. Ospreys."

"How's Lambert?"

"A man of one motto."

"Nothing to hope for from any promise, nothing to fear from any threat," he said, laughing a little. "He hasn't changed that tune since he was fifteen."

"You want to take a look?"

"Yes."

I slid the sketchbook across the table. He took in each page. Finally, he sat back and folded his arms. "These ospreys are highly recognizable," he said.

"What about the harlequins?"

He looked at the harlequin ducks, four or five of them. Pointing to one, he said, "This captures a harlequin's nature. But what I most admire is that it doesn't resemble *every* harlequin. It's got its own character as well. But these others fall short."

"Short of what?"

"Of your best harlequin. You told me yourself, Fabian—all these drawings you do every day, you've got a standard

38

to uphold. But you don't always know the standard until you look over your day's accomplishment, drawing by drawing. For my money, today's best is this last harlequin. And the ospreys."

"I've got a commission. *Maritime Monthly*. Crows, and whatever ducks I prefer. They sent an advance. That's a first. A one-dollar advance."

"It's their confidence in you, that dollar."

"There's a lot of people drawing birds in Canada."

"That's some sort of attitude, I suppose. Better than none at all."

"Okay, I'm pleased."

"I said once to Lambert that if a bird, even a buzzard, spoke to me in a dream or nightmare, I couldn't ever shoot another one."

"How'd Lambert reply?"

"Lambert said that he didn't dream, so didn't worry about such things. Then he added that if I did have such a dream and it stifled my hunting, he'd get a new hunting partner. He boiled it down to that."

"A practical man."

We heard my mother come out of her bath.

"Before I go in, I'll let her stare out the window," my father said. "At the lighthouse. Or more likely the stars. It's a clear night out."

Then, as I had heard it said when two people fall silent at the table, an angel passed.

"I know this is a curious aside," he said, "but your mother's the only woman I've known or heard of who dresses for bed in more layers than she wears during the day. She makes a man work at it, all right. Our wedding night was like that, and it was unseasonably warm. Just about this time in September."

He said all of this with some humor in his voice, tinged with resignation, and when my mother appeared in the doorway, he cut himself short, then winked at me.

"I overheard clearly," she said. She did not seem angry at all, only about to state a fact. "It's not so much against feeling cold, the layers, as it makes me feel girlish and secure. And it helps me to sleep."

My father stood up. "Look at that, will you?" he said. "Fabian and me sharing coffee and father-and-son talk, and you fresh from your bath, and suddenly a new revelation about what you wear to bed. A simple life still leaves room for being surprised, doesn't it, Alaric?"

"I'll bet Margaret Handle's a lightly clad sleeper," my mother said, looking past us out the window.

She was wearing thick woolen socks folded over once into reverse cuffs of equal width. She had on red long johns under a cotton nightgown. Over the nightgown, she wore a faded white robe. With her right hand she held the ruffled lapels of the robe together at the neck. Her left hand was deep in the one pocket.

"I'm going to bed now," my father said. As he left the kitchen, he kissed my mother on her forehead.

I prepared tea for my mother, then said good night.

In my bedroom I put on my nightshirt. Then I noticed the photograph. It was in an ornate frame of darkly whorled wood, on the table next to my bed. I kept little else there: a sketchbook, matches, lantern. I got into bed and turned the lantern down to a faint. I took up the photograph and looked at it closely. I had absolutely no idea whom this face belonged to, or in which country in the world she lived.

The next thing I was conscious of were the words "Knock, knock," which is what my mother usually said after she had knocked on my door. I had fallen asleep with the photograph facedown on my chest. My mother looked pleased. I quickly set it upright on the table.

"The picture is of your fourth cousin," she said. "Her name—dear thing—is Cora Holly, of Czechoslovakian descent, like your father. She's a cousin on Orkney's side, by way of England. She lives in Richibucto, New Brunswick, a coastal village like ours."

"What's her picture doing here?"

"I just *knew* you'd ask that. Well, your father and I are interested in her. In your marrying her, more precisely."

"What?"

"That Margaret Handle, whom you've been sleeping with. You know what people say, that she's better to visit than marry."

"What people? You're like someone gossiping with herself."

"Calm down, Fabian. Think Cora Holly over, will you, darling? All I ask is that you turn your thoughts to her, for my sake, for your father's. And of course eventually for yours. Because it's our understanding that even the lovely face in that photograph hardly does Cora justice."

"When's the last time you saw this Cora Holly?"

"I've never seen her."

"And the mother and father?"

"Pavel and Klara? Well, let's see. It would be twenty years."

"And given that, how'd this photograph get here?"

"Well, Klara and I have been exchanging letters."

"You've kept it a close secret."

"When the mail comes in, you look for letters from Mr. Sprague. You don't ask for anything else."

"True enough."

"Cora is keen on marrying you as well."

She closed my door.

It took two full days to repair the *Aunt Ivy Barnacle*. The crew was made up of myself, Boas LaCotte's nephew Giles, and my father. I spent hours next to my father, hammering, prying, planing, caulking, sanding, painting, yet he never once mentioned the photograph, and neither did I. He did, however, reminisce about a group of Beothuk Indians he used to see as a boy. At the outset of the conversation, I told my father that in my history primer all we had were watercolor facsimiles of Beothuks paddling, fishing, tattooing their bodies, smoke-drying fish in domed huts, staring out to sea.

"Well, nobody ever got a photograph of a Beothuk," he said. "A book might say they all died out in the early 1800s, but I swear I saw a few stragglers after that. Those Indian faces were not, I guarantee you, commonplace. And you

could tell Beothuks from Micmacs and Eskimaux. A few
—Beothuks, I mean—seemed lost stumbling drunk in the
century itself, a sad sight. The ones who ventured into the
general store, then run by Romeo's father, came to buy
fishhooks, not to converse. There was one old woman I
remember in particular. She bought the hooks. She'd say,
'I'm baptized. I want fishhooks.' I don't know if it was true."

"Which thing?" I said.

"About her being baptized. Anyway, she looked shabby
and was polite. The others just stood staring at the floor."

"I wish I could've seen them."

"Enoch here has Beothuk blood, and that's believable,"
my father said. "Try and find cheekbones like his elsewhere
in Newfoundland. Other than in Margaret's face, naturally.
Enoch can say words in Beothuk. *Mammatek*—that means
'house.' "

"You pronounced it wrong," Enoch said, annoyed. He
had been eavesdropping from his chair, which he had placed
near the rail of the *Aunt Ivy Barnacle*. He had been on deck,
writing in his leatherbound log, sharpening pencils with a
strop razor.

"Enoch," my father said, "what's Beothuk for 'bird shit'?
You told me once, but I forgot."

"*Sugamith*," Enoch said, emphasizing the first syllable
about twice as loud.

"Enoch can resurrect some truly ancient words," my father said. He admired this.

"Tell Fabian about the parrot," Giles said.

Enoch jumped down. He was a stocky man, with a vise-grip handshake, wisp of beard, black hair slicked with grease; he had to clean the inside rim of his pilot's cap with rubbing alcohol.

"See," Enoch said, warming up for a long tale. "This Beothuk twosome lived off by themselves, north of Witless Bay. 'North' is as accurate as anyone knew. This was back when Orkney and I were kids. Back before we even had a local doctor."

"We'd try and stop bleeding by putting cobwebs on it," my father said. "Or turpentine of fir."

"My mother knew a secret prayer to stop a nosebleed," Enoch said. "Anyway, when I say the Beothuk twosome lived off by themselves, I mean a location meant to shun a bear. You didn't see them for a long time. Then, one day they'd just show up in the store. To buy flour, fishhooks, whatever.

"They owned a parrot. A lice-ridden bird, green with some yellow. The old man, hell, he could've been part of my direct ancestry, he had a beat-up coat. French-made. The parrot rode there, clamped right on with its claws to his shoulder. The parrot spoke a lot of Beothuk words. I think whole sentences. I don't have the foggiest where they got the parrot. But they'd clipped its wings and cut its tongue and it liked to say Beothuk words to any audience. And of course it spoke parrot garble, naturally.

"The twosome had a fishing camp out where Lambert Charibon's trout camp is today, along the Salmonier River. When they died—rumor had it on the same day—they were found at their camp. Some trouters notified the church.

"Now, the reverend at that time was named Clemons.

Broderick Clemons. He performed the funeral. Rainy day, a few curious onlookers, but who knew how to grieve correctly for them? To grieve on their behalf?

"Clemons took money from the church till, and there were later complaints about this. He had two grey slabs put over their graves, with the first verse of the Lord's Prayer chiseled in.

"Afterwards, Clemons adopted the parrot. He'd stay up late by lantern light, writing down Beothuk words in a ledger. He kept the bird in a room behind the pulpit. To many, it seemed rancorous to worshippers in an uncalled-for way—but you'd hear the bird squawking and carrying on during sermons. 'Hey, hey, hey, hello, hello, *Nonsut, Demsut!*' That's as close as I can recall the pronunciations.

"It echoed all throughout the church, belfry to pews. Clemons never muzzled the bird, either. Who knows why? *Nonsut, Demsut*—everyone figured those were the two-some's names. They may not have been, though. Who knows that either? It might've just been the mad ravings of a parrot in Newfoundland lonely as hell."

At dusk on the second day of work, I was sanding a new cabin plank when I jammed a long splinter clean through my glove, lodging it deep in the base of my thumb. It was a stupid accident, out of tiredness, and when I reported it to Enoch, he gave me a swig from his flask of whiskey and said, "Quitting time." At home I soaked my hand in hot water. It took my mother fifteen or so minutes to work the splinter out. She dabbed on iodine, then set the splinter on the table to show my father.

45

We had a late supper of sea bass, lettuce and tomatoes from my mother's garden, which produced almost through September.

"How's the hand?" my father asked.

"I can feel my pulse in it."

"Nothing to die for, now, is it."

"Did we get paid?"

"Two separate stacks of money, Canadian. Yours is in an envelope, in the potato cupboard."

"I'll use a little to buy inks."

"And groceries. You're still part of this family."

"All right."

"Don't let that hand get infected or you won't be doing much bird drawing, I'll tell you that."

"I saw Margaret along the road. She knows of an ointment in Romeo's pharmaceuticals that'll ease the pain better than iodine. She kindly said she'd pick it up for me. I'll visit her later."

"Margaret ease the pain," my mother said. But it sounded like an abbreviated request of her own and embarrassed her. She turned to the stove.

I was in bed by eight-thirty, thinking about an early morning of sketching ducks at the tidal flats, when my mother appeared in the doorway.

"I washed the fingerprint smudges off the glass," she said, referring to the photograph.

"I didn't notice."

"Well, *notice*." She sat on the end of my bed. "That Cora Holly's got a mesmerizing face, don't you think?"

"I wouldn't use those words, no."

"What's your opinion, then?"

"I'd say it's a face the photographer caught just right to favor it."

"Do you suspect that the Hollys chose an uncharacteristic likeness to represent their daughter?"

"How could I know that? I've never met them. I've never met this Cora Holly. You and Father never once mentioned their family. And then this photograph shows up."

"It *arrived*, Fabian. It's part of a correspondence between hopeful parents. Don't fool yourself. There's no one normal way in this world to meet a bride. It can happen in all sorts of surprising ways, really. I could tell you stories. What's important for you to know is that Pavel and Klara are honest people. I can vouch for that. And I noticed that you didn't stuff the photograph in the rubbish."

"The frame is nice handiwork."

"My next question is, can you believe that curiosity might be the first part of passion?"

"I haven't thought about it."

"Did your own mother just now saying the word 'passion' embarrass you?"

"I don't think so."

"It means a lot in life, Fabian, passion does. Especially if it's absent."

"Maybe that's a thing you'd say to Father."

"Let me educate you here." She was annoyed. She shifted uneasily on the bed, squaring herself directly in front of me. "Once in a while I say something to you that I purposely choose not to say to Orkney. And what I *do* say to him, in private, is none of your business in turn. Kindly move that photograph back from the table edge, will you?"

My mother closed her eyes; she sometimes gathered her thoughts so intensely that she all but sank into sleep. This was a sort of interlude I was accustomed to.

Breathing lightly, propped up by one arm, her hand pressed into the blanket, she suddenly trembled—and I mean that the bed shook—as if she had compressed a night-long fever chill into a single moment. I all but got the quilt out of its cedar chest at the end of my bed to cover her up, it was that convincing. I recalled, then, a sermon that Reverend Sillet had given. He had quoted someone, a martyr, blind sage, someone, to the effect that in the lifelong vigil for redemption, each show of faith in the face of torment and doubt was a reprieve from madness. At the moment of hearing that, I had especially clung to the word "vigil." I thought that the word fit my mother. That her life was a vigil. Though waiting for redemption for which sin, which trespass, exactly, I could not say at the time, nor could I say now. Passion for what, or whom, I did not know. Later, of course, I thought it all applied to her adultery with Botho August. Yet as time passed, I realized that Botho August —that one man—was finally too narrow and convenient a way to consider my mother's emptiness, her longings.

Opening her eyes then, my mother absently turned her wedding ring, rubbed her hands over her face, and said, "I'm tired, darling. Good night."

"Good night."

All through my life at home with my parents, I knew that my mother's sadness (that is the word I always fall back

on) had a grip on her. I did not know all of the ways it
worked, or all of the things it made her do, but I felt its
existence early on. Some days in our house you could
breathe it like air. I had felt it as a child, and by adolescence
regarded it as permanent. I think back on the dozens of
conversations we had had at the kitchen table after supper,
my father asleep or working half the night at the dry dock,
the dishes cleared, me drinking coffee, my mother sipping
tea. I had often wondered if I had missed what she had
intended as most intimate in her observations, opinions,
advice, even in her very occasional teasing. I have come to
the conclusion, with bracing regret, that I had. Further-
more, I believe that on certain topics she would detect a
blank or at best a puzzled look of incomprehension on my
face and be disappointed in me. I suppose this is true for
any son, but when I look back, certain declarations become
my mother—"I neither champion nor repudiate my life thus
far," she said one evening. "I mostly feel stuck somewhere
in between."

"I just like to wake up early, wash my face, and get out
and draw birds," I said in reply. "Maybe I should be more
brainy and philosophical."

"No, no—lucky life for lack of that," she said.

My mother had a clear, resonant voice. She articulated
like a schoolteacher. She was graceful, it was nice to
watch her walk. She said what was on her mind, though
her boldest assertions were often followed by "Now,
where on earth did I get *that* thought? Obviously that's
just the kind of girl I am!" She would blush, as if she
had had a revelation not only about her own character but

about what she was truly capable of saying to her son.

From as far back as age five or six, perhaps earlier, I remember that she demonstrated great empathy toward me, though she'd never allow me to play out my catastrophes or confusions for too long, or whine, or wallow in self-pity. Her pet phrase was "Get on with it, then." Once in a while this became an extended meditation: "I'm quite impatient with people who tell me they're going to do something and don't at least try. You get all caught up with their enthusiasms, and then things change and what have you got?"

"Do you have anyone in mind?" I once said. I think I was fifteen.

"Fabian, be polite to your mother. When I'm thinking out loud, just hush up and listen."

I dutifully listened then, but she would not say another word. We fell silent. And I heard gulls. Once again, it seemed that in our house when you turned away from talk, day or night, with the windows open, the keening of gulls marked every passing minute.

As for her brief, dry laughter, it seemed more of an accompaniment to her silence than an actual change of heart. It scored up her forehead with deep wrinkles, and caused her to cup her hands over her mouth, as if trying to hold it back.

"My grandmother always said heavy hoop dresses strengthened your back and stayed your posture upright, but when I wore them, my back always ached. It was like taking off a barrel every night. I just had enough," my mother once said. By and large, most women in Witless

Bay dressed alike, skirts and blouses made of serge or woolen cloth. The skirt bottoms were flat at the front waist, but tucked up high and full in back, all sewn with tiny stitches. To make such a dress was detailed labor, and most every girl could sew one by age ten. Mostly the sleeves were puffed at the shoulders and tight-fitting at the wrists. We had muddy and dusty roads, and women had to lift their skirts while walking. As a boy I recall washing and polishing my mother's shoes nearly every day from the spring mud and summer dust. In summer, women generally wore "winseys," lighter, more ruffled dresses, except when doing outdoor work—salting, potato scraping, gardening, and the like—when they wore housedresses covered with rough burlap aprons, or aprons made of burny cloth.

Some of the time my mother wore such local clothing, as she called it. But deep down she had another way of thinking. "You may not realize it," she said to me, "but when I stroll into Gillette's store, or to church, or anywhere, I feel that I have the soul of a world traveler. I've just stepped off a schooner, and lo and behold, look at this odd little village we blew off course to! You may laugh, but I cannot begin to count how many days this lie to myself has got me through, Fabian." She sighed and shook her head at her own invention. But I knew, too, that there were more nights than I could count when my mother had stayed up until morning light, working on one new dress or waistcoat or other.

As for her manner of dress, I had the impression that she as much organized clothes on her person as merely wore them. She was an expert seamstress. She made most of her own dresses, shawls, and vests. She preferred somewhat odd combinations of color. This, to me, was less an eye for fashion—there was only the fashion of Witless Bay, and the occasional magazine—than a composition of thought that wore her inside. She would spend a ritual half hour or so standing in front of her closet, riffling through dresses, greatly amused. "How do I look?" she would ask, whirling, modeling a familiar dress combined with an equally familiar vest or shawl. "If you say 'interesting,' I'll know I've failed."

She spent a good deal of time alone. I thought of her as someone who knew how to do that. I did most of the grocery shopping, errands. Even in summer she had an indoor pallor. Coming home from the dry dock, I would see her crouched in her garden and think, My mother's outside— though this tends toward exaggeration, because in fact she did go on long walks, some days more than one. And she would row a dinghy out into the harbor. She would pack a lunch and row out, staying all afternoon. She did that two or three times a summer.

I cannot say she had one close friend in Witless Bay, no one she called that, at least. People were, as I have mentioned, friendly to her. Romeo Gillette was flirtatious, which my mother took in good humor. Otherwise, she would be matter-of-fact in her visits to his store, unfailingly polite, measured in her inquiry as to his health, and so on. She was pretty much that way with everyone. By the summer route—a horse path through the meadow, then through Giles LaCotte's apple orchard—it was less than a mile to the store. Yet my mother's appearances on the store porch or in its cluttered aisles were few and far between.

She was in 1911 still a very pretty woman, I thought, though perhaps the accumulation of estrangements from my father and from family life, combined with her storm-in-a-bottle emotions toward Botho August, or a hundred other factors had begun to tighten her features. Crow's-feet webbed out at the corners of her eyes. She had bouts of arthritis that no liniment seemed to relieve at all; then, quite suddenly, the pain would disappear.

She used skin creams from France. She kept them in a separate cabinet in the pantry. Her skin was a forthright vanity, though she would take only a few moments each evening to massage cream in around her eyes, on her fore-head, the backs of her hands. And she would leave the door open when she did. I once mixed hues of white and pale grey paint in order to match the color of one of her skin creams, a color which reminded me of a sky I had seen one day at Portugal Cove, when I had painted a dozen or so murres heading fast toward a cliff. For three nights of paint-ing in a row I referred to the open jar of cream on my desk, returning it to the pantry before I went to bed.

At about eleven o'clock, late for me to be awake, after that long day's work on the *Aunt Ivy Barnacle*, I replenished the iodine on my thumb. I had gone to visit Margaret, but she had told me that Romeo had run out of the special ointment. We stood in the apple orchard kissing for a long time, then parted.

In my room I set my lantern on the night table. Lantern light made it seem as if a bonfire glowed to the left of Cora Holly. My curtains shifting in the breeze, the moonlight, all flickered shadows across the framed glass. In the photograph, Cora Holly stood in front of a shed. There was cordwood stacked nearby. She wore a dark sweater over a darker dress, and fur-lined white snowboots. Her knees showed. Her lips were pursed into a smile. She had made fists and held them outward close to her waist. Her hair was tucked under her fur hat. She had, I thought, a mature bearing for someone her age, which I guessed was fifteen. In that I was wrong. In the photograph she was sixteen. All in all, it struck me that Cora Holly was barely tolerating the moment. This made me laugh. I was convinced that it was true. I had a random thought then: *She's had her photograph taken, and I haven't.*

I took my magnifying glass from its drawer. The glass had been a present from Margaret Handle. I saw that the shed door had metal hinges inlaid with some kind of intricate leafy vine, and I imagined that the photographer had used their detail to gauge his focus. The focus was good; still, the shed's roof had a ghost line. I was almost certain it was a meat-drying shed, though—so if its woodstove was cranked up, then the ghost line was most likely steam rising from the roof's snow. I put the photograph on the table. I lay awake a long time, wondering how Cora Holly was being convinced to marry me.

3

M o r s e   C o d e

On October 1, 1910, the *Aunt Ivy Barnacle* brought in a copy of *Bird Lore*, which had my drawing of a common raven on its cover. I stood staring at it. "There's another envelope for you," Romeo said. It contained a check for the cover rate, two dollars Canadian.

"Any letters for my mother?" I said.

"Here's one again from Richibucto," Romeo said. "Handwriting is a woman's, I've noticed all along. That puts to rest the notion of Alaric having a distant paramour."

"Can you cash this?"

"Sure thing."

Romeo took care of the checks from Halifax, where *Maritime Monthly* and *Bird Lore* had their offices. Looking at my cover, he said, "Congratulations. When one of your paintings adorns an official postage stamp of Canada, I'll brag to everyone that I handled your banking. Maybe a stamp saying, 'Welcome, Newfoundland, the Newest Province!' Then one of your birds, a Newfoundland bird, hovering over the coast."

"That really would be something."

Having the raven so prominently featured inspired my working dawn-to-dusk, seven days a week. It was unseasonably warm. Migratory birds were lingering. In October, I completed watercolors and ink portraits of diver ducks at Bay Bulls. Half a day's walk to Cape Broyle, I sketched harlequins. I had a weeklong stint with yellow-bellied sapsuckers behind LaCotte's sawmill. I went north to the spruce crags outside Petty Harb, filling two sketchbooks with grey jays. I had hoped to earn ten dollars in October. That was my goal. It was an amount I had simply snatched from thin air; one minute I thought, Ten dollars is a lot of money, then immediately decided to work toward it. I had all this ambition. I'd fall asleep five nights a week at my desk.

"I think you're trying to earn back as much as you pay out to Isaac Sprague," Margaret said. "To make a clean break from him eventually."

On Tuesday and Thursday nights, Margaret and I slept together. I suppose this arrangement was to our mutual satisfaction, since almost from the start it did not vary. I would not ask Margaret if she ever spent nights with someone else. I would never ask her that. After all, Witless Bay was a small village, so I presumed I would hear, if there was anything to hear, and most likely would get such news from Margaret herself. In turn, she must have known I was faithful to her. Though on the night of October 19, 1910, when I finally told her of Alaric and Orkney's efforts to arrange my marriage, she said, "To even consider it is a betrayal." This revealed deeper feelings than I had heard before, though I'd known they were there.

Five nights a week, then, we would keep our distance. But during periods when Enoch was up the coast, overnight in St. Anthony or Twillingate, where he would sleep in his bunk on the *Aunt Ivy Barnacle*, or Bonavista, where he would stay with his sister, Sevilla Pierce, Margaret and I would spend from early Tuesday and Thursday evening until breakfast the next morning together. And she would seldom sleep.

There was a chowder restaurant, Spivey's, in Witless Bay. It took up the ground floor of a two-story house, set back from the water about a hundred yards. The owners, Bridget and Lemuel Spivey, had moved to Witless Bay from Trepassey in December 1899. They lived upstairs. "We spent the exact turn-of-the-century drunk as skunks," Lemuel told me. "Putting up wallpaper." Spivey's was especially popular on "Family Night," as it came to be known, which was Sunday. I had taken my mother there for her thirty-eighth and thirty-ninth birthdays, my father joining us after work at the dry dock. Enoch, Margaret, and I had supper there now and then as well. That always went smoothly. We counted on Enoch to spice up the conversation with news from his mail route. He was an even-voiced, tireless raconteur, who began any number of accounts with "I just hap-

pened to hear" or "I happened upon," as though interesting
events and people more or less fell into his lap. Anyway,
during supper with Enoch we would hear about places we
had not been to. We all got along. Outsiders might have
thought they saw a family.

One night at Spivey's Enoch said, "When are you two
getting the rings? I'm authorized to marry people shipboard, if you'd prefer to stay out of church."

Margaret cut in. "We haven't got a fix on that yet, Pop,"
she said. She placed a hand on Enoch's shoulder and
squeezed, looking at him sternly. He never broached the
subject again, at least not in front of me.

Tuesdays and Thursdays, then, Margaret and I would
eat at Spivey's. We would be out in public. The restaurant
had one large room crammed with tables of assorted shapes
and sizes, mostly square tops that seated four. A window
on either side of the door took in a view of the dry dock,
part of the flats, and on out to sea. Gulls swooped close or
attended the gateposts, as though begging scraps through
the window. The gulls would stare in. On any but the
warmest nights, however, the glass finally drew cold from
outside and warmth from the kitchen or woodstove, and
the windows would completely fog over.

Bridget Spivey presided as hostess and the only waitress.
She would shout a welcome to you at the door, then point
to an empty table, if there was one. She was a short, lithe
woman in her fifties, and would move quickly from table
to table, scribbling orders, fastening each slip to a string
with a clothespin. Lemuel, the cook, would pulley the slip

close enough to read it through the small order window. He would be back there, expertly maneuvering the cramped space between stove and shelves and kettles, despite taking swigs of cooking sherry. He was about six foot two, with a pudgy face, deeply clear blue eyes, and a head of unruly brown hair, all mops and brooms, as they say. He was slovenly. Yet Lemuel had sophistication in his bold humor. He would burst through the kitchen's swinging door, tap the metal tray with a spoon, call out, "Presentation!" and then hold the tray above his head. He would walk to someone's table, lower the tray so that the guest could savor the aroma. He would inhale dramatically, then set down the tray, revealing a lobster under the cloth napkin. Sometimes this drew applause, usually Bridget's.

Now, Boas LaCotte, like all the regulars at Spivey's, had seen Lemuel perform any number of times. One Thursday night, I recall, the place was packed. There had been a three-day blow, sleet, freezing rain, and people just wanted out of their houses. Margaret and I took a corner table. At a center table, Boas sat with his wife, Mercy, and their nephew Giles. Mercy and Giles ordered sea bass. Boas ordered lobster. That morning there had been a small fire at the sawmill, little damage to speak of, but it all had put Boas in a foul temper. When Lemuel lowered Boas's lobster, Boas said, "Goddamnit, Lemuel, I didn't pay for bloody Shakespeare!"

LaCotte's indiscretion, which flew in the face of Lemuel's grandiose way of showing gratitude to a paying customer, hushed Spivey's to the last person. Lemuel answered right away. "You haven't paid yet at all," he said. He stared stone-faced at Boas. "And what's more, this lobster's on the house."

Lemuel picked up Boas's mug of beer, held it high, and said, "Here's to Boas. For the skill of being a one-man fire crew this morning, and saving his own ass from debtor's prison!"

A few mugs were clinked, but given the certain tension it was a halfhearted response. Boas, a tall, somewhat gawky man with a lean, weather-beaten face, was so stymied that he could only put on his short-brimmed cap and center himself in his chair. Everyone knew that Boas was tight-fisted about money, far past any practicality, yet he was scrupulously honest as well. These two forces in his char-acter seemed to collide at that moment. His face collapsed; the only thing worse for Boas than being overcharged was not being allowed to pay what was rightfully due.

Lemuel slapped his knee, sending up a cloud of flour. "It's the biggest goddamned lobster of the night, too!" he said. He set Boas's mug down hard.

As Lemuel stalked toward the kitchen, Boas hung his cap with great deliberation on his chair, sat up stiffly, and said, "I won't enjoy one bite and I'll leave a tip double the bill!"

"Suit yourself!" Lemuel said. The kitchen door swung back and forth. Inside, Lemuel called, "Order up!" and set two plates of steaming halibut on the counter. Bridget said, "Thank you, dear," and held one plate above her shoulder, the other near her waist, as she moved to a far table. Boas cracked open a claw. Lemuel had not gained, Boas had not lost, nobody was changed. Everyone turned back to their meals and conversation. They were in the only restaurant in Witless Bay.

October 19 proved to be a memorable night. It was just after dark, about eight o'clock, when Margaret and I got back to her house from Spivey's. Margaret and Enoch lived between the sawmill and Helen Twombly's cold-storage shack. Theirs was a stilt house situated amidst boulders at the end of a tidal inlet. It was painted rust-red, its roof shingles black. The rooms were small; there was a kitchen, dining room, two bedrooms, a sitting room. The attic's high ceiling had three thick, knotholed beams. Enoch kept sea maps scrolled against a wall. Margaret worked at a spruce table in the attic. She kept records for the *Aunt Ivy Barnacle*, kept the books for Spivey's, LaCotte's sawmill, Gillette's store. She had all the financial records filed in packing crates. In school she had been good at math, top honors, and, as I've mentioned, had been tutored in bookkeeping by Mrs. Bath.

The sitting room was just off the kitchen. It had a loose-spring sofa and a rocking chair, and a bulky ship-to-shore wireless on the table.

"My father taught me Morse code as a kid," Margaret once told me. "We used to talk in it at the supper table. Pass the peas, pass the butter, all in Morse code, though you can't get certain homey details. But you could tap out the weather, say, or a little gossip. I'd tap the table with my spoon. Tap, tap, tap, tap. Then he'd tap, tap, tap. Very stormy seas, he'd say. My boat's in trouble. I'm going to capsize. So long, fare thee well. Then I'd rush over to him and hug him and save him from going under. We had a lot of fun."

One night, when we thought that Enoch was not coming home, Margaret woke me up and said, "Listen." We heard the wireless clicking in the dark. "That's my pop. He's just offshore."

"God, I'll get dressed and out of here."

"No, he says he's sleeping on the boat. He's too polite to intrude. He must have seen his own house lights. Maybe he looked up here through binoculars and saw you walking by a window. Who knows?"

The wireless clicked again.

"What's he saying now?" I said.

"Asked if I'd row out some hot cocoa first thing in the morning. I think I might do just that."

Soon after we got to her house on the night of October 19, Margaret went in for her bath. When she came into the bedroom, she was drying her hair with a towel. She had another towel wrapped around her. She poured a shot glass of whiskey. "Salut!" she said. She would say that even before she drank a glass of water. She slugged back the whiskey. "Want some?"

"One glass. Then I've got something to mention."

"Can it wait?" She opened the towel, quickly closing it again.

"After you hear it, you might have wanted me to wait."

She took off the towel and set it on the chair by the window. Lingering naked right in front of me a moment, she then put on a freshly laundered nightshirt. I finished my drink, then sat back against the headboard. Margaret sat cross-legged at the opposite end. She poured a second glass for herself.

"You'll take this how you want," I said. "Alaric and Orkney have got the idea to marry me off."

Margaret took this in without expression. "I'd spit out this whiskey," she finally said, "but what a waste. Who's the lucky girl?"

"My cousin. Her name is Cora Holly. She's from Richibucto, New Brunswick."

"A first or second cousin, she'd give birth to something untoward."

"Fourth."

"That's far enough away in blood. I didn't know you even had New Brunswick relations, Fabian. Whose side?"

"My father's."

Guttering the candle with a wet finger, Margaret lay close to me. It was dark out now. Pulling my shirt away from my belt, she unbuttoned it to the waist. She situated my hands on her hips, under her nightshirt, then turned fully toward me. She whispered, "To even consider it is a betrayal."

Right then, I should have moved my hands up or down, let the subject fade and the whiskey work into us both in the most useful way. Yet I said, "You noticed I brought my day satchel along?"

"Bird sketches to show me, I figured."

"Her photograph's in there."

Margaret rolled from the bed. My hands felt suddenly cold. She fumbled in the dark. When she found the satchel, she carried it into the dining room, then sat in a ladderback chair and lit a candle. She was as beautiful as ever in that light, I will not forget it. She took out the photograph, moved the candle close, and stared. She turned the frame over, removed the backing, slid out the photograph. Then she picked up the salt and pepper shakers, walked to the window, propped the photograph between the shakers, lifted the window, and stepped back out of my line of sight. I heard a drawer open. And then the house exploded in gunfire—she fired three shots, bursting the pepper shaker, pulverizing the photograph. The house and my ears rang with the shots.

"Jesus, Margaret! Somebody might have heard that!"

"So what if they did?"

I smelled the gunpowder in the room. She placed the revolver on the dining-room table.

"They'd say, Well, Fabian's shot her, or more likely, she's shot him, to save him from a stupid life," Margaret said. "Once they decide which—all cozy in their beds—everything else can wait until daylight."

"More likely," I said, "they'd think it was Boas LaCotte shooting at raccoons."

Margaret sat on the bed. "Gunshots making people think that things are just going along per usual," she said. "Sure enough, probably just raccoons." She yawned as though it were some other woman, in another house in the village yawning.

"They—I mean Orkney and Alaric. What should I say happened to the photograph?"

"I'm here now, in this bed," Margaret said. "I've just done something out of pure emotion, from being upset. And all you can worry about is what to say to Momma and Poppa! Okay, just say I got an urge for target practice and Cora Holly volunteered. Or, if you'd like, I'll march over first thing tomorrow morning to report why this girl's missing from your house. I'll stand on your porch. Alaric will be in the doorway. I'll say, 'Fabian slept with me last night. He brought the photograph of a total stranger. I took out a revolver.' "

I have to admit that we tore at each other that night. Margaret drank whiskey, moaned, frightened me a little, just in the way she would do something she had never done before, say, "There, that's a fact of life," and not let up. Her words labored up from deep in her throat; it was barely Margaret's own voice. By dawn she was into her second bottle. I had begun to use a begging tone, almost, asking to come back that night.

"No, Fabian. Thursday. Not until Thursday."

"Where'd you learn those things?"

"I learn most everything from my own thinking them through. I was saving them for a future time, and then, halfway through last night I thought, What the hell."

"Margaret, listen."

But she interrupted, her voice slurred. "Now you know what it's like to stay up all night," she said.

"I couldn't help myself."

"Don't fret about it too much, Fabian. I'm just working my way through you, right on out of Witless Bay eventually, same as you are, vice versa."

"There's love between us, though, Margaret."

"That's easy to say, when everything around you this minute is so familiar. The bed, the smells, all of it."

"I don't want the picture frame back."

"Generous in the wrong ways, as usual."

Nightshirt on now, Margaret leaned back against the bedroom wall. "I've never had my photograph taken," she said. "Not at that age. Not ever. Not at goddamned *all*."

Then I got dressed and went back to my house. I drank coffee and drew birds all day.

Two weeks later, after a supper of cod, soup, and bread, I made coffee for my father and me. "Did you enjoy the potato-leek soup?" my mother said.

"Well, you noticed I took a second helping, didn't you?" I said.

"The Hollys, in their most recent letter, mentioned that potato-leek is Cora's very most favorite. I suppose that, in a way, I made potato-leek tonight in Cora's honor."

"Here's to Cora Holly, then!" my father said, knocking his coffee mug lightly against mine.

"The idea is that I should marry her because we both like the same soup?" I said.

"The *idea*," my mother said, "is quite simple. It is that it's intelligent for fiancés at such a distance to develop a bond in advance. And soup is as natural a thing to start with as any."

"Did the letter say that Cora was *passionate* about potato-leek soup?" I said.

Without so much as a glance or utterance, my mother left the kitchen.

My father stared after her. "Marrying a woman you've known all your life," he said, "Margaret, for instance. Now, that *could* turn out badly. To marry your fourth cousin, come in sight unseen from Richibucto, granted, that's the opposite end of the stick. But it's still marriage. Still the same stick. It's your God-given privilege, and the woman's, to choose without fear of the future or the unknown."

Back in the doorway now, my mother cleared her throat loudly. "That's it in a nutshell, then," she said. "Orkney Vas sounding pious and philosophical as Reverend Sillet himself. What your father, here, Fabian, considers marriage: the unknown."

Granted, it was a rare loss of restraint, but my father slammed the table with his fist. The coffee mugs jumped.

"It's just *words*," he mumbled, as though convincing himself. His face withdrew a moment, then he took a deep breath. "There, well," he said. He mopped up the spilled coffee with a cloth napkin. "Nothing to die for, now, is it."

"I'm awaiting an apology," my mother said in a clenched voice.

"Till hell freezes over," he said.

"I'd like to see that very day," she said. "It would provide an interesting change."

"We're not conspiring against the boy here, Alaric," my father said in painfully measured tones. "All I meant was, marriage is not to be feared. It's meant to be everything else, maybe."

"I've got work to do," I said, standing.

"A cup of tea, please," my mother said, her voice stripped of sentiment. "A cup of tea first, before you flee Cora Holly's presence at our family table, back to your birds."

My father, shaken by what had transpired, rummaged in the mud room, emerging with a raincoat, gloves, and two hammers. "The *Ryland Barney*"—a schooner in for all-night repairs—was all he could manage to say. He shut the door quietly behind him.

"The repair crew will use so many lanterns," my mother said, "you could see the glow from as far away as the rookery cliffs, below the lighthouse. It's like a false dawn. I've seen it. It's like that."

In fact, I did not go back to my desk right away. Instead, I made tea for my mother and sat across from her at the table. For a few moments it was odd; she gripped the table edge, bracing herself as though expecting an earthquake. She held on tight. Then, relaxing her grip, she looked at me. "I didn't ever intend for you to have memories of things gone on in this house like the ones you'll now have," she said.

"I'll have lots of different kinds."

"Bad memories shout the loudest, for the longest, my mother used to say. More lemon, please."

I cut a lemon in half, then squeezed a half's juice into her cup. She clasped her hands around the cup.

"I'll now proceed to subtract what harsh messages just flew between you and Orkney and me," she said. "I'll subtract them from the rest of our conversation, here, right now."

"Fine by me."

She absently rubbed the other lemon half against the back of her hand.

"Ouch!" she said, suddenly using a girlish voice, pulling her hand away. "There's always invisible cuts."

"The smell of lemon juice at night. That'll be a memory."

"It is rather exotic, isn't it? You know, I told the Hollys that we were close, you and I. Do you think that's true, darling? That we're close."

"I think so. I like to think so."

"We try, don't we, each in our own way."

"Yes. But, Mother, these letters going back and forth between you and the Hollys. They discuss my future, but I don't get to read them. And I don't sense, deep down, that you even think that's peculiar. You bought a new letter opener especially for them."

"I purchased it with money from a shawl I'd knitted for Mrs. Harbison, who housekeeps, as you know, for Reverend Sillet."

"The letter opener's not in question here. Your devotion to the letters is what."

"Well, I'm very up front in my letters to the Hollys. I told them about your birds, for instance. Why, I'm all but writing your biography to them. That's a devotion, I suppose, yes. Of course, I didn't maintain that you were a scientist of birds. Rather, a serious artist. I did add, for practicality's sake, that you could repair any boat. I said that not just to please them but because it's true, and it's a truth that should please them."

"A lot has gone into these letters of yours, hasn't it?"

"I bend over the table just the way you do, I've noticed. Though I reprimand myself for my posture."

"Have you felt well, Mother? You've seemed—that your mind's wandering."

"A mind can't wander and come up with a shawl as detailed as the one I made for Mrs. Harbison."

"Detailed as letters can be."

"Those as well."

"I'm a grown man. I sleep with a woman right in the village, which everyone knows. I work. I bring in money. I'm saving to leave Witless Bay. No secrets in any of this. And then one day it turns out that my parents have made a decision for me. On my behalf, to put it generously. Yet I'm not really consulted. I'm more or less told. I'm led into it. It comes to me like news about somebody else's life, except it's not, it's mine. Suddenly the house is filled with this *name*. Cora Holly. And the sad, aggravating truth is, as time goes by, I all but mean hour by hour, I'm numbed between the craziness of it and the enticement. And I don't know why. It's like being crippled with desire."

"Margaret told me she shot up the photograph. She came right over and said it. I told her it didn't matter, since Cora's presence was fixed in your mind. And that we could always get another photograph."

"Please, don't bother."

"Look, Orkney and I see some basic facts. You're old enough for marriage, one. Margaret—"

"Leave Margaret out of this."

"That'd be my hope exactly. But it's hardly possible."

"You have never once invited her for supper."

"Fabian," my mother said. She sat back in her chair. "It's between Margaret and me. Perhaps it's not logical, as if logic ran the world one minute of any day. Or fair. Perhaps it's something I see in her that I despise in myself. I've given that some thought. Whatever it is, it was powerful from early on and won't abate. When I see you and Margaret together, I should feel that you look sweet. That you look sweet together. I should. A son would want his mother to set aside hostility and cantankerous opinion, if only for the sake of his own self-respect. I know that. And I apologize. And I should have done so long before now. But toward Margaret I can't change. I simply cannot."

"Well, I haven't proposed marriage yet."

"Has marriage come up?"

"Enoch brought it up."

"He's a good man."

"Knowing Margaret, she'd do the proposing anyway, not the other way around. She'd ask, and if she didn't like the way I said yes or no, or the look on my face, she'd take the proposal right back."

"Basic fact number two. Orkney is willing to pay for the wedding, as far as he's able to contribute. The bride's father has certain obligations, but Orkney has stubborn pride in this event, and he wants to let the Hollys know he's no pauper. He's arranged a trip to Anticosti Island for feather birds. He says it could be lucrative. He's got buyers already alerted. Lambert Charibon will be in on it. He always has hunted on Anticosti with Lambert. They'd go early next summer. We had in mind that all of us would go down to Halifax for the wedding. Perhaps next October. The Hollys know Halifax quite well. They love the idea of the wedding taking place there. In one letter, Klara called Halifax 'romantic,' and I got the distinct feeling she used the word from experience. Now, Enoch Handle would have to take us on the mail boat. That may prove awkward, what with him being Margaret's father, I mean. But it would be a fact of life. He might well not speak to us along the way, but my bet is he'd take us nonetheless."

"Halifax is pretty much the same as the moon to me. I've never been either place."

She reached into the pocket of her robe.

"Here," she said, holding out a piece of blue stationery, folded once over. Opening it, she let loose a piece of string with an O shape at the end. I picked it up.

"It's Cora Holly's ring size," she said. "Romeo Gillette's got a catalogue of rings. I've notified him of our interest."

"Romeo let in on our family business on purpose. Now, that's a new one."

"Fabian," she said, holding her hand over mine. "The first few times we seriously talked about this marriage were bound to be awkward. But you wait and see, we'll get better at it."

"How would I support a wife?"

"The Hollys have family money, enough to hold you until you get started."

"You're describing our married life as if it's already in motion."

"There, you see how natural it sounds?"

4

Botho and

Alaric

Early on July 2, 1911, my father left with Lambert Charibon for Anticosti Island. Shortly after supper on the same day, my mother took up with Botho August.

All winter the *Aunt Ivy Barnacle* had been in dry dock. With Enoch home, Margaret and I used the spare room adjacent to the Spiveys' kitchen. Bridget and Lemuel refused our offer of payment. Given that the restaurant was open until nine o'clock, we would stretch our meal and talk until the Spiveys went upstairs. Then we would go into our room, set our shoes at the end of the bed like tourists. Tourists in our own village. Sometimes we would have breakfast with Lemuel, who would be up working at 5 a.m. He would move kettles around and wake us.

November, December, January, February, March, April, May. No letters from Isaac Sprague. No letters from the Hollys, either, but my mother spoke of Cora every day.

The morning my father left, my mother prepared por-
ridge, poached eggs, scones, and coffee. I went out to look
at my father's travel weather. To the north-northeast, sun-
rise had streaked the flat clouds with crabapple light; south
along the coast, black rain clouds seemed to leaven in the
updrafts. The wind carried the smell of codfish up from the
flats. I could picture it down there: a dozen or so families
standing at outdoor tables—the Jobbs, Austers, Benoits,
Corbetts, Barrens, Parmelees, and others—dressing out fish
for salting. They might be saying, "Codfish are a bit early
this year but we'll take them when we get them, eh?" Talking about last year's harvest, the year's before that, the one
before. My father and I had worked codfish crew once, when
I was thirteen. Every night, sitting in his chair at the table,
he would stare at the blisters on his already calloused hand
and swear off the job. But he would get me up at three the
next morning, and the next, until that season ended.

When codfish arrived they did so in abundance, but it
averaged only about two or two and a half weeks with the
trap. The sun broke through about four-thirty, traps would
be set by that time, and trapping and jigging would be kept
up until eleven or eleven-thirty at night, or even past midnight. When it got dark, cod-oil lamps were lit. You had a
glimmer of light then, enough to clean the fish on deck if
you chose. After the codfish slacked the trap, it had to be
taken up, hauling eighty-pound grapnels out of twenty-five
or so fathoms of water. This went on, over and over, from
Monday through Saturday. Jiggers alone were used for
another three weeks. After the middle of August, the last

of the fish were dried. The whole catch might be five or six hundred quintals, there being 112 pounds to a quintal. Around the first week of October, the last of the export schooners would arrive to pick up the fish. After the fishing, the laying out of fish in neat rows, the salting, drying, stacking, hauling in carts and wheelbarrows to the wharf; the pay was at the rate of $100 Canadian for a quintal, some years $125.

At the breakfast table, my mother looked out the window and said, "There's Lambert now." She opened the door. "Hello, Lambert."

"Hello, Alaric," Lambert said. He nodded at my father and me separately.

"I'm sure you already had breakfast," my mother said. "Would you care for a second one?"

"No, ma'am. I'll wait out here."

"That's all right. Ours is usually a house where visitors don't come all the way inside."

My father had known Lambert all his life. They were both born and raised in Buchans, in the center of Newfoundland. "When Lambert was in his twenties," my father told me, "he was all temper. He served jail time for brawling, assault, inflicting bodily harm, and other categories of violence. Then, when he got to thirty, he was beaten nearly to death up in St. John's. And stabbed. It was a foreign sailor he'd insulted who did it. After he got out of hospital, you could say he was a reformed man, mostly."

Around my mother Lambert was painfully polite; I do not think that he could look any woman directly in the eye, though. He was burly, and he had the widest sideburns I had ever seen. Except for a horseshoe shape of curly brown hair, he was bald. He had a wide, doughy nose, bad teeth, and oddly a rather delicate smile. I would have to call it painful, too, his smile. He usually had on worn black trousers held up by a rope belt, high boots, a calico-lined undershirt, and one of the two checkered shirts he owned.

He stood on the porch facing the wagon. Romeo Gillette had loaned the wagon and horse to Lambert, so that he and my father could haul their supplies to the wharf.

My father finished his breakfast to the last. He and Lambert loaded up burlap sacks, my father's shotgun, shells, spare boots, two coils of rope, each attached to a three-prong hook. Lambert got up into the wagon seat and kept the horse calm by murmuring, "There, okay, okay now," over and over.

I stood near the kitchen door. On the other side of the table, my father kissed my mother on her forehead. I sensed a deep, yet deeply strained tenderness between them. "You haven't been to Anticosti in five years," she said. "You'll of course be careful on those cliffs."

"What will you do the rest of the day?" he said.

"I'll have tea," my mother said. "That first. Then I'll get properly dressed for gardening. Then—let's think ahead now. Yes. Then it'll be lunch, and the afternoon will require separate planning, won't it?"

"And for supper?" my father said.

"I think perhaps fish. If Fabian goes to the market, or out in a dinghy. I'll ask him to. Fabian?" She turned to me. "Darling, can you buy a fish for supper, or catch one?"

"Yes," I said, without looking at either of them.

"There it is, then," my mother said.

"And if Fabian doesn't get to it, despite promises?"

"Some idea for supper will come along," she said.

"I've always been overly interested in day-to-day routines, haven't I?"

"Not overly."

Then my father stepped up to me. We shook hands. "It can't please you, the particular fact I'm off to kill birds," he said. "A lot of birds. Mainly puffins and auks. Anticosti's the best place to get hundreds of birds in a reasonable amount of time, especially given I don't want to shotgun high numbers of puffins offshore of Witless Bay, now, do I? That wouldn't be local etiquette, eh? With any good luck, I'll have money when I get home. And that's what my going to Anticosti comes down to, doesn't it? Enoch's given us a fair price for passage there. It's pocket money for him. He won't have to report it. That's a privilege he's due, from seniority.

"Anyway, about birds, Fabian. I'm going to shoot any number. So is Lambert. I'm saying this because I want you to hear that I know exactly what I'm doing and why. It's my choice, this way, to earn money. Your wedding is the beneficiary, but you don't have to like that. I've tallied up costs in advance, the travel of us all down to Halifax, hotel room, food. I think that I can realize such costs from killing birds. Finally, it all depends on your going through with marrying Cora Holly, but I'll hear about that news one way or another when I get back. And when I get back, I'll tell you whatever you want to know: total numbers killed, prices obtained, the weather on Anticosti. You just ask. I'll tell it all, or part of it, or nothing. The birds'll be gone by then. I'll just have the burlap sacks left. And the money."

"Map me out your travels," I said.

"We'll go past Trepassey, then across Grand Bank. Stop at Cape Ray overnight. Back out in the morning across Cabot Strait, weather allowing. And then across the Gulf of St. Lawrence to Anticosti.

"We'll be working the rookery cliffs all over the east, southeast, and north of the island. But we'll have to go into Port-Menier right off first thing to register our intentions, get a license, pay the fees. There's a hotel in Port-Menier, the Gaspé North. The original, the Gaspé Royale, is in Quebec, Canada."

I nodded. "See you when?"

"I'd guess late September, thereabouts," he said. "Depending on everything that affects a trip like this."

"Well, goodbye, then."

"Take care of your mother."

He walked out to the wagon. He climbed up and sat down. He looked small next to Lambert. Lambert clicked his tongue, flicked the reins lightly across the horse's rump, turned the wagon from the weeds the horse had been nibbling, down the road into town. My father waved over his head without looking back.

"What'll you do today?" my mother said.

"I'll go past the burntland about two miles, to a barrens. North of Mint Cove."

"Oh, everyone's talking about such faraway places this morning. I'm wistful. Maybe I should go somewhere different, too. Visit my long-lost sister in Vancouver, for instance. Anyway, darling, why the barrens?"

"Because a journal wants water pipits, and the barrens is popular with that bird."

Yet I did not make it to the barrens. When I reached the burntland, a stretch of scrub pines and stumps, I saw a three-toed woodpecker right out in the open and got all caught up with it. It was a male, with a large yellow crown patch and black wings. The black barrings on its side reminded me of the rough shadings and texture made when I would rotate a pencil against paper to sharpen it. I sketched its comings and goings all morning. He was foraging two stumps about twenty yards apart. Hammering, echoing, sometimes in quick bursts like Morse code, other times in a single thrust, perhaps impaling a bark beetle with a perfectly aimed blow. Every now and then he let loose a cackling call that befit some general notion of insanity, while flying in erratic dips and glides, scrawling the air. I knew that I could never capture that motion on paper. After working up a dozen or so sketches, I walked to Romeo Gillette's store.

There were no customers. Romeo was at the metal scale weighing nails, dividing them into quarter-, half-, and one-pound bags, which he lined up on the counter. I bought some bread and a piece of cheese, then sat down on a barrel to eat lunch.

"Did my mother mention a catalogue?" I said.

"She mentioned wedding rings some time ago. I showed her a selection."

He pointed to a stack of catalogues at the end of the

counter. "Third one down, I believe," he said. "Turn the stool facing away from me if you want privacy. I can't leave these nails."

Sitting on a stool at the counter, I took out the piece of string with Cora's ring size on it. But I saw Romeo glance over, so quickly put the string back in my pocket. I studied the rings in the catalogue. There were close-up illustrations. Some of the rings were on ring fingers. There were floating faces of women admiring rings on their own or other women's hands. On a few pages there were grooms. Romeo saw me staring. "The grooms all look pleased, don't they?" he said.

"Page after page of rings."

"Mind-boggling, isn't it? How many choices."

"I've marked a page here. I want the last ring in the last row, the simple one to the right. I'll leave the ring size with you. It's on this string."

I put the string on the counter.

"What about your ring, Fabian? Did you forget, you get married, you both get rings?"

"I'll need a piece of string."

"Just take one off the spool there, end of the scissors and knife shelf."

I cut a piece of string, tied it around my finger, knotted it off, set it next to Cora's string.

"That ring decision didn't take too long," Romeo said. "Well, poor Margaret's heart is going to break like a wave on the rocks."

"That's one guess," I said.

He slid more nails onto the scale, which needed oiling.

"You know the laws of human nature and Newfoundland are not for mortals to figure out. My father used to say that. Course, that was after his heart seized up, when every minute was a confusing puzzle to him."

"Margaret's sure a puzzle." I wanted both to end the conversation and to get deeper into it. "She's so full of human nature, I doubt ten men could figure her out."

"You might feel alone in the over-all predicament, which is why you just invited nine other men in."

"It was just a number at random. It didn't mean anything."

"If you say so."

"I say so."

"Well, Margaret quite possibly can fend for herself, once you're married down in Halifax. That's a choice she'll have to make. And fate will play a card."

"Which choice do you mean?"

"Choice of a man to be with; there are eligible men about. A choice, if a young woman has imagination. There's a good man. A bad man. There's a number of in between men. There's giving up entirely, then the very next day getting surprised. There's—"

"That's a long enough list."

"I see you don't like the thought of Margaret with somebody else, eh?"

"Did Botho August pay for Margaret's Canada-made stockings?"

"Yes, he did. If she told you that, she told you the truth.

What's more, I mentioned that to Enoch and he paid Botho back the cost of the stockings."

"Margaret never told me that part."

"Margaret, Margaret. You know, a year before my wife, Annie, passed on, rest her soul, she came home one night from cards. You recall how Annie got together with Dorris Letto, Dara Olden, Edna Forbisher, Mary Kieley, and sometimes younger ones such as Alice Heltasch and Margaret Handle? Hearts and Draw Fives were the most popular games. Or Old Maid, the card game that migrated up from Halifax or down from St. John's. Well, on this particular night, it was Old Maid. The ladies brought bread, tea, and Margaret had her customary flask of spirits in tow. The game was held in the Lettos' kitchen.

"Annie told me what happened.

"The cards were being handed along, you know, how the rules dictate. And suddenly Margaret lets out a whoop and pounds her fist on the table. Then she crumbles up the Old Maid card and pops it directly into her mouth! Chews it. I mean, swallows it right down.

"Margaret then says, 'Oh, girls, well, I'm sorry. I'll have Romeo order another deck from Halifax at my expense. No, I'll have him order two. One for us, one for me to keep in reserve.' Then she dabbed the corner of her mouth like she'd nibbled a cookie with tea."

"I'm sure it was a once-in-a-lifetime moment for all of them," I said.

I watched Romeo weigh nails. I thought of what my parents had told me about his life. He had never intended to run a store. He had inherited it in the aftermath of his father's heart attack. Actually, Romeo was all set to become a doctor. As a young man he had attended two years of medical college in London. Recognizing a chance to have a permanent doctor in Witless Bay, and because Romeo was so well liked, Reverend Weebe (he had succeeded Clemons, and later on Sillet took his place) put out a local call for funds. Finally, enough money was raised for Romeo's steamer fare and tuition. He was about halfway through his studies when Dalton Gillette was stricken. Once notified, Romeo booked passage to Halifax on the first steamer he could afford, then took the mail boat home, all of which took four months. The only thing he had bought in London was a new suitcase.

At first, Dalton could move only his eyes and feet. He could swallow, too. Romeo said that heart attacks allowed for unpredictable combinations of mobility in the human body, and that things might change day by day. "The mystery of it's way bigger than the science of it," he said. After a few weeks with his son, however, Dalton rallied to where he could stand up and sit down, piss on his own, chew down forkfuls of meat, and say a few logical sentences, which more or less lurched out of him. Romeo spent hours reading books to his father. At meals he would cut up Dalton's food into small bites, search for fishbones, hoist the spoon or fork to his father's mouth, then wipe it clean with a napkin.

Romeo made over a storeroom into convalescent quarters. He hired Annic Stuyvcsant to work the counter, and a year later Annie, a lovely, clear-thinking woman with a mischievous sense of humor, married Romeo. It was her second marriage; a brief scourge of smallpox had widowed her at age eighteen. By and by, Annie got the store's financial records in order and took over as manager, while Romeo attended to his father, saw to inventories, and was the general stock boy.

Using two years of medical training and a lot of intuition, Romeo thought up ways to try to funnel Dalton's frustrations, his unwieldy temper, into a healing force, part of which worked and part of which did not. He would walk his father back and forth across the room, hundreds of times in a row. He made Dalton read out loud, even if at times he could not get past the first sentence. He made Dalton lift a fork, even if there was no food on it. "We'll get you back to your old self," Romeo would say. "Or almost."

Right up until age sixty-one, when he was stricken, Dalton was a rambunctious figure in Witless Bay. He referred to himself as a brigand. I remember later looking that word up in the dictionary that Isaac Sprague had sent me and laughing out loud. Dalton's own wife, Romeo's mother, was named Ethel Kitchener. She had been Helen Twombly's closest friend. Ethel died one night in her sleep, no one knew from what. "Ethel was a private person," Dalton said. "She died in a private way. I prefer being the widower of Ethel than a husband to anyone else, even in my imagination." And Dalton never did remarry.

He had once been on a ship to South America. When he ran the store, he would often greet a customer with "Buenos morning!" or "Buenos afternoon!" But he said it in a way that avoided his showing off too much, because he had thought to match one word of Spanish with one of English. On the wall behind his counter was a mottled anaconda skin stretched out in a glass case. "As I was touring the river Amazon," he was fond of reporting, "it slithered aboard my dugout canoe. But it did not debark!" He would make a chopping motion as if wielding a machete, and laugh boisterously. In fact, Dalton's laugh had its own reputation. It was like an odd musical composition; it began with a tentative humming, then burst forth in donkey brays, sometimes ending up with a coughing fit.

Dalton was of middle height, with fine ink-black hair and bright blue eyes that caught you off guard if you had been too convinced of his character by his long, sad face. He was a world away from dour. And never was there a more direct inheritance, bone structure to steady gait, hearty laugh to love of imported shoes, than between Dalton and Romeo. So strong was their physical resemblance that it was easy to imagine a line of nearly identical faces going centuries back to the heart of England, the country of their ancestors, the place Romeo hated so much.

After months of grueling and loving work, Romeo got his father to where he could take a walk every day, and his favorite place to do that was on the cliff path behind the lighthouse. "My father's a stubborn man," Romeo had said. "He dares his own sense of balance, just him and his walking cane." And then of course Margaret ran into Dalton on her bicycle. Word had it that Margaret walked the bicycle all the way to the wharf, down the dock, propped it against

the *Aunt Ivy Barnacle*'s cabin, told Enoch what had happened. Enoch walked with her up to Gillette's store. Enoch
left right away for St. John's and brought back Mitchell
Kelb.

Back to the day that my father left for Anticosti. I mentioned it was July 2, Margaret's birthday.

Having left Gillette's store, I bought a sea bass from Peter
Traynor, who had just come in from dory fishing in the
Bay. I brought the fish home wrapped in straw. Then I
went back to the wharf. I sat with my sketchbook, trying
to capture how cormorants perched on buoys, fanned out
their wings like a closet rack full of black neckties, drying
them in the sun. How they held their beaks gaped open.

In his letters Sprague had insisted that I work with birds
I did not particularly enjoy looking at, and cormorants were
that. "I have one student who at first could not bear the
sight of any long-necked waders," he wrote. "Herons,
egrets, and so forth. After two years, she draws them beau-
tifully and the question of likes or dislikes is no longer
there." Yet for some reason I portrayed cormorants as
spectres, grim, foreboding out on the buoys. Warning what,
I did not know, but I had turned cormorants into superstitions of my own making. In my drawings of this bird
Sprague found "an irksome prejudice. Granted, cormorants
can look eerily like a fossil bird come alive in your harbor,
there. Nonetheless, they are worthy of everything but your
poor drawings of them. Yours are indeed poor. I request
five pages of cormorants, seen from every possible angle, in

order to get your thinking right about this bird. Bird art must derive its power from emotion, naturally, but emotions have to be tempered and forged by sheer discipline, all for the sake of posterity."

I was fairly succeeding with ducks, shorebirds, crows, ospreys. I failed miserably with cormorants. No journal accepted a single one. Can a person truly hate a bird? I do not know, but I hated my failure with them. Once I even dreamed of Margaret shooting cormorants from her bedroom window, picking them off one by one from buoys and stanchions. In real life, though, I am sure she never did that; she shot only what she needed.

Anyway, by dusk on July 2, the sky was clear except for stretches of washboard clouds. I walked home. I opened the door. And there was Botho August sitting at our kitchen table. My mother had set three places for supper, though Botho's plate was not at my father's customary spot. Botho had apparently brought a music box, a miniature merry-go-round bedecked with painted ribbons. The salt shaker rode on it. The music box was working a plunky tune, but when I walked in my mother frantically reached to stop it. Botho reached to prevent her hand. Their hands touched and my mother drew hers back as if from a hot skillet.

Botho had a boot off. He looked at me, then at the other boot, which he then pried off with his toes. "Ah, there, much better," he said. "I had a stone in there."

My mother gave a short sigh, then watched the music box wind down to a standstill.

"I'm going to be employed by Mr. August," she said.

"On a part-time basis, and out of his own pocket," Botho added, though he spoke only to my mother. Annoyed, he had flattened his voice as if they had rehearsed the moment and my mother could not remember the first simple thing they had agreed to tell me.

"In the lighthouse?" I said.

"That's where Mr. August works, yes," my mother said. "It'll do me good. I'll feel useful, in a new way. I often go on my morning walk past the lighthouse, when I do go on a morning walk. Now I'll simply change that to an evening stroll, stop in, sit at the wireless. Mr. August has agreed to teach me how to talk to the schooners, by beam and wireless."

"We'll take it slow at first, then get to the more complicated work," Botho said, still looking only at my mother. "It's good for the village. What if I drop dead on a foggy night. Who's going to help boats out to sea? I need an apprentice, eh?"

"I'll learn to work the light, the foghorn, all the apparatuses," my mother said. "It interests me. It would be rare and useful knowledge for a woman, this day and age, even if Mr. August doesn't drop dead."

Botho wore suspenders over a faded denim shirt tucked into his trousers, better suited, I thought, to colder weather. His hair was neatly combed. His way of dealing with tension was to splay his fingers open, taut against the table, like a man about to play the piano, and press down hard until the tips were white. He held his hands that way, staring at my mother.

"This boy doesn't like me, Alaric," Botho said.

"He's not a boy," my mother said.

"He holds a fierce grudge from Thanksgiving at Romeo Gillette's table, when I said a thing to him. I can't remember what I said. I've been told I'm not polite."

"I told you that," my mother said.

"I'll eat at Spivey's tonight," I said.

"Good. All the more fish, potatoes—let's see, what else?" Botho said. He leaned over and opened the oven door. "Cake. All the more for us. Enough for three's enough for two."

"I worked to catch that fish," I said.

"This time of year you can whistle a fish from the harbor," Botho said. "Besides, I saw you buy it. I was at the wharf. You didn't see me, maybe. But I saw you. I saw you buy the fish."

"No, you didn't see him, either," my mother said to Botho. "I *told* you that Fabian bought the fish."

"I'll eat in the restaurant," I said.

"This is your house, too," my mother said. "You don't get exiled to Spivey's. Darling, please sit down. We have a guest you don't care for is all. That happens in a life."

"Once too often," I said.

"Fabian, please. Wash up for supper."

"I've seen you in that dress in church, Mother." She had on a light blue cotton dress with a white lace shawl. "But just now, I don't recognize you in it."

Storming from my house, I bypassed Spivey's and went directly to Boas LaCotte's sawmill barn. It had been a favorite refuge since childhood, a hideout. Whenever Lambert was away from the village, yet not at his trout camp, he left his crippled owl, Matilda, in LaCotte's care. I did not know an owl's life span, but this one seemed very old to me. In the barn, Boas kept it tethered by one scaly leg (the other leg had been mangled in a muskrat trap) to a sawhorse. It was on the sawhorse now. The barn had high rafters. The floor was littered with wood scraps, chips, sawdust, random planks. I loved this barn most early in the mornings, when sawdust in the air suspended sunlight in swirling eddies and traced the sun's slantings from the roof to the ground.

When I stepped into the barn, the owl shuffled excitedly along the sawhorse, its wings ruffling loudly, lifting it up a few inches. It rolled its head in its socket, then tore at a mouse Boas had nailed by the tail to the sawhorse. The owl spread a clipped wing like a magician's cape over the mouse, revealed it, covered it again. The owl usually got worked up when a person came close.

I sat there until dark, then took a lantern from its shelf, lit it, found a piece of scrap paper, took a pencil from my pocket, and began to sketch the owl. It was a frenzied effort, though. I was just killing time. Botho's presence in my house, let alone on the very day my father had left, had skewed my thinking, violated every notion of propriety. Yet I had not been fully able to grasp the forebodings. How could I? It was enough, just then, to be shocked at the sheer audacity of the circumstances. I had had to flee my own house, where suddenly I could not breathe the same air as Botho August. I did not know how to think about all this.

I did not know how to think about anything, except what I discovered minute by minute. I stopped drawing. I sat there. The owl picked apart the mouse. It got totally dark in the barn.

Finally, I returned home. The house was dark, my mother gone. No note. No message scribbled down. I made a cup of tea for her out of habit, out of misguided hope that she had only gone for a walk with Botho. Her new evening stroll. But of course the tea was long past cooling by the time I nodded off, head down on the table. In the morning I had just coffee for breakfast, leaving a note saying I had gone to work at Portugal Cove.

On the way to Portugal Cove, I stopped at Margaret's house. She was in the attic working on accounts.

"I had a cake waiting," she said. "It was my birthday and you forgot I'd invited you for cake, or else you remembered, which is worse for your not showing. You're a worm under a rock, Fabian. I had a cake."

"It was my original evening plan. I looked forward to it, Margaret. Truthfully. But then this other—"

"And no gift, either. No gift last night, and from the looks of it, no gift now."

"It's true."

"You look about as repentant as I thought you'd look, which is not at all. What, did Alaric say, 'It's not exactly a national holiday! Come help me with the dishes'? Fabian, I do not forgive you."

"I'll make it up to you. What happened was, I got home yesterday for supper—"

"I saw you yesterday, at the wharf, as a matter of fact. I was up the wharf a bit, talking with Imogene Malraux, who'd just broken her finger and had it in a splint. I didn't know you could break your finger just hanging up clothes. God Almighty, you situate your hand wrong between a blouse and a clothespin and everything suddenly changes. What a stupid life this is."

"Did you see Botho August at the wharf?"

"No, I did not."

"Anyway, I got home. I walked into my own kitchen. And who is sitting at the supper table?"

"Botho August."

"The same."

"Well, some days life has no big surprises, eh?"

"He was about to eat supper with us!"

"Your father gone to Anticosti?"

"Yes."

"Sit down, Fabian. I'll set aside my disgust about my birthday for five or so minutes. Sit down, on my lap if you like. Your voice is off-kilter."

"I'll stand, thanks."

"What happened next, pray tell?"

"He had brought my mother a music box."

"A music box. I see. And?"

"I left the house. I stayed in LaCotte's barn awhile. I went back home. Nobody was there."

"Well, such excitement. But it would have been as exciting with me last night, in a different way, naturally. When you got home was there any food left on the plates?"

"Margaret, what are you talking about?"

"That you're making me a detective here."

"Oh—I'm sorry. I'm—"

"God, okay, *now* I see. Your mother and Botho."

"Yes."

"She wasn't at breakfast, I take it."

"Right."

Margaret jotted down a few figures in a column, tucked the pencil behind her ear, pushed her hand through her hair, then looked at the floor.

"So, that's it, then," she said softly but clearly. "Alaric's an adulteress."

"Is that what you think?"

"It's either true or it isn't. I'd bet it's true."

"She never once, not *once*, mentioned his name in our house."

"Now I'm utterly convinced it's true."

5

Helen Twombly

All summer, right up to the day in October, in fact, when my father came home, my mother spent every night in the lighthouse. The change in my life had been immediate, strange, disturbing: the truth of it spun me sideways and backwards. One moment, I could almost shrug it off as her passing fancy for Botho. The next, her adultery battered my senses. In the rare times we were alone together in the house, she would sing lyrics or hum tunes I had never heard. Their source had to be Botho's gramophone records. The songs were part of my mother's new world, a short distance away in the lighthouse. It was a kind of secret music, because it meant more to her than I could fathom. She knew I could not bear to hear the songs. She had seen me actually clamp my hands over my ears. I would leave the room. She sang them so I would leave the room.

We had set up a strict pattern of avoidance, my mother and I. We fell into it; it had gone unspoken. One day there is a family, the next day there is not. I needed even a make-shift philosophy about it. One night, I decided that her infidelity was a result of her sadness, therefore inevitable, ill-fated, and nothing could change that now. Yet looming up ahead was the prospect of my father's coming home, which I both longed for and dreaded beyond reckoning.

I drifted into eating at Spivey's every night. At first I merely looked forward to it, then came to rely on it, just to not eat alone. Lemuel, who must have known about my mother and Botho, avoided the subject. After about the twentieth night in a row of my sitting at the same table, he said, "So, my cooking's finally got you mesmerized, eh?"

I went weeks at a time without drawing or painting.

One night in late August I actually met my mother as she walked to the lighthouse and I walked home from an after-supper coffee with Margaret. I had seen her lantern up ahead. It was awkward. I did not know at what distance from my mother to stop.

Finally, we stood an arm's length apart. "It's a nice night out," she said. "Ten thousand stars in the sky exactly. I counted them."

That very phrase was one she would say to me as a boy, and it had always made me laugh and think that it was true, she had actually gone to the trouble to count stars.

"I don't like any of the songs you hum in the house," I said.

"Well, all right, now that I'm aware of it, I'll stop."

"You were aware of it before. I just finally wanted to say it."

"Fair enough. But of course, when I'm standing at the sink, or making tea, they still go round in my head."

"Nothing I can do about that."

"You could knock me senseless with a pot. Look, I'm still your mother. I've still got all the feelings toward you I ever had. It's just that now I've got new feelings for some-one else, Fabian."

"And toward my father?" Yet I did not want to hear any answer so I began to walk away.

"Fabian, I forgot to mention—"

I stopped. She waited for me to turn around.

"Margaret Handle left her nightshirt in the house. I was tidying up and discovered it. I washed it and hung it out to dry."

"She'll wish you hadn't."

"Tell her you did it, then. I don't care." She nervously smoothed her hands down the side of her face. "Well, I'm neither early nor late for work, but I'll be on my way. I was just up to visit Helen Twombly's grave by moonlight."

A few weeks earlier, during supper at Spivey's, Margaret had said, "If we keep it to Tuesdays and Thursdays, I'll sleep at your house, generous soul that I am. I'm used to an empty house, whereas one gives you the jitters. I'll help you out."

That very night in my kitchen she unpacked her night-case. I did not know she even owned one. She took out a toothbrush and a bottle of whiskey. She took two glasses from the cupboard, filled them, and we sat at the table.

"I prefer that we sleep in your parents' bed," she said. "I'm sorry—do you still consider it your parents' bed?"

"I don't know."

"Well, think about it in any spare time before we go to sleep. Hey—look what I brought!"

She reached into the case, taking out a deck of cards.

"This is an Old Maid deck," she said. "Have you ever seen this hag close up?"

"No."

Margaret swallowed the last of her whiskey, then poured a second glass. She fanned the cards out on the table, located an Old Maid, and set her apart.

"Don't eat that card for dessert," I said.

"Oh, you heard about that, did you?"

"Romeo told me."

"It's not the sort of game to enjoy by yourself. It's bad enough with a crowd. Want to play?"

"No. I don't know how, and don't care to learn."

"A bit goddamned touchy tonight, aren't we. It's just a game for the ladies, is that it? Well, what do you want to do, then?"

"Sit here. Sit here and not think out loud."

"Not think out loud about what?" She finished her drink.

"I've got money worries. I've been using up my savings at Spivey's. There's been no work at the dry dock. I can't seem to draw. I owe on commissions rendered in advance. I've spent that money. I've lagged behind. I've got money worries."

"Yes, and what with the rings on order."

"No—no, actually—" These words slipped out. "Actually, the Hollys—"

"Are paying for the rings? How pathetic."

"You'll finally hate me for Halifax, won't you?"

"Probably I will before you go there. I've felt some hate already."

"You are a blunt woman, Margaret."

"Fabian dear, I'm only exactly as blunt as life is, forgive the preachy sentence. You're going to marry a stranger. Your mother is adultering nightly. Your father's got one hell of a homecoming in store. How much more bluntness do you want?"

"What I want is not to talk. I want to sit here not talking."

"Well, what am I supposed to do here, twiddle my thumbs? Whistle on the open bottle, *whew whew whew*, or what?"

"My mother has some books. Would you like to read a book? There's a shelf of them. There's things to read in this house."

"All right, then. I'm more than content with that brainstorm. God Almighty, there's a lot to pack into a night, isn't there? A book, a bottle, *whew whew whew whew*"— she blew shrill whispers on the bottle. "And then there's your very tough decision as to which bed we sleep in. I'll look forward to resolving that. Well, we'll meet up in one bed or another, anyway, and you'll show me what you've painted—you are going to paint for a while, aren't you?— and I'll tell you about what I've read. Two little school kids on a nighttime adventure. All right. Finish your drink,

there, my friend. Momma's working late and Poppa's elsewhere. And I'm about to go deep into my reading."

"You finish mine."

Margaret picked up my glass and took it into the living
room. She sat in front of the bookshelf and ran her finger
along the spines. I went into my bedroom, mixed paint in
two jar tops, and took out a piece of blank paper.

I did not look in on Margaret, did not hear her out in
the house. In an hour I had gotten well started on an ovenbird. The ovenbird is in the warbler family. It has olive-
colored wings and tail and upper body, but its belly is
heavily streaked in black. You often saw ovenbirds walking
on the ground, as I had that week behind the sawmill,
though sometimes they perched on low branches. I thought
it was easy to detect a human word in their call, *teacher
teacher teacher*, each repetition louder than the one before.
Maritime Monthly had advanced me two dollars and would
pay another two on receipt of ten ovenbirds. I badly needed
the money. This new drawing was coming along nicely. It
was best to keep at it. But Margaret knocked.

"We could start in your bed, and later move to Orkney
and Alaric's," she said through the closed door. She was
talking louder than necessary. "The bottle is empty, and
reading is hard work, it turns out. Or: we could start out
in their bed. There's more choices than you might think,
Fabian."

"Come in."

She opened the door. "Thank you," she said. She had
doused the lantern wick, and in the vaguely moonlit kitchen

a ribbon of smoke wavered up. She had on her nightshirt.

"We can start out in here," I said.

"All right, then. At least that's a decision."

She got directly under my sheet and blanket, pulling them up to her chin. "Cozy, cozy, cozy," she said. "If you want, just go on with that bird. I'm perfectly content. I'm worn out from reading, though."

"No, I'm through for now."

"Fabian, there's a second bottle in my overnight case. Be a dear, will you?"

I got the bottle and handed it to Margaret. She took three swigs, then set the bottle on the floor next to the bed.

"All of that reading hurt my eyes. Would you turn down your lantern?"

I guttered the wick and went into the kitchen. I washed my face, dried it with a towel, then brushed my teeth and took off my clothes. I had never done that before, undressed in the kitchen. I put on my nightshirt, laid my clothes across a chair, and got into bed. Margaret took a long drink.

"Fabian," she said, her voice cracking slightly. She hesitated a moment. "I bet you think that Witless Bay is so small, whatever goes on people will hear of it. Sooner or later, but eventually."

"If you're referring to my mother and Botho, yes, everyone surely knows about it. I don't get stared at in Gillette's store, though. Some days it all bothers me worse than the day before."

"No—I meant *me*. Something about yours truly, Margaret Handle."

She began to cry, racking sobs broken only by moaning and deep sniffling and coughs. It just took me aback. I stood, then sat down again. It was such powerful crying that it turned her face into a child's; not just any child's, but it was her face in Gillette's storeroom, so many years back, when Romeo had slapped her. To me it was that face exactly, and it had the effect of jumbling together all the years I had known Margaret. She wept in a way that seemed beyond comforting. She sat straight up then, facing away from me.

"What's going on here?" I said. "I don't get it."

"No, you don't."

"Maybe you shouldn't drink more just now."

"Fabian, do you know whom I consummated with, one time, before you came along? My first time."

She took a drink, then a deep, ratcheting breath. Somehow she was speaking clearly now, and there was a terrible sadness in her voice, and it seemed a strength beyond my comprehension for her to speak at all.

"None of my business," I said.

"That's correct. But something you don't know about can still affect you."

"Don't talk in circles, Margaret. It's not like you."

I reached out to touch her shoulder, but she could not see that. She was still turned away. I pulled back my hand.

Now, turning, she looked at me. "I *mean* Alaric's way of treating me."

"She hasn't liked you since you were a little girl."

"Well, it got worse for a reason in particular."

"What reason?"

"A year before you and I started up together. Before our Tuesdays and Thursdays. Before that." But she could not catch her breath and stopped talking. Then she outright moaned, "Oh—" She wiped her face with the hem of her nightshirt, then looked into my face.

"Fabian—listen carefully. From Botho August's bed, you can see so far out across the water. It's—"

She kicked the bottle across the room, clutched herself, rolled back and forth on the bed as though poisoned. As though the memory had poisoned her. "It's all hopeless," she said. "You're hopeless, Fabian. Get out. Get out of the room now. Go away."

"I'll sit here with you. I'll make us coffee."

"You're such a child. You just don't know how to think about what I've just told you, about me and Botho August. Well, it'll all sink in. You'll finally understand that Alaric knows what happened between me and Botho, and that she's jealous of me. Of my past with him."

"One night is not a *past*."

"It is to Alaric, now that she's in love with Botho."

"Not love—I doubt it. Not that."

"Well, I can't expect you to grow up all in one night."

"I'm no child. Confused as one—"

"By the way, Alaric has some interesting reading. And not on the shelf. Behind it. In a shoebox, like a mouse would nest in. Letters are all neatly stacked in there, Fabian, tied in string."

Margaret took some deep breaths, calming herself.

"Those are my mother's letters."

105

Now Margaret took on a sneering, mocking tone, quoting a letter: "Richibucto is *such* a lovely place. Alaric dear, you simply *must* visit us here sometime. Of course, our home is yours."

"Those letters are private."

"God, I could vomit."

"Did you put them back?"

"Such a child," Margaret said, her voice trailing off. She closed her eyes, slowly got under the covers again, and in a moment was asleep.

I made coffee. I stayed up all night, not drawing.

The following morning Margaret was sick with a hangover, fever, vomiting. She woke mid-morning, had a few sips of tea, and got back into bed. "Don't speak to me," she said.

My mother, of course, did not come home for breakfast or lunch. I drew at the kitchen table, looked in on Margaret, to find her either in a fitful, sweating sleep or glaring at me. "Get out!" she would say. "Don't look at me!" My mother stayed away for supper. After dark, I persuaded Margaret to try a cup of rice broth. She sat at the table in her night-shirt. She looked wretched and pale, and seemed to have only enough strength to lower her face to the broth. "Don't watch me eat," she said. I had to wait in the living room.

"I'm through," she called.

I went back into the kitchen. "All right to look at you now?" I said.

"I don't give a good goddamn."

We heard footsteps on the porch; the door opened and

in came my mother, waving an envelope. "Oh," she said, taking in Margaret's presence. Glancing at me, she tucked the letter into a bag containing a loaf of bread and a bottle of milk.

Margaret rubbed her temples with her thumbs. "Your son here, Alaric, and I were sharing soup like an old married couple," she said. "Care to join us?"

My mother sat down, still holding the bread and milk. "Margaret," she said, "I've got something to tell Fabian of direct consequence to his future, if you please."

"Got a new letter from Richibucto in hand?" Margaret said. "I read all the others. I'm interested in keeping up, you know."

"A private moment with my son," my mother said.

Margaret looked at me. "Fabian," she said weakly, "I'll need some help to our bed."

Margaret leaned against me as we walked into my room. She sat on the bed. "I considered swooning, but didn't want to give Alaric any entertainment. God, I drank enough last night to kill an ox. I had two of the worst nightmares in history, then your soup. I'm deathly ill in the house where the mother hates me. But you know what? Just look at *you*. You seem worse off."

Then we heard my mother break into a sea dirge, alternately singing the lyrics and humming.

"Alaric likes to kill sailors, she sings those dirges so often," Margaret said. "I heard her singing one near the church the other day. She didn't know I was close behind. She likes a song that leaves widows and orphans."

107

We heard: ". . . the tenth of November, a storm come hard, oh, oh, into Bleak Joke Cove."

"Bless her heart," Margaret said. "Just a few moments back in her own house, she breaks into song."

My mother did not have a good singing voice, not important for dirges; she seemed to force a lower octave, and she forgot words or cut songs off on purpose.

Yet something else interrupted her this time. There was a voice calling with great urgency at the kitchen window. "Fabian! Margaret! Fabian Vas!"

I stepped into the kitchen. My mother looked at me with blank panic.

"Even if he knew the truth, Father wouldn't call out my last name," I said. "And how would he know to call for Margaret here?"

My mother opened the door. Romeo Gillette stood there in his rain slicker, hat, and galoshes, all streaked with water. The wind was up. "This rain blew in suddenly," he said. "It's not a squall yet and might not be."

"What's wrong?" my mother said.

Romeo took us all in: Margaret in her wrinkled nightshirt, leaning against me, my mother raking her fingers through her hair. "Peter Kieley," Romeo said, "was working late at the wharf. He saw Helen Twombly row out. She got into a dinghy. She had bottles of milk with her. The harbor's now almost entirely fogged in."

"She wants to end it," Margaret said. "The poor thing just does."

"Who's to say?" Romeo half-shouted, then calmed himself. "Not you. Not Reverend Sillet. Who's to say that? Who's to allow such a thing to happen?"

"I'll get a lantern," I said.

"Hurry, then," Romeo said. "She was my mother's best friend."

Romeo turned from the door and was quickly out of sight in the rain and darkness.

"I'm going, too," Margaret said. "I'm going with you, Fabian."

"Don't be stupid," my mother said. "You're in no condition to be out there. You stink of vomit, Margaret, and you can hardly stand up."

"Go back to your lighthouse, Alaric," Margaret said.

Margaret went into my room and got dressed. I heard her coughing. She came out wearing one of my sweaters over her own clothes. "Is there a spare slicker?"

"Rain gear's in the pantry."

"Botho August could be of some help in this," Margaret said. "Tell him to get his light going."

"I'm sure that somebody's got to him already," my mother said. "There's fog out, he'll be alert to it."

"Tell him, anyway."

My mother drew her eyes to slits, held the bag of groceries like they were all she owned, then fled the house.

Margaret and I set out a few moments later. We walked half-blind in the fog toward the lighthouse. The rain had let up some. When we passed the lighthouse, its beam was off. No lantern in any window, fog swirling around the housing.

At the steepest incline above the wharf, we stopped stock-still, listening to voices from down below, though we could not make out the words.

"I hate to think of Helen out there now," I said.

"She's made a choice," Margaret said. She coughed hard. "Poor woman wants to end it. There's no one left to talk with is what she told me, just last week. I went to visit Helen more often than you might have guessed."

"She liked you."

Each of us held a lantern. We made our way down.

At the wharf, familiar sounds—voices, rainy drizzle on tarpaulin, masts creaking, dories knocking against each other—all seemed to struggle through some thick garment of fog. Life on the wharf felt ghostly.

Margaret bent over coughing. I had linked my arm in hers, so bent down with her.

"They should just leave Helen alone now," she said. "Okay, I'm fine, let me stand up."

"They won't leave her alone."

We heard a dory shove off. "Get the lantern turned up—" And suddenly the dory materialized out of the fog and glided right past us, close to the dock. We saw the faces of Boas LaCotte and Giles LaCotte, almost familiar in the opaque light.

Soon the harbor was a scatter of lanterns floating above the water, face level, shoulder level. Helen had surely extinguished her own light by now, if she had brought one to begin with.

Margaret and I located a dory and climbed in. It did not matter to whom it belonged. The oars were under the thwarts. We set our lanterns between us on the middle thwart. Guided by other lights, I rowed. The long night of drifting began. The vigil began.

Throughout the cold, dark hours the fog held, and like survivors of a shipwreck in lifeboats, people called out their names, names that wended through the darkness with the force of grim affirmation, of astonishment at this common experience. "Peter Kieley—" a voice said. It was repeated, then answered: "Peter Kieley, this is Harry Delacroix." It started up then, this consensus of rowers, like a children's round of overlapping verses, except devoid of music and playfulness. "Harry Delacroix, this is Elmer Wyatt." Then: "Elmer Wyatt, this is your brother, Sam Wyatt."

And then: "Where's the goddamn lighthouse beam?" I do not know who called that out.

Margaret and I heard a dory close by. We heard oars dripping. An oar's length away, Reverend Sillet now held his lantern up near his face. I had always thought of his face as a place where mannerisms resided: overly anxious grins, clownish frowns—a face that overdid emotions. It was a wide face, whose tics were distracting. I think Sillet knew this, because he had moved his pulpit a considerable distance back from the front pew. He was, however, a man of great seriousness, too, because he would cloister himself in his library, the midnight oil burning. He was rather portly, physically very strong, agile. He was about fifty-five, with pronounced jowls, thinning grey hair, dark brown eyes with thick eyebrows. His voice was gravelly. Neither of us had ever made much of an effort to know each other.

In the dory, Sillet moved his lantern closer to us. "Ah,

Fabian, Margaret, it's you," he said. "You know, being out here has given me an uneasy thought."

"What's that, pray tell?" Margaret said.

"That Helen is the only one of us still alive. That she's really back on shore, tending to her bottles. And that, lured and harried forth by the terrible illusion of her suicide, we are all now drifting in purgatory. That Witless Bay Harbour was purgatory all along, only we didn't recognize it as such."

"I don't like your imagination," Margaret said, racked then with coughing. She spat. Barely croaking out her words, she said, "If I had your imagination, I'd slip overboard. Fabian—row away from him, right now, please. He gives me the jitters."

"I'm taking you back in," I said. "Helen's probably caught her death out here. No reason for you to catch yours."

We rowed back to the dock and Margaret climbed out. Standing on the dock, she said, "I'm going to my own house."

I rowed out again, looking back once to see Margaret's lantern fade.

"Richmond Fauvette, this is Oliver Parmelee." Oliver's voice and slapping oars were nearby. "Oliver Parmelee, this is Fabian Vas."

I do not know at what hour people began to return. They had searched the harbor high and low and still were not giving up, only stopping their search for the remainder of the night. Yet I did not go back. For some reason I stayed in the dory. There is a kind of peacefulness that exists only after other boats have left. I felt that now. In an hour or so, the wharf was to my north. The rain had stopped. I could see the first tinges of light on the horizon, sun filling the clouds from the bottom up. There was a cormorant on a buoy. It had its wings outspread, hoarding, I thought, the early warmth. There was a gull on each post of the old dock, the one with rotted slats and posts and underpinnings; it had been rotted for years and was Margaret's favorite place as a child to ride her bicycle.

I had been gazing off into the distance when I heard a hollow clunk against the hull. Leaning over the side, I saw a milk bottle. I placed it in the boat. I got my bearings. I was at the mouth of Caroline Cove, halfway between Witless Bay and Bay Bulls. I had drawn bitterns and teals here. I was a hundred or so yards offshore. I took up the oars and rowed toward a line of boulders and flat rocks to portage.

Almost immediately I saw Helen's dinghy. It was wedged into a sandbar. Farther on were rocks jutting from the water. Small waves slapped against Helen Twombly, who was curled on a ledge of rock. One high-topped shoe drifted, though still fastened by its lace to her ankle. She used to tie the laces above her shoe tops, crossing them twice, then making a bow. Some sort of twisting or tossing must have removed her shoes, I thought; Helen must have gone through something awful to have had that happen. My second thought was, What Providence is this? Yet the phrasing was not mine, not mine at all. It came from the Bible or maybe one of Sillet's sermons. I felt ashamed and stupid. Here I was, out all night, then I'd found the body of someone who was already old when I was a boy, hardly common experiences. You would think an original utterance would get into my head. But all I could finally think of to do next was fit Helen's shoe back on.

The shrieks of the carrion gulls quickened my blood then, and I rowed to Helen. Closer now, I could recognize her flower-print dress, though it was sequined with dry salt. Vines of kelp, slick leaves shining, festooned her legs, strangling her waist and arms. Sand flies buzzed loudly in droves on her face and hands. I anchored, tying up with a tow rope. I went ahead and forced the shoe over Helen's bloated foot. The deep gash on her cheek was stitched with flies, her skin bruised but otherwise drained of color. Still, she had a human expression, and if I could describe it one way, I would say that she looked puzzled. I said, "You got even smaller," but that was all.

I took out a jackknife and cut away the kelp, then hoisted Helen into the dory. I could cover her completely with my raincoat. I rowed home. The current ran across the bow, so it took a long time.

On the dock in the distance, Giles LaCotte, Romeo Gillette, and Oliver Parmelee were preparing to set out again. I shouted to them. They waved. I was too exhausted to do anything but row steadily. I knew that they could see I had something in the dory, a cargo. When I got near the dock, Romeo saw the shape and said, "Where was she?"

"South. At Caroline Cove."

I tossed the rope and Oliver caught it. He pulled us in, then tied up. Lifting Helen, the men did their best to keep her inside the raincoat. They laid her gently on the dock.

114

"I'll go tell Sillet," Romeo said.

"No. I brought in this news. I'll tell it to him."

I walked directly up to Sillet's house, a two-room white house with a black roof located directly behind the church. He was in his yard, washing shirts with a scrub brush and washboard, leaning over a tub.

He saw me and said, "Mrs. Harbison's day off. I don't usually get this familiar with my shirts, other than wearing them. By the way, tell Margaret that under the circumstances last night, I forgive her her harsh words."

"Forgiveness won't register with Margaret. Not from you. She just won't care."

"So be it. What's on your mind?"

Looking down, he scrubbed a shirt.

"I've brought Helen Twombly back. She drowned."

"Lord have mercy. Where is she now?"

"Laid out on the dock. There's people with her."

"Terrible, terrible accident."

"Accident" seemed the one perfectly wrong word.

I went home. The house was empty. I changed my sheets, heated water for a bath, and bathed a long time. I made coffee and sat in the living room, thinking about Helen.

In an hour or so Sillet came by to return my raincoat.

"Helen has no heirs or relatives whose address we know," he said. "I'll manage things from here on out."

I do not know all the reasons, but just then I had an unusually narrow tolerance for Sillet. "That's one of the things the village pays you for," I said.

115

"That temperament comes from finding a person dashed on the rocks, poor boy."

"Maybe so."

The funeral was held on August 3, 1911, late in the morning. My mother came to our house and put on a black dress with a black shawl. The shawl was lacy and reminded me of one worn by a Spanish lady who, in a magazine, sat ringside at a bullfight.

"I understand that you found Helen," she said. "An experience like that must have unraveled you."

"It was unusual, I'll say that." I had on my church suit and was polishing my shoes. "There's been a lot of those lately."

"Someday you'll sort them all out."

"I might not sit with you at the funeral."

"I imagined not. But do please acknowledge my presence, Fabian. I don't much care about keeping up appearances. At this point that obviously would be folly. But do acknowledge me, please. Quite simply, it would show good upbringing. It would show politeness—at least that—in the face of adversity."

"I'll bring you a plate of food at the testimonial."

"That would do nicely."

My mother went on ahead. I waited for about ten minutes, then followed her to church. Though the temperature was fairly cool for summer, the sun was strong, the sky all but cloudless. When I got to the church at about eleven o'clock, the pews were almost all filled. I managed to get mourners to slide down, allowing me an aisle seat in a middle pew. People stood inside along the walls as well, others leaned in through the windows or sat on the porch or stood outside near the open door. They all could hear Sillet.

Helen's coffin, covered with flowers, had been placed across two sawhorses directly in front of the elevated pulpit. Francis Beckett, a top-notch net maker, was playing the organ. At the last moment, three horse-drawn wagons pulled up and about two dozen Moravians from Renews climbed down and stood together off to one side of the church. I do not know who reported Helen's death to them, but I was impressed that so many had come. The women held black umbrellas against the sun. Among the Moravian men was Jarvis Bellecamp. He had been Emile Twombly's friend and partner in a number of enterprises, including bee farming. He was in his eighties and was the only person I knew of whom Helen had visited on a regular basis. The Moravians' minister, Sander Muggah, had stayed in Renews.

There were only a few practising Moravians in Witless Bay, and of course they had to travel down to Renews to worship. Catherine Jobb was one, as was Archibald Benoit, while both Catherine's husband, Thomas, and Archibald's wife, Florence, were Anglican and in fact made a practice of sitting next to each other in Sillet's church. With their religion having traveled down from Labrador, the Moravians were a mysterious lot to me. Through gossip and some mention in school, I had gathered a few facts about Moravians, whose church's real name was the Church of the

Unitas Fratrum, or Renewed Church of the Brethren. They were known as "God's singing people." They had different services that consisted entirely of singing. For instance, in a Saturday-evening meeting, Sander Muggah would sit down and start the hymns himself, and there might be ten or fifteen hymns in all, and then people would go home. I had heard that most Moravian ministers were good singers. I had heard that Moravians used fiddles in church, accordions, and even brass bands, all of which struck me as lighthearted. But at Helen's funeral they were all dressed in dark suits and dresses. I noticed an accordion in one of their wagons, hanging from the seat, and thought that maybe someone had played it along the road to Witless Bay. The Moravian children kept to the wagons, well behaved, talking quietly amongst themselves.

I sat next to Ruth Henley, the undertaker's wife. At one point she craned her neck to look down the center aisle and out the door. "I didn't know that Helen had befriended so many Moravians," she said to Rebecca Newton in the pew behind us.

"Befriend one, befriend all," Rebecca said. "I think that she respected their God's house more than ours."

Because of the large crowd the temperature in church quickly rose past comfort, and it seemed that all at once hand-held fans bloomed all down the pews. Eight women in my pew alone were working fans near their faces: Ruth Henley, Mekeel Dollard, Chelsea Webb, Lisa Flood, Clarissa Lindon, Edna Forbisher, Mary Kieley, and Olive Perrault. Reverend Sillet himself went through three glasses of water in less than half an hour. My attention flagged in the heat, but I recall that in his eulogy Sillet described Helen as a "dogged, otherwise-minded woman, contrary, opposed to the general sentiment of any given moment—and therefore a rarity, a source of deep yet unpredictable delight."

I truly wanted to like what Sillet said, because I liked Helen so much. And I could see where he had attempted a loving remembrance through honesty. Deep in my heart, though, I felt he had fallen short, that he had patronized Helen in death, right there in her coffin, which was made by Giles LaCotte in his father's sawmill. As an unbridled rage toward Sillet rose in me, I was relieved when he finally moved on to the idea of prayer in general. I knew that his eulogy was nearly at an end.

"We talk of inexorable laws," he said. He poured a glass of water from a pitcher and drank it all the way down without stopping. He wiped his brow with a handkerchief. ". . . but without any interference with the fixed order of nature, may not the spring be touched, away and above all general laws, in answer to prayer which brings the result that the believing heart craves for. The law of prayer is real and potent as any other. 'Ask and ye shall receive,' and so long as tragedies exist in human life and tears fall on the faces of the dead; so long as want and woe and suffering mark the path of humanity, so long will prayer continue to ascend to the ear of the All-Merciful One.

"Amen," he said.

"Amen."

He paused, drew in a deep breath, then nodded to Mari-

Lyma Fsjikskedjal, who was sitting in the frontmost pew. She was a tall, beautiful Norwegian woman in her late thirties. She rose gracefully—the back of her dress was stained with sweat—set down her fan on the pew, and walked up the two stairs to the organ, which had a vase of flowers on top. She placed one hand on the organ, the other on her chest. Francis Beckett began to play and Mari-Lyma sang:

> *Oft hath the sea conferred Thy power,*
> *And given me back at Thy command;*
> *It could not, Lord, my life devour,*
> *Safe in the hollow of Thy hand.*

Mari-Lyma had a soprano voice and was in perfect pitch despite the heat and the sadness. The highest notes lifted her chin slightly. When she finished the third and final verse, she closed her eyes, opened them, and returned to her seat. She picked up her fan.

In the silence immediately following Mari-Lyma's hymn, the vaguely discernible sound of gramophone music drifted into the church. No matter how loud the gramophone's volume, no matter how windless a day, music could not have carried in from as far as the lighthouse. Botho August must have brought the gramophone to the high meadow behind the church, cranked it up, and played his dirges. His and my mother's dirges.

In a short while the murmur of conversation started up, and I heard two entirely different sentiments.

"If Botho August hadn't been dallying all night with Alaric Vas, we might've had the lighthouse's help and found Helen in time," Abner Pittman, a man I had always liked and had worked with, said in a loud whisper. He sat in the pew in front of me and now, for the first time, suddenly seemed aware of my presence. "I'm sorry, Fabian," he said. "I should've kept what everybody's thinking to myself."

The second comment came from Elias Cutter, two pews back and to my left. He had leaned forward and said to Romeo Gillette, "Well, Reverend Sillet didn't slide backwards in my esteem for that eulogy."

"Neither backwards nor forwards in mine," Romeo said.

Then both men stood up, and along with everyone else filed out of church and walked to the field behind the general store for a testimonial and lunch.

Mrs. Berenice Elgin and her husband, Davey, had set out tables, and Bridget and Lemuel Spivey supervised the placement of food and drink. "The Moravians will eat, all right," Davey said within my earshot, "but they'll prefer to sit at one table together." The Moravians' table was at the north end of the group of tables.

Then it began. At any point in the afternoon, I would say that almost every man, woman, and child in Witless Bay was in attendance, if only to pay brief respects, have a plate of food, and then go home. Platters of lobster, codfish stew, trout, potatoes, parsnips, and fruitcakes were on a separate table and people helped themselves. I carried a plate of food to my mother, who sat at the table farthest from the Moravians. I saw Margaret leave the church, but did not see her sitting down or milling about afterwards. I figured she had simply decided to go home, or off to drink by herself, perhaps to sit on Helen's cold-storage shack. We had agreed to meet at Spivey's that evening. Reverend Sillet more or less blended in, and Romeo took up the role of a kind of master of ceremonies.

He was dressed in a formal black suit and neatly pressed white shirt, and wore a black beret, the only beret in Witless Bay. There were too many children shouting, crying, running about, too many separate conversations rising and falling, too much over-all commotion for Romeo to command everyone's attention. Yet he managed quite well with the three or four tables nearest to him. I sat four chairs away. He tapped a glass and shouted, "This testimonial for Helen Twombly has commenced!" Things did generally quiet down then, a few screaming children were carried off, and Romeo tapped the glass again. "Anyone care to begin? A prayer might be in order."

Adele Harrison, a woman near Helen's age, stood up across the table, assisted by her niece, Rhea, who remained standing as long as her great-aunt did. Rhea held Adele's elbow with one hand and put her other arm around Adele's waist. I recall looking at Adele's plate. She had taken the smallest helpings of food I had ever seen an adult take, a few bites of meat and peas. For her advanced age, she had a remarkably strong voice and did not take a prayerful tone. "In 1905," she said, "on the Feast of St. John the Baptist Day, which people up in St. John's celebrate in a colorful way . . . I was visiting my grandchildren there. I'd decided to take a walk by myself down to the harbor. It was a very cold day. And that's when I saw with my own eyes an iceberg in the shape of the Virgin Mary. Well, why in hell was it so bitterly cold so nobody else was there to witness this? I don't know. I didn't even risk trying to convince my thick-headed daughter of what I'd seen. When I got back home to Witless Bay, I asked myself, Who'd believe me, let alone grasp the meaning? . . . Helen Twombly. And to this very moment, Helen Twombly was the only one shared my secret."

Adele and Rhea sat down. The Moravians said "Amen" in unison.

"Was that a prayer?" Romeo said. "I'm not suggesting that it wasn't, Adele."

"It was a personal reminiscence," Adele said, "to offset the sort offered by Reverend Sillet, who was embarrassed to have Helen in his church."

"Well, thank you, then."

Apparently what Adele had said had wholly sufficed, because nobody else offered a second testimonial. Looking around at silent faces like an auctioneer, Romeo sat down, and an afternoon of steady eating, drinking, and talk followed.

It was threatening rain now, though not foggy at all. Yet at about four o'clock the foghorn sounded a single, long blast. There were perhaps a hundred people still gathered, and while nothing could entirely sober the drunkest, the foghorn did silence everyone for a moment.

Soon Botho August appeared at the top of the grassy

incline in clear view of the tables. He held a whiskey bottle and had obviously been drinking. I stood and looked at my mother. She covered her face with her hands.

Botho dropped to his knees. He had on a suit but no socks or shoes. He tucked his head to his chest, clutched his knees, and tumbled to within feet of the Moravians' table. None of the Moravians moved from their chairs. Botho got slowly to his feet, grabbed a breast of quail from Jarvis Bellecamp's plate. "Ever drawn one of these, Fabian?" he said. He stuffed some quail meat into his mouth, then spit part of it out.

"Before I did those somersaults," he said, slowly shaking his head back and forth, "I planned on holding a grudge for nobody inviting me here to this testimonial."

"The whole village was naturally invited," Romeo said. "There wasn't a thought to print up a special invitation for you."

"Well, no matter," Botho said. He picked up a bottle of wine, cocked his head back, held his mouth open in an exaggerated O, and dribbled in the remaining few drops. "I feel a lot better now, anyway. It may be of interest to the truth"—he steadied himself, hands flat on the table—"to the *truth*, to inform you, my dear neighbors, that Helen Twombly came to me with her intentions."

My mother set out toward our house. Rocking on his heels, Botho squinted and watched her leave. He turned back and spoke more or less at Romeo.

"We had a little chat, Helen and me, early on the day she died," Botho said. "In that regard, count me as an accomplice to her drowning, but at her own request. Keeping the lighthouse beam off, as I did that night."

Botho then fell over onto the Moravians' table. More precisely, his head shattered Jarvis Bellecamp's plate.

Jarvis got up and said, "We've felt welcome, anyway." He nodded to his families and began walking toward the wagons. In only a few moments, the Moravians' wagons made a dust-up down the road, south.

I was one of the last to leave. Well after the dishes, spare food, and bottles were cleared, after the other tables were taken in, Botho remained sprawled across the Moravians' table.

Helen was buried next to Emile. A light rain had begun. By dark, Spivey's was packed to the last table. I think Lemuel even brought a few chairs down from his own dining room. Margaret had saved me a place at a corner table. I got a cup of coffee right away. I drank it, then suddenly needed some air. "I'll be right back," I said to Margaret. "You go ahead, order anything for me."

I walked back to the Moravians' table. I sat next to Botho. He groaned, yet did not fully wake. I could hear rain right on Botho's back, on the table, and out on the sea.

By the time I got back to Spivey's, my clothes were soaked through. Margaret had finished her meal. "Where'd you go in such a hurry?" she said.

"To look at Botho August close up."

"Not a pretty sight, I imagine." She took out a little flask and poured whiskey into her empty water glass.

"He's ruined a perfectly good suit."

125

6

The Murder

It was a chill morning in mid-September. I had not slept all night. In fact, from just after supper I drank coffee without letting up, a binge unlike any I could remember. At dawn I made my way to Margaret's house. I knew that Enoch was away to the north. I pounded on her door until its rough wood chafed my knuckles to bleeding.

"I hear you!" she said. "Hold on! A girl's got to wear clothes to the door!" The door opened. Margaret had on her nightshirt. "No surprise it's you, Fabian."

"Please row out with me to Mint Cove. I need you to figure out for me what's on my mind."

"Why there in particular?"

"Past the lobster boats nobody's around."

"Just us school kids sharing nasty secrets, eh?"

"Just us, yes."

She left the door open. I saw her slip on a raincoat and galoshes, then take a revolver from the desk drawer.

Once outside, she shifted the revolver from one pocket to the other, slowly, so that I would see it. Looking at me, she shrugged. "Scoters have stayed late this year, I'm sure you've noticed," she said. "And I've got nothing for supper."

The wind was up, but we could hear the cries of gulls in the air. As we made our way down to the wharf, we locked arms and stumbled a bit because of the fog. Near the wharf, we heard dories knocking against the pilings.

"Let's use that one," Margaret said, pointing to a dory. It was secured to a bollard on the embankment. A spare oar was under a tarpaulin puddled with rain. Leak water pooled at the bottom. The rail was chalked with gull droppings, ground in by gulls walking it. We climbed in and faced each other.

"I think I'm coming down with something," she said. Her nightshirt was hiked up. Her raincoat was open. Her face was flushed, sweaty. Spools of her hair lay tamped against her forehead. "You don't look at the peak of health, either."

"I drank thirty cups of coffee last night."

Margaret rowed. Mint Cove was about half a mile to the north. The name itself was wishful; even on a day as brisk and clear as that one broke, the wind going seaward, the cove reeked of rotting kelp. Halfway to the cove, Margaret let the boat drift. "Such a lovely courting date you've asked me on, Fabian. And so early in the morning. I guess you just couldn't wait to see me, eh?" She ran a finger along the rail, chalking it up. "A little behind each ear," she said, daubing it on as though it were perfume.

"Wash that off."

"I'll do no such thing."

The outline of land was forming, scrag spruce, cliffs; puffins, guillemots, razorbills every which way, like confetti against the dark rock face. There were a few lobster boats out, and Margaret rowed far clear of them, then secured the oars. She placed the revolver on her lap.

"Over there," she whispered.

She pointed to where a gather of common scoters rested on the swell. She took out a handkerchief full of bullets from her pocket, loaded, spun the cartridge, then laid the revolver back on her lap. She stared at me, rubbing her thumb with her other thumb.

"You've painted pictures of scoter ducks," she said, "and now we're out to kill some. But that hero of yours, Audubon, he did the same."

"It's true, he didn't always paint from life."

She suddenly pointed the revolver at my face, then swung it around, aimed it at the distant lighthouse, and said, "Bang! Bang!"

Lowering the revolver, she turned and saw that I was shaken.

"Fabian, for God's sake. Here your father's off to Anticosti, hoping to earn enough money for your stupid goddamn arranged wedding, to that fourth cousin they foisted on you. Meanwhile, your very own mother is shacked up with Botho August. Up there playing gramophone records. Cozy, the two of them. And she hasn't been at your breakfast table since Orkney left."

"Those are facts I swallowed a ways back."

"And they've torn you up inside. You can borrow this gun any time you like."

Her arm fully stretched, she popped a scoter straight on. She rowed to it as the others flurried off, then settled all at once ten or so yards away. She lifted the dead one on the flat of an oar, then dropped it into a wooden bucket.

"What say we name this first little dead bird Mr. Botho August?" she said.

"Let's not name it anything. Margaret, maybe I could stay with you tonight, even though it's one night early."

"Afraid not. I prefer keeping it to Tuesdays and Thursdays like always. It keeps life familiar." She held out the revolver. "Care for a shot?"

"No, I'll watch."

"Just as I thought."

As easily as if they were mechanical ducks floating in a carnival moat, Margaret picked off five scoters in quick order. She reloaded. The bucket was now crammed full. She emptied the birds into a burlap sack. She buttoned her raincoat to the top and shivered.

"I'm coming down with something for sure," she said.

"Maybe I should row back."

"No! If it's a fever, I want to work to make it worse as soon as possible. The sooner it gets here, the sooner it'll leave, is my opinion. Maybe I'll swallow some of that powder from Gillette's pharmaceuticals later on, that makes me piss off-color. Fever or no, I'll expect you tomorrow night. I'll go on sleeping with the village idiot. Mostly for pity's sake."

She yawned. Wiping the revolver with the hem of her nightshirt, she waved it in front of my face. "As for this, let me know your decision, if you can make one."

She rubbed her arms. "I feel something aching up in me now," she said. "I want to be at home. Get a fire going and dry off my clothes from this fog. Maybe clean the ducks. A hot bath next, and some sleep. And I don't—*don't*—want you to come with me."

As she rowed even harder than usual, I said, "Margaret, I love you."

She let loose a wild laugh. "You love me, but how's that work? You're getting wed in a hotel in Halifax. You told me that to my face, remember? Now, be sure and write me a postcard, delivered by my father, telling me the exact room number you and your bride honeymoon in. So that in the future I can bed down some lummox in the same room. Long, long after I've forgotten you, Fabian, but not the room number. I'm good at numbers, you know, being a bookkeeper. Plus which, I've always wanted to visit Halifax."

Margaret was getting dressed. She liked to dress in front of me. It was the evening of September 28, 1911. We were going to the annual dance, held in LaCotte's barn. As she slipped on her red dress with a black lace collar and lace at the hem and cuffs, she looked at me and said, "Cat got your tongue?"

"No. I'm just thinking of something Helen Twombly told me."

"And what's that?"

"That you liked her superstitions, and even heeded one or two."

"They might well have been superstitions. But Helen all but ran her life by them."

"I know this. She told you that if you want to cause somebody ill fortune, you take dust from your shoe, then throw it over your shoulder in the direction of that person. Helen said you listened closely to that. Then you bent right down, fingered up dust from your shoe, and tossed it, and a fleck of something flew right back at you. You got a mote in your eye. And you were shaken by it."

"Old coot could talk a blue streak, couldn't she."

"Who'd you intend the curse for?"

"That's my woman's secret."

"For how long?"

"Till I die." She twirled around. "Do you like my dress?"

"Your hair's done up nicely, too."

"Fabian, do you know who made this dress? Sewed it by hand?"

"No."

"Alaric Vas."

"That's not true."

"It took her three full weeks to make this dress, right up there in the lighthouse. My father paid her handsomely for it. It was his gift to me, for no reason at all. Not a birthday. Nothing."

"I like the dress. Let's leave it at that. I was talking about Helen, anyway."

"To dream of a wedding is a sign of a funeral. That's another one she told me."

"When you heard it, did you dream of a wedding the same night?"

Margaret moved to the far wall and leaned against it.

"I worried that I would," she said. "So I stayed up all night. That's how you get around certain dreams. You don't sleep."

"You're one of a kind. I won't meet someone like you again."

"Better or worse, that's true."

She locked her arm in mine and we walked to LaCotte's barn.

There were no decorations other than lanterns. Moths fluttered around them; moths seemed to live a second life after summer for a while in barns. An elevated plank band-stand had been constructed, as it was each year. Francis Beckett sat at the piano. The pulley ropes and dolly used to haul the piano to the barn were set off to one side. Elmer Wyatt stood rosining his fiddle, plucking the strings, bring-ing it close to his ear in a kind of private communion, tuning, fitting it to his chin. Oliver Parmelee stood next to the piano, an accordion strapped around his neck. When Maurice March, the second accordionist, who had come in from Renews, arrived, the musicians huddled around the piano, going over the evening's selections. Beckett had written them out on a piece of paper.

When Margaret and I got there, it was about 7:30. "This herringbone jacket of my father's itches around the neck," I said. There was a half-moon, and a sharp breeze off the sea. Inside the barn you still needed a sweater or jacket. Couples were milling about the dirt dance floor.

"I read a romance in Mrs. Bath's library once," Margaret said. "The heroine was going to a dance alone. I read quite a few romances when I was a girl. I noticed that heroines liked to be alone, or at least knew how, but that life didn't *leave* them alone. Anyway, in this one romance, she was going to the dance alone. She wasn't downhearted about it at all. Because she had a silk dress on. She liked how it felt against her skin. She thought that wearing a silk dress, you didn't need a dance partner. It was already like dancing with someone, silk pressed against you, the two of you moving through the air."

"How'd that book turn out?"

"I forgot the rest."

Near eight o'clock, Botho August and my mother sauntered right past us and stood in the center. To my knowledge, it was the first time they had stepped out together in public.

"My, my, look at them," Margaret said. "Love birds and everything."

"Looks like it."

"Well, maybe dancing will put you in a better mood."

"I won't dance."

"Suit yourself, Fabian. Fine. But I'm here with Alaric's son, who's promised to his cousin. Alaric's here with Botho August. Truth is truth, and all eyes are open. Besides, this is a local dance, not Judgement Day."

The band struck up "Amazing Grace," though done in waltz time. Twenty or so couples got to dancing. Next came a jig, "Mother Carey's Chickens." During it a lot of children hopped about, but as soon as the jig ended, they heard a slow number, "Jesus Shall Preside," featuring Wyatt's melancholy solo, and they retreated to the hay bales and under the bandstand. This piece droned along and the band seemed to fall in and out of tune. It was halfhearted. Maurice March's accordion playing stalled, slurred, cranked up again as he tried to catch the rhythm. He looked embarrassed.

Margaret got annoyed. She walked up to Francis Beckett and said loudly, "My request is, leave religion out of the rest of this night."

She pulled me onto the dance floor. "Don't look so blinking sour," she said.

"I owe it to my father not to dance on the same floor as them."

When a lively reel started, couples moved around us, yet I remained fixed in place, staring at my mother and Botho. They took it as a slow dance. Arms entwined, eyes closed, they were barely moving.

"This barn's clearly no place for a mother's son," Margaret said, giving my chest a slight push. I went over and stood by the door.

Margaret then cut in on Dara Olden, who was dancing

with Reverend Sillet. Dara looked insulted, huffed, then walked briskly over to join Catherine Jobb and Mekeel Dollard by the water glasses and pitcher.

Margaret pressed herself to Sillet's chest. She took the lead, and Sillet more or less stumbled about, trying to keep back an arm's length, finding it impossible to do so. Margaret wrapped her arms tightly around him. Sillet was sweating. Lifting the hem of her dress to his face, she gently tamped his forehead, then rubbed the bottom of her dress roughly over his entire face.

The band stopped playing all at once, except for March, whose accordion trailed off in a long, mournful wheeze.

"Adultery spices up an evening, doesn't it?" Margaret said to Sillet.

Sillet finally broke loose, stepped back from Margaret, his head shaking in a sudden spasm, his teeth clenched. In his barely restrained pulpit voice he said, "And what name shall I call you by? Making a spectacle of yourself."

Margaret put her fists to her forehead, closed her eyes tightly as if in deep thought. Opening her eyes, she said, "You can call me harlot, if I can call you the word that's in *my* mind."

"I'd rather you didn't," Sillet said. He turned and walked over to get a glass of water. Mekeel Dollard poured it for him.

Margaret now looked at Botho and my mother. She walked over to them. Clutching my mother's face, she kissed her on both cheeks. Looking at Sillet, she said, "Love thy neighbor."

Then, loudly, she said, "Fabian—shall we go home to bed now?"

I was fast out the door. "You wait for me," Margaret said. As we walked toward my house, the band struck up a different reel.

On my porch, Margaret said, "God help me, but I do believe Sillet's in love with me." We stepped into the kitchen. "I'll have to live with that long after you've gone to Halifax."

Hours after we had been to bed, Margaret apparently had gone home and come back, because she woke me and said, "Here's the revolver." She placed it on top of my dresser. "I've cleaned and oiled it. I do that now and then. Everything neat and clean and in its place."

I threw on a nightshirt and took the revolver to the shed. I wrapped it in rags and wedged it under a floor plank.

When I came home from sketching ducks at a tidal flat on October 5, I found my mother preparing supper. This alone would have surprised me enough for a lifetime. Yet when I set down my satchel on the table, she said, "Orkney's home. Not in the house yet. But definitely back from Anticosti. The mail boat tied up early this morning. Did you know already?"

"I was north of here all day."

"Well, he's home. I'm making a family supper."

She took a letter from her apron pocket. Her hands were trembling. "I want to read this to you," she said. "It's the letter I had with me the night that Helen drowned."

I sat and she took the pages from the envelope.

"I'll skip some," she said. "The Hollys have made the necessary arrangements. They'll meet us in Halifax on October 23, the day before the wedding. There's to be a rehearsal."

She hesitated, then looked up from the letter.

"That's not much time to get acquainted," she said. "I suppose in the best of worlds, though, getting acquainted is what a life together is for."

I slumped in my chair, nodded as if I understood, then shrugged, gestures by which I repudiated myself.

"Just look at your face," she said. "You'd think somebody was shackling you to the mail boat, Fabian. You're a volunteer, finally."

"Please just go on reading."

"She suggests—let me see here"—my mother set the first page aside, glancing over the second—"we use a justice of the peace, to avoid offending anyone's religious sensibilities. They're Baptists, apparently, however *that* happened. And I told her that we were practising Anglicans. They've reserved a room for themselves, another for Orkney and me, a third for you and Cora. On a separate floor, naturally. Klara says the Hagerforse Guest House is lovely. There's a park directly across and oak trees lining the street. What a pleasant place it sounds like, Fabian. What a pleasant, serene place to sleep your first married night, in the city there. Klara goes on to say that they'll leave Halifax the morning after, first to sightsee at Peggy's Cove, then up to Prince Edward Island for the beaches. Weather allowing.

'We are drawn to autumn beaches without sunbathers,' she says. And then they'll go home to Richibucto."

At the same instant we looked up to see my father standing in the doorway. He may have heard part of the letter, I do not know. We did not hear the door open. No doubt I had left it unlatched.

"Oh!" my mother said. It was like an utterance from a ventriloquist's dummy, hollow, and she even moved her hand woodenly to her heart.

Without meeting our eyes, he dropped the tightly bound bundle of burlap sacks to the floor and immediately picked them up again. He carried the bags to the pantry. He stood there, facing away from the kitchen, silent. I heard him catch his breath. I do not know exactly what I had expected, though it was not that he would be as clean-shaven, his hair so neatly combed. He did have on the same clothes as when he had left months earlier, allowing for the wishful delusion that no time had passed. Though even so, his clothes appeared to be freshly washed and ironed. Then I fixed on his shoes. He had on new shoes. I thought that I even recognized the pair, from Gillette's store. They had been on the third shelf to the left of the counter, above the galoshes. I had even once thought of buying them for my father. I had almost asked Romeo to set them aside. They were black, with slightly raised eyelets. Since his return to Witless Bay, my father had bought new shoes, yet they were not laced up. This oversight was a detail that gave him away. He was not quite himself.

My mother tapped the salt and pepper shakers together.

My father turned and walked into the kitchen. Leaning against the door, he said, "Here's the places I'm offered to stay while I think things over. Until this thing gets settled in my mind. There's the bunk on Enoch's boat. No, I turn that down. And Romeo Gillette's offered me his sofa. And there's the spare room at Spivey's. You know the room, Fabian. I've just washed up there, and it would do nicely. I guess it's my turn there, eh? I'm partial to it, anyway, because I haven't slept in a real bed in months. You see, I didn't have a *choice*, one bed or the other, on Anticosti. So that's it, then. I've made up my mind. I'll stay at Spivey's. For a week, say. And, Alaric, I'll expect you not to be in this house after that, not that you have much of late, anyway."

The pepper shaker cracked, scattering grains on the table. My mother's hand was bleeding.

"And what kind of man are you?" he said to me. "To allow this humiliation to go on."

"Leave Fabian out of this," my mother said.

"How's that possible? He's sitting right here, not deaf and dumb."

He went out the door, down the road to Spivey's.

"I'll take the music box with me," my mother said. She stood up, washed her hand in the sink, held a cloth napkin to it. "He won't get that."

"Father doesn't even know about any goddamn music box, Mother. But he did get told about you and Botho. Maybe from Enoch. Maybe Romeo."

"I've hurt him deeply, Fabian. I have not kept a clean marriage. There's no turning back."

Except for cracking the pepper shaker, she had kept a tense composure; now, however, she went into her bedroom and I heard a lot of commotion. She cursed, then smashed an object against the wall. I looked around the kitchen. On the counter, lemon rinds were drying. My mother stayed in her room. I imagined her curled up on the bed, a jolted stillness at the heart of the house.

I looked in on my mother an hour or so later. She was asleep. The music box lay in pieces on the floor. It was just after dark. I walked to Spivey's. I sat on the porch until the last customers, Mekeel and Paul Dollard, came out. "White horses on the bay tonight," Paul said, referring to the whitecaps breaking into foam on the rocks. They both offered tight-lipped smiles.

"Good night, then," Mekeel Dollard said.

"Good night."

I stepped inside. Bridget was clearing dishes. Lemuel was sponging a table.

"He's in his room," Lemuel said. "You eat supper? Because if you haven't, neither has Orkney, and it's easy enough to send you back with a tray."

"Not hungry, thanks."

I knocked on the door and opened it. My father had set his shoes on the floor next to his old pair of boots. He had polished the boots as well. He lay on the bed, a pillow over his face.

"It's me. Fabian."

"This pillow is Bridget's advice," he said. He lifted the pillow away. "She claims a cool pillow against your face can change your disposition. Good if you need sleep."

141

"Things with Mother changed without warning."

He set the pillow on his chest. "—that all these years should come down to infidelity. Christ, how pitiful."

He placed the pillow behind his head.

"—in the register of births," he said.

"How's that?"

"Your mother's maiden name."

"What about it?"

"Her name before marriage was Alaric Banville."

"I knew that."

"That's how I'll refer to her from now on. Alaric Banville."

"All right. That might help."

"Don't be goddamned stupid, son. Nothing helps. Life's taken a downward spin. I'm brain-sick. It's all got me so riled and full of murderous hate. Toward both your mother and Botho August."

"That's put directly."

"Enoch Handle told me he once delivered a man who was criminally insane. He'd done some awful deed up in St. John's, and Enoch was delivering him to a hospital sanatorium away from civilization. There was a British constable along. The man in question was locked into a straitjacket. I mean padlocked—like this—"

Wrapping his arms tightly around his chest, my father demonstrated, adding a look of anguish. It did not strike me as an imitation. It was more as though he had become the man himself.

"You feel like that now."

He stood up. "That's the goddamned point, Fabian! If I stepped from this room for a minute—now—I could *do* something. I'm capable. And what's more, I might not regret it."

"Well, I'd regret it."

"Don't protect them. Some citizens can't be protected."

He looked at the wall, then back to me.

"On Anticosti—" He reached into his trouser pocket, taking out a slip of paper. "I wrote it all down, not to forget. Three hundred six puffins. Two hundred twenty-eight auks. All the deliveries and haggling done. The wedding money's in the till, a secret place away from Alaric Banville."

"I don't see how we can travel as a family down to Halifax."

He stepped over to me, put his hand on my shoulder, and squeezed, then sat down again on the bed.

"It's a former plan," he said. He stood up, walked a few steps to the chair. "A plan from a time months back, when we were a family. Or so I thought. Back then, we'd worked something out on your behalf. So now we can proceed as though we're honoring a promise. Do you want to go ahead with marrying Cora Holly? That's my question, here and now."

"Would it please you?"

"Nothing could, wholly. But that would, more than anything else I can think of."

"All right, then. Yes."

"Yes, but with very little conviction in your voice."

"It's just that it sounds like a brutal journey to me. Hatred between you and Mother, going down to my wedding that way."

"It could well happen that we stare from the rail in different directions the whole journey. It could. It could go exactly how you might imagine it. But my small advice is, save imagination for marriage itself. I'm still in favor of it —marriage. God strike me dead, but I am. Even allowing the fact that Alaric Banville has sent ours to hell. Now leave me be. Get out. I'm tired."

I shut the door behind me. Bridget and Lemuel were upstairs. There was a clean tablecloth on each table. The soiled ones were piled in a corner. Out on the porch, I heard the rusted weathervane. I walked to Margaret's house, but when I got there I saw that she and her father were having a late supper. They were laughing. I stood back from the house, watching them through a window. I went back to Spivey's. I sat on the porch. I walked past the lighthouse, home.

My father did not wait a week. Three nights later he came to our house. My mother had sequestered herself. I had been out each day trying to draw birds, but as far as I knew she had not been back to the lighthouse. It was late, around eleven o'clock. I was lying fully clothed on my bed. It was raining hard. The roof, the chimney, the shingle-roofed shed each registered rain with a different sound, and there was spillage out of the eaves. My door was open enough to see the blurred figure of my father go past. I got up and went to my door. He had tracked in. He had not bothered to take off his raincoat or galoshes.

"You want a miracle?" my mother cried out as a greeting.

Their bedroom door slammed, but I could still hear them.

"Do you want some angel from on high to save you from humiliation?" she said. "Do you want to kill me? Do you want Reverend Sillet to put me in stocks so you and everyone else can spit on me? What is it, Orkney? Do you want me to drown myself in the sink? What would satisfy you? What would make it worth your while that you ever came back?"

She kept the questions flying, and I thought there would be no end to them.

"Should I cut out my heart? Should I write 'I'm sorry' a thousand times on the blackboard?"

At one point my father shouted, "I'll kill you! I'll kill myself!"

"That solution's a little too generous toward Botho August, don't you think," my mother said hoarsely.

"I'll kill him!"

As for me, these were hours of bewildering helplessness and fear. Such a violent argument can turn a house inside out, let alone a mind, and there seemed to be no way to intervene, and no way to slow my heart down. It could have fairly beat out of my chest. What was perhaps most unpredictable was that the air choked with accusation, the guilty questions, the silences all emboldened me. It all emboldened me, maybe in the most senseless way, yet it did. I went to the woodshed, took up the revolver, and from that moment forward the revolver was part of my fate. As I walked to the lighthouse, I heard the foghorn. Three extended blasts. In a manner of speaking, I had perfect knowledge of everything to come, because I had said out loud, "You've got a gun." I named the thing I held, and even having done so did not cast it aside. I tucked it into my belt under my shirt. And then it was as though the rain drowned out the sound of my own thinking, all reason, any hope at all. I was accompanied by dumb silence and rain.

At the lighthouse I made my way along the picket fence. I watched as the beam swept and flattened out on the sea. I thought of how many times I had stood watching this from a cliff. How the beam caught a trawler, miniaturizing it like a toy boat on the full yellow moon, the firmament surrounding. Black. How the kittiwakes and gulls flicked darkly through the beam. At such times, you had to figure that Botho August would see these night birds, and that the trawler crew saw them as well—the night birds is what they had in common between them. I remembered Romeo Gillette saying, "A ship in trouble is exactly the same distance from the lighthouse as the lighthouse is from it—a simpleminded fact, except if you're shipboard and about to capsize, that particular fact holds out no hope whatsoever. You simply hate the lighthouse keeper for being safe and warm, and mostly for you having to rely on him. And yet you pray he's in top form."

Looking up to the yellow-lit third-floor window, the living quarters, I moved closer. Despite the rain I could make out that Botho August was expertly puppeteering the silhouette of a donkey against the opposite wall. He must have been sitting beneath the window, and had arranged the lantern in the best position to allow for hand shadows. He had come down from the housing for some entertainment, and he was not alone. One of the donkey's ears drooped, and the silhouette of a hand considerably smaller than Botho's lifted it up again. The hand disappeared and the ear flopped over. This routine was repeated eight times. I counted them.

At that instant all of the elements of the entire unnerving night thus far gathered and sent some kind of poison up to my brain. I took Botho's frivolity as a personal insult. He could not know this, of course. He could not know that out on his lawn I was so addled, had such disdain for him, that I was suddenly short of breath. Holding the revolver tightly in my right hand at arm's length, steadying it with my left, I slammed a shot through the window. I walked to the door, stepped back about ten yards, and waited for Botho to show.

The door opened and Botho peered out until he saw my figure in the yard.

"Who's that? Who's there?"

He had on his galoshes and nightshirt.

"Fabian Vas," I said.

As he stepped from the doorway, I heard gramophone music coming from upstairs.

"Is that a revolver in your hand?"

"I shot the window out just now."

"There's glass all over the floor. It's rained-in, too. It's a goddamned mess."

"Fine by me."

He looked at me a moment. "I didn't force your mother to visit me so often," he said, "just like I didn't force Margaret to be here now. She did it on her own volition. She wasn't bewitched. She walked up the stairs on two feet like anyone."

"You've done damage."

He sighed deeply, puffed out his cheeks, and made a loud blowing sound. "Congratulations on your forthcoming marriage," he said. "Why, just earlier in the evening, Margaret told me. We'll make a little toast later on, clink glasses and the like."

Botho lurched toward me. I shot him in the neck. The bullet spun him sideways, and by the time he turned back to me he had clutched his neck and appeared to be strangling himself. He took his hands away and inspected them. He rubbed them together like a child washing his hands with rain. Then, with awkward deliberation, he searched for the entry hole as if he might simply stop it up and be saved.

Loudly the gramophone music scratched to a halt. I shot him in the stomach.

He slumped to his knees. "I'm shot," he said.

"This was supposed to happen. It's what I came here to do."

"I'm shot in the body, Fabian. I'm just the lighthouse keeper."

"You're more than that."

"How old are you? How old is my murderer?"

"Twenty."

"I don't suppose you'd say goodbye to Alaric for me, whom I loved, if I could anyone." He wheezed.

"No, not in good conscience," I said.

He could barely talk now. "Imagine that," he whispered, "—a murderer's good conscience. You're going to visit Mr. Ellis."

Since childhood I had heard any hangman, Canadian or otherwise, referred to as "Mr. Ellis."

Botho was curled in the mud. It was pelting down rain.

"Mr. Ellis will be the man breathing good air right next to you on the scaffold." He was now half facedown in the mud.

I think that it was near one o'clock in the morning. Retching blood, Botho jerked his head back and forth, then lurched forward as though loosing his earthly form. This was followed by a sharp intake of breath, as though he was trying to suck it back in again. The bullet had lodged near his shoulder; it had not damaged his throat, and he could still utter, "I'll pay the devil my soul twice over to watch you hang." That sentence seemed to take an eternity to work its way through. I all but felt his grimace clamp down on my heart; blood bubbled along his lips. As he spoke those last words, his eyes had wandered crazily, which somehow made his prediction of my fate less plausible. Still, looking away just then, I was suddenly bent over with a true or imagined bodily pain and overpowering dread. If saying a thing more forcefully than it is felt makes it an outright lie, still, I dropped to my knees, knelt over Botho, drew his face close to mine, and confessed: "I'm glad I did this. And that's what I'll have to live with, however long I do live." His eyes rolled back, his Adam's apple seemed to

149

lock like a gear fitting. I thought surely he was dead. He was leaking into the mud and grass. I saw the bullet hole and powder burn through his soaked shirt. An image came forth, of myself as a small boy on my knees by my bed. I said the Lord's Prayer.

I stood, dropped the revolver, and fled without thought to LaCotte's barn, like an animal crazed by cold rain. The harpy voices of my mother and father quarreled in my ears. When I got to the barn I crouched in a corner. I breathed sawdust. The bile of fear and confusion rose in my throat. All in a few moments' time, I was the most local of convicts. Pinned to the dark by the wretched gaze of Charibon's owl.

7

C o f f e e

Mr. Ellis, Mr. Ellis, Mr. Ellis, I kept hearing,
but there was nobody else in the barn. As the remainder of
the night passed, it turned out that I was pursued only by
my father. The rain had stopped. I heard his voice: "Fabian?" He stood in the doorway holding a lantern.

"Over here."

The owl fluttered, made a small screech, caped open its
wing.

"Fabian, don't panic now, son. I'm keeping my distance
here. Now listen carefully. Your mother has packed our
bags. We're leaving for Halifax. It's best we go right now.
Down to the mail boat. We'll take things as they come."
He forced a strict calm into his voice. "Right *now*."

I hurried alongside my father to the wharf. Enoch had
lit so many lanterns on board that from the top of the wharf

their diffused light made it look as if the *Aunt Ivy Barnacle* was on fire. When we reached the dock, I saw that my mother was already there. She had on her raincoat, and the hem of her nightgown could be seen. She looked tired, pale, as distraught as I had ever seen her.

"We woke Mr. Handle up," my mother said. "We marched right into his house, imagine that. Imagine a neighbor doing that. Still, in this emergency, we remained discreet. We didn't wake Margaret."

Enoch drew in the tie rope. My father and I stood at the rail. My mother stayed mid-deck.

"Fleeing the village you were born in," my father said.

Enoch of course had for years full knowledge of my mother's dislike for Margaret. Still, for the sake of civility, if nothing else, in advance of a long journey he said, "Alaric, you repair to the bunk. There's blankets. You can go down there now."

My mother did that. Enoch climbed into the steering cabin. He idled up the *Aunt Ivy Barnacle*. Then he maneuvered us out into the harbor. Now fog was breaking into drifting wreaths and patches, and in the very first wash of daylight we gained open water. A half mile or so west of the harbor, Enoch steered south.

"Coffee's up here," Enoch said.

He had the engine full throttle, humming evenly. He kept things always finely tuned, oiled. Water churned and fanned out behind us. A few gulls rode the bow.

My father screamed something incoherently into the wind.

"Orkney there said there'd been a killing," Enoch said. "He didn't mention who's dead or who did it. He put money in my hand, and now I'm taking you to Halifax."

Hands gripping the wheel, Enoch looked at me. "What is your life now?" he said. "Christ, what a sad day."

He fiddled with the wireless. "Botho August, this is Enoch Handle," he said loudly, so I could hear. Then he tapped it out in Morse code.

He sang:

> *On the tenth of November*
> *as you all may well know,*
> *in the year nineteen-ought-two*
> *on her last trip she did go*
> *where she leavèd Dog Tooth Harbour*
> *about 3 p.m.,*
> *with a strong breeze from the south'ard*
> *for Lamb's Head she did steam.*

When he finished this verse from "The Wreck of the Steamship *Bella May*," he said, "Fabian, I know who's dead."

Now, concentrating on the sea ahead, he broke into another song, then abruptly stopped. "It's a Beothuk song," he said. "You can't possibly know what it means. It's talking to the dead. You can't talk to the dead through a wireless. You have to do it another way."

As he took up the song again, thick with consonants, it shaped his mouth oddly. *Hod-thoo, corah soob, puth-a-auth.*

153

I recall the sounds. He would translate in bits and pieces, as though English had just somehow broken through: "Sorrow, sorrow, sorrow," catch himself, and return to Beothuk. The song was eerie, yet agreeable to the ear. He sang loudly, riding it into his private world, then it was over. "Pour me a cup of that, will you?" he said.

"Enoch, in the eyes of the law you're an accomplice of sorts."

"Maybe so. For now, though, I consider myself a paid employee. That and nothing else."

I studied Enoch's face. His expression did not betray guilt, worry, or even doubt, as far as I could tell. In volunteering to help us get out of Witless Bay, he had cast aside personal pride, future shame, and fear of legal consequences. Eventually, too, Margaret might say, "Pop, you delivered a murderer to his bride." Or perhaps my mother was right in the first place: that Enoch viewed this journey, now graceless and desperate, as a fact of life, nothing more, nothing less. I did not ask.

"I just hired on," Enoch said.

By 7 a.m., three hours out of Witless Bay, the sky was cloudless. My mother had kept to the bunk. I saw that she was buried under the blankets. The Hollys' letters were neatly stacked and tied with a string on the nightstand nailed to the floor.

"We'll tie up at Cape Broyle shortly," Enoch called out. He pointed to a few stilt houses.

And then I understood. He was going to take us through

his regular routine of mail pickups. He knew that the wedding was set for October 24. It was now October 9. Given reasonable postponements for gales, mechanical troubles, or other unforeseen circumstances, there would be time. I stood next to my father. "Do you think he's slowing down so the law can catch us?" I said.

"I think he doesn't want to waste a trip."

We anchored at Cape Broyle. Enoch cranked down the dinghy, then rowed it in. He stayed about an hour. He returned with a stack of mail and a few packages. In addition, he brought food aboard. In the small pantry below-deck, he unwrapped hot scones from a cloth. He returned to the wheel. "Get off, you shit birds!" he shouted. Two cormorants flapped from the bow, then flew low to the water. He took us out to sea.

As we entered the current the water darkened. At the rail, my father said, "How'd I even start to look for you in the first place, you might well ask."

"I figured you went to confront Botho August. I heard you and Mother fighting."

"Botho was still breathing when I got there. He was still alive when I found him, son. I thought it was a miracle, considering he'd been shot three times."

"Twice."

"No, you're wrong."

"I shot him in the neck and then in the belly. I might not have been clear-headed, but I could count to two."

"One in the neck, that's true. One in the belly, also true. The final truth is that to the left of his heart, if you'd rolled him over and looked down on him like I had, was a third hole. Seen clear as could be, because the rain had washed him like a baby's bath in Eden."

"I killed a man and now I feel nothing toward him."

"I called up into the lighthouse. I heard a scratching sound, maybe that goddamned gramophone. I took Botho's pulse. It was now gone. I hurried back to our house. Alaric was facedown on the bed. 'Botho August is dead,' I told her. 'I think it was Margaret who did it, maybe Fabian.' She started packing suitcases without a word. A frantic person. Where did she think we were going? In a short bit, though, she walked into the kitchen and said, 'It's up to Enoch Handle now.' And then I knew what she meant. I got out the money from where I'd hid it, in the woodshed. We woke Enoch. Then I found you in the barn. And one other thing to tell you."

"What's that?"

"At the lighthouse, when I looked up, I saw Margaret in the window."

"Botho told me she was with him. I don't have to hear it again."

From October 11 to October 13, we rode out a storm just north of Lamaline. Late on October 14, we tied up at Lamaline, at the southernmost tip of Newfoundland. "I'll go into town now," Enoch said. "I'll be back in the morning. What about cribbage? There's a set in the pantry. Or else one of Margaret's Old Maid decks, it's around here somewhere. We used to play it. You don't even have to talk to one another, playing that."

"Just go on ahead," my father said. "We'll do fine without cards."

Enoch rowed into Lamaline. My mother retired right away to the bunk. On a sudden impulse my father started to mop the deck and steering cabin. He worked the mop furiously. He reached into every crevice and corner. I climbed on top of the cabin and began to sketch red knot and dunlin. In the waning light I could still see them darting and foraging alongshore, their plaintive voices drifting out, if the breeze had caught them just right. My father finished his mopping. He stood beneath the roof. "Sore shoulder for some reason," he said. "I'll rub in some liniment and call it an early night."

The sketch paper seemed to hold the last light. I heard the dunlins but now could barely see them. The villagers of Lamaline lit window lanterns. It was a peaceful moment.

I heard a dull thud down the rail, about halfway along the boat, where the lifeboat was secured. I climbed down and moved, mostly by touch, along the rail, trying to focus my sight. When I managed to do so, I recognized my father rowing away. As he approached shore, he entered the reflected light from the nearest stilt houses. He carefully tied up the lifeboat. He did not have any sort of bundle with him. He struck a match, which moved like a firefly to the wick, and then his lantern was lit; it made its own small pool of light on the water. He held the lantern up near his face. He stood like that for a moment or two. He turned toward Lamaline. It was the last time I saw my father.

In the pantry I brewed coffee. My mother was awake, I think, though she kept her eyes closed. I took the coffee up

157

on deck and drank the entire pot. I grabbed the mop and for hours repeated the cleaning of the *Aunt Ivy Barnacle*. I stayed up all night. I brewed a second pot. I watched my mother sleep. I ate cold scones. Toward dawn I got violently ill, and crammed coffee grounds down my throat to make it worse, which it did; I vomited over the rail. I lay flat out on deck. At first light, I woke my mother. She groaned from sleep, sat up, and said, "What?"

"Father's gone into Lamaline."

She climbed down from the bunk and stepped to the small woodstove. She stirred the ashes, added kindling, lit it, took up the bellows, and drew up a blaze. She put in two small logs and placed the teakettle on top of the stove. "You look like death warmed over," she said. When the kettle whistled, she brewed tea. She carried her cup to the porthole and looked out. She took a sip.

"I think that if we look—knowing Orkney as I do—we'll find that he's left us money to get by on in Halifax."

She set down the cup, walked to her suitcase, snapped it open. An envelope lay on top of her sweater. She slid out a stack of money.

"I'd feel better if we paid the Hollys back for the rings, wouldn't you?" she said. "It's only right."

I went up on deck. I hoisted a bucket of seawater, splashed a few handfuls on my face. My mother came up the stairs.

"I do hope that Enoch brings scones again. I'm starving," she said.

"Where do you think Father is?"

"Orkney? Oh, into Canada somewhere, I imagine. I doubt he'll venture a foreign country. Into Canada, I'd bet."

My mother went back down and changed her clothes. When she emerged again, with a different sweater on, I said, "Look!" We saw Enoch rowing out, and he had a passenger on board. As they approached, we saw that it was an elderly man. He looked to be at least eighty. He was wearing a black sweater, black trousers, galoshes, and a cap. Leaning over the rail, I held out my hand and assisted him up. His hands were knotty and strong. His face was stubbled with beard and there were tributaries of veins on his sallow cheeks. He had flat blue eyes. Open-mouthed, lips tucked back over his yellow teeth, he was panting. He forced a few words between ratcheting breaths.

"So this is the one you mentioned, Enoch," he said. Enoch stood next to the man. The man poked me in the ribs with his whittled cane.

"I'll make introductions," Enoch said. "Fabian and Alaric Vas, this is Avery Mint. The cove's named after his family. I suppose you didn't know that. Anyway, I told Avery here that if he could muster the strength to come out this morning, I'd reward him with something he's never seen first-hand close up." Enoch turned to Avery. "Well, Avery, there he is, a bona fide murderer. Imagine it, Avery"—Enoch was all but shouting into Avery's ear—"my daughter not being good enough to marry a murderer. In his and his mother's and father's minds, at least."

"Hell, I'd marry her in a minute," Avery said. "I'd rather have that pretty girl kill me in bed with a heart attack and get my entire savings than have her spend one hour with the likes of this one here, Enoch."

"Thank you for saying as much."

"Some murderers," Avery said, "if they're truly remorseful, you can see it in their eyes or hear it in their voices. I don't see remorse in this boy's eyes. Remember the Cobb murder?"

"In Renews, 1890," Enoch said. "Yes, in fact I had a close look at the man who killed Sandy Cobb, named—"

"Laslow Sprunt," Avery Mint said. "A miserable worm.

"Still and all, Sprunt tried to do himself in with a bedspring in jail—at least he was tormented enough to do that," Avery said. "I'll give him credit."

"I agree," Enoch said.

"Well, I appreciate you showing me the boy here," Avery said. He poked me twice in the stomach. "Are you remorseful, boy?"

"It's the least I can do, considering all the nights you've put me up in your home," Enoch said.

"One more thing," Avery said. "Can you fetch that barnacle scraper and get my back with it?"

Enoch took the barnacle scraper from its nail and scratched Avery's back, up and down.

"That's got it," Avery said.

Enoch helped him back into the dinghy. He rowed Avery home. Avery slowly walked up the slope into the village. Enoch noticed the lifeboat. He looked up into the village, then turned back to the lifeboat. He maneuvered it into the shallows. He tied the dinghy to it and, with the dinghy in tow, rowed back to the *Aunt Ivy Barnacle*.

On deck, Enoch said, "Him being husband and father alike, I imagine you weren't apt to stop Orkney from leaving. Did he kill Botho August? God knows he was all anger and blame, much of it righteous."

"You're not the law, Enoch," my mother said.

"I didn't really care to know, anyway," Enoch said. He held up a basket. "Scones, jam, more coffee. The people of Lamaline have always been generous to me."

As it concerns the rest of the passage, memory comes in fits and starts. Maybe we remember, anyway, by selectively forgetting, and vice versa, though that sounds preachy. Then again, some of the things you try most to forget come back and ambush you, often in your calmest moments. I do not know. I do recall thinking on board the *Aunt Ivy Barnacle*, however, that Enoch was smuggling my mother and me into a deeper incomprehension of our lives. We seemed more confused by the hour. Enoch was our keeper. Standing on deck with Avery Mint, he had acted on his true harsh opinion of us. He had pronounced the word "murderer" with real disdain, almost as if he was about to spit. And yet, during the rest of our journey, he remained polite, if distant. Now and then he would sing in Beothuk in his cabin.

Perhaps our days on the *Aunt Ivy Barnacle*, coldly dreamlike, exhausting, perplexing to the heart, menacing to the soul, should have been a chance for even a provisionary forgiveness. Instead, we avoided one another like the plague. We ate whatever Enoch brought on board. Using a cod jig I fished off the rail when we anchored or docked in harbor. At

night, standing at different places, we would stare at village
lights, as if each passing hour deepened our homesickness as
well as the fear of no longer having a home. What was the
future, Halifax being just another bitter unknown?

After Lamaline, we stopped at St.-Pierre on the strait to
the Miquelon Islands. We traveled in rain across to Glace
Bay, Nova Scotia, then along the coast toward Halifax. The
Aunt Ivy Barnacle was filling with mail for the outside
world.

The evening before we reached Halifax, I drank coffee
for two hours in a row and had an attack of memory so
powerful it nearly flung me overboard. I would close my
eyes and see the same thing over and over. Not a vision of
Margaret with Botho in the lighthouse. Not Margaret and
me at some childhood escapade, or anything whatsoever to
do with innocence. What kept returning to my mind with
increasing clarity and detail was a time when Margaret and
I went ice fishing. I think it was about three years earlier
—in March.

We had met by happenstance in Gillette's store. "Fabian,"
she said, "I've got a shanty all set up. Why not come out
with me? You can't possibly have anything better to do."

From behind his counter Romeo jokingly said, "If you
don't, Fabian, I will."

"That's enough reason right there," I said.

We walked in bitter cold to Margaret's house. I saw the
shanty just about where the inlet in front of the house met
the sea. We walked over the ice and went in and sat on
opposite slats. Margaret added a split log to the small wood-

stove set up off the ice and it quickly got warm inside the shanty. She took out a flask and drank from it. The jigging pole was fixed to its stand—no luck yet.

"I was remembering a song today," Margaret said. "All day so far I can't get it out of my head. I think it's from my mother. I think she sang it. 'There's no love/true as the love/that dies untold.' That's the refrain. I think that's true. Do you?"

"I'm not sure I understand it."

"I know what it means. It means, once a third person— outside the couple in love—knows about the love, it's diminished somehow."

"Are you talking about us?"

"I could talk about us if you want me to. But I wasn't. Not really. I was talking about the song. It's hot in here." She took off her coat, then slipped off her sweater and unbuttoned her shirt partway down. "Aren't you even a bit uncomfortable, Fabian? It's warm in here."

"I'm fine, thanks."

"You're fine, but you're thickheaded as a stump." She kissed me and laughed.

"Margaret, an ice-fishing shanty is not a romantic place."

"You do something romantic, the place you do it in becomes that."

"You've been thinking too many thoughts today is my impression. People shouldn't take apart a song like you do, Margaret. People should just sing a song and feel it. You took apart your mother's love ballad—which got you sad. It's sad enough without adding sad thinking to it."

163

"Well, that's me, isn't it? Everything reminds me of everything else."

"Yes, it is."

She buttoned up her shirt. "Consider today a missed opportunity, Fabian. Because that's what it is. It's not Tuesday or Thursday, even. I was willing to break a rule. A shanty's as good a place to be adventurous in as any, five below out. It'd be memorable." She put her sweater and coat back on.

"I might have tried it out here with you, Margaret. Given a little time—I'd have warmed up to the idea. Possibly."

"That's easy for you to say once I'm all battened up again, in all these layers."

"Besides—look. There's no place to lie down in here. This is a fishing shanty, Margaret."

"I heard about a couple did it, her sitting on his lap."

"Who was that?"

"Oh, some couple I heard about firsthand, from the wife of the couple herself."

"Which wife? Who? Where does she live?"

"I'm sworn to secrecy, Fabian. But the couple lives in a place small and tidy as Witless Bay, only farther south. What's more, they didn't get any special knowledge from a city or anything. They figured out about each other's laps on their own."

"If I think about it, I'll figure out who it was."

"You should be thinking about *it*—not *who*."

"Just now I'm cold. I want to go back. I'm going back."

"Goodbye, then. I'm staying. I feel lucky. I'm going to catch a fish."

Then I went back home.

I do not know why that day, of all days, kept plaguing me, kept repeating itself in my thoughts. Maybe because it was such a clear example of how I shrank from any given moment of enticement. There had only been a yes or no, right there. Whereas I could have offered a third choice. We could have found a bed somewhere. No, it was more than that. I should have proposed marriage. I was only seventeen. But I should have proposed. I would have learned why that particular song tore Margaret up so much. I would have learned who that couple south of Witless Bay was. I would not be making this journey.

I drank more coffee and my thinking got even more jumbled, until remorse and longing made me crazy. I had to do something—anything. I went down into the bunkroom. My mother was asleep. She had been sleeping at odd hours. I took up the Hollys' letters. I was going to tear them up one by one and throw them off the rail. But I hesitated. Then I slid a single letter from the stack and took it up on deck. I could not know what the letter contained. I had not read any. I tore it up without reading it and threw it to the winds. It was such a desperately small gesture, considering that suddenly this whole voyage to be married in Halifax felt like a betrayal of Margaret—of the years we had known each other. I closed my eyes, the day at the ice-fishing shanty came back even more clearly. I kept my eyes closed and went through it again.

Just after dark ocean light glimmered and the sky was showing stars through hazy clouds. I watched murres arrive out of nowhere. We were a good mile from the coast. The murres whirled above the boat, moved along with us as though they comprised a spectacular mechanical kite, towed by an invisible string. I had my lantern and sketchbook out. I had just drawn a rough sketch of the murres when the engine coughed to a halt. I heard Enoch say, "There's no problem—sometimes I just like to drift a moment or two."

I moved closer to the cabin and saw that he was talking with my mother.

"That's a nice freedom," she said. "To be out at sea. Besides, what can a minute—even an hour—mean on such a long journey?"

"Not much, unless you're in a gale."

"I heard you talking and singing in Indian." She had her raincoat draped over her shoulders.

"If you think in a language nobody else knows," Enoch said, "well, that's my definition of true privacy. Nobody else to argue with. Just you and your God."

"I'd hate to be alone with Him. I'd rather be on a boat full of people who despise me than alone trying to talk with God."

"Look at you, Alaric. You're all dressed up with nowhere to go."

She held open the sleeves of the raincoat. "It's my wedding dress. We had so little time to pack. What to take, what to leave behind, because I didn't think ahead, really. I didn't know the relation of this journey to my outerwear, you see. Would it be warm or cool in Halifax? What shawls to bring. Now that I've had a chance to open the suitcase and see what wardrobe I'd salvaged, I discover that I must have gone into my closet and snapped up my wedding dress. For the life of me, though, I don't remember actually doing that. As you can see, it's not the traditional white bridal gown but one of my own designs. Much simpler. And notice, after all these years the moths have spared it."

"Margaret will wear her mother's wedding dress someday."

"Enoch—I'm sorry."

"No apologies needed, none accepted."

My mother put the raincoat on, buttoning it to the top. "Enoch, I'm going to end it here and now. I'm going to slip overboard, and I don't want you to counsel me to the contrary. My past has thrown a dark shroud over my future, and I don't wish to live anymore. All's lost, Enoch, you understand. I'm a shameful presence. It's intolerable."

"You're tired. Worn out, is all."

"You've started to counsel me, Enoch. Please don't."

"Why even tell me your plan, then?"

"Because I need to tell you a last will and testament."

"That should be in writing. There's a pen and paper in the pantry."

"There's no time. I'll tell it to you. What I leave for Fabian, what for my sister. It's not much to remember. I'll make a short list, and that'll have to suffice."

"Hold on a minute. Let me get something."

He set the wheel and rummaged around the cabin. "Here," he said, "try some of this."

"That's the filthiest-looking pipe. Not at all a gentleman's pipe. What's in it?"

"Beothuk Indian brain medicine. Old as cavemen, I imagine."

"I'm not sick, Enoch. I've thought this through."

"You only want to slip overboard."

"That's my clear choice."

"Well then, this potion might make it easier."

"It looks like some sort of tobacco."

"Think of it that way. Or any way you choose. It's not hocus-pocus, Alaric. I may be the only one still knows the natural recipe. It's a secret handed down and down. You pulverize it, tamp it, like this, see. Then you light it." Enoch struck a match. "And breathe it in through this pipe. People have had similar woes to yours for centuries, you know."

"Can you die from smoking this?"

"Alaric, I'm not going to kill you so that you can't do yourself in, now, am I?"

"I suppose not."

My mother put the pipe to her lips, drew in deeply, coughed, gave it a second try. "This is foul," she said. She tried it again.

"That it is."

"Can you tell me anything worthwhile?" she said. "A story from the past, from before all of this—behavior. From a time when there was some hope."

"I don't know any stories like that, Alaric. Every Indian story I ever heard as a kid, Beothuk, Micmac, had human failing. It had fear and evil figures and ghosts that caused great trouble. Hungry ghosts. Unhappy—miserable ghosts. Cantankerous for eternity. Spiteful, too. And you could hardly take a walk without death leaping out at you. In those stories, people clung to the day-to-day. A dog barking, a trick played by a coyote, or staying warm, cooking food, things like that. Because just outside the village was the world, and that was a place of unknowns. You ventured too far out to sea, for instance—"

"Go ahead, say it. You go right ahead. You venture too far from what's day-to-day, you'd perhaps drown. Or drown yourself. Well, that's right. And I'm going to slip over-board."

"After you get some sleep, maybe."

"You see, it's been so hard, Enoch. What with everything. What with one thing or another, that damn most recent shawl to finish for Mrs. Dollard. For instance, that shawl —and for what? For a pittance. And then there's the leering of Reverend Sillet. His leering at me, like I was the only harlot since the Bible. Did he ever bring me up in a sermon? Did he ever use me as an example? Did he refer to me in a sermon on harlots?"

"I haven't been to church in some time."

"But did you hear of him doing as much? People tend to tell you things. They confide in you. They give you letters and they tell you things."

"No, Alaric, I never heard of Reverend Sillet mentioning you in church, no. Not by name. I'll personally ask him not to, if it'll make you feel better. Alaric, you might want to lie down now. You look awfully tired. I'll set out my coat for you. You've got this arduous plan, you know, and you'll need some strength to carry it out. Even to lift yourself over the side. That'll take some strength, even to lift your own weight. It's just now dark, so there's plenty of time. Plenty of time left tonight."

Her voice now trembling, she said, "When I'm dead, you just wait and see, Sillet will use my life as an example." She was barely whispering now. "He does that sort of thing, doesn't he? He even makes people from the Bible seem like his very own confiding friends, have you noticed? Like he knew Job and Ruth and the others personally, and then he goes and takes the privilege of his pulpit to gossip about their intimate lives. He'll open my marriage up to the congregation. Mark my word."

"Alaric, you sleep."

"I am tired just now."

I stepped into the cabin and saw that my mother had drifted off. She was curled on the floor. Enoch draped his coat over her.

"A cold wind is up," he said. "In a while we'll move her down to her bunk."

"I was listening in."

"There's still fifteen or so hours of water between here and Halifax. We'll keep a close watch on her. But I think she'll sleep at least till mid-morning. That's my guess. This stuff either wakes you up more than you've ever been or puts you out the same."

"You did a good thing here, Enoch."

"I'll bet Alaric won't think so." He started up the engine, and we set out night-traveling to Halifax.

8

My   Marriage

Mid-afternoon on October 24, we arrived at Halifax Harbour. Enoch brought us right alongside the wharf. On the dock next to ours I saw the *Doubting Thomas*. I tapped my mother on the shoulder and pointed out the other Newfoundland mail boat. "Somehow, when you get out in the world like this," she said, "coincidences get more frequent." There had been a drizzling rain that morning. A man dressed in galoshes and a black frock coat was pushing a wide broom along the pedestrian walkway that led to the commercial fish stalls. I had never before seen a broom used to push water back into the sea, except on board ship. Children were fishing in groups of two or three from all of the ten or so docks in sight. There was a general air of activity, the unloading and loading of crates, longshoremen shouting up and down decks and loading platforms, fish wagons, ice wagons, pushcarts rattling along cobblestones, gulls keening, darting here and there for a fishhead one of the children tossed aside. A cat was curled up in a wheelbarrow near some grain sacks; the sacks leaked grain-colored juices. On the north side of the harbor was a stone quay with a wagon road leading up into Halifax. The sharp odors of fish, wet burlap, and lumber filled the air. From on deck we could see all along the wharf, the granary silos, the ascending levels of commercial buildings, on up to the residential streets. We stood next to our suitcases.

"At the guest house," my mother said, "let's at least try to be civil to each other. Let's at least try and masquerade as people who still know each other, if for nothing other than Cora Holly's sake, meeting her in-law for the first time."

"Let alone her husband."

"The Hollys don't have the slightest notion of the worst part of our lives. My most recent letter to them kept wholly to the future."

"The future may be the worst part."

My mother and I each picked up our suitcase and did not move. It occurred to me then that we had left my father's suitcase in the bunkroom. Enoch set the plank and we walked down and stood at the bottom. "I'll be staying at the Princeport Hotel," Enoch said. "It's about ten blocks from the Hagerforse Guest House. Let me know when you want to return, whoever's going back, though it wouldn't surprise me if I go back alone." He lugged down one sack of mail, secured a wagon to take him and the mail to the postal depot. He threw the sack into the wagon. He handed the driver some money. The driver walked with Enoch back on board, and each of them retrieved two sacks of mail. Enoch made no introductions. He did not look at us or say a word. It was as though we were not there.

We walked to the end of the dock and up the street of fish stalls for a moment. My mother then set her suitcase down. "I'm still your mother, Fabian. No matter what else I've become. No matter what longing you have to disown me. I'm your mother," she said. "The most important thing to me—you should believe this—is that this wedding christen a new life for you. A new, exciting, and better life."

"I murdered Botho August. So what can you possibly be talking about?"

"Ye of little faith, and still, things may turn out for you."

She bent down, laid her suitcase flat on the cobblestones, snapped it open, and took out a cloth wrapping with a hard, rectangular object inside, which she handed to me.

"It's the Garganey for Cora Holly. I took the liberty, given that we were in such a hurry."

I followed my mother to the nearest fish stall. The peddler was a tall, stoop-shouldered man in his fifties, with thinning white hair and a deadpan expression.

"Can you please direct us to Robie Street?" my mother said.

He was arranging fish on a bed of ice. He looked up at my mother, then at me.

"Just off the boat, eh?"

"Just."

"Which boat? Not French, not Russian, no sir, you speak God's English, with some evidence of Newfie in it."

"Is a certain background required by you to get directions?"

He laughed as my mother stiffened. "From Newfoundland, then. Journey in from British Territory first class, did you?"

"On the mail boat," I said. "The *Aunt Ivy Barnacle*. Maybe you've seen it."

"I know all the ones that come in here. I know both the Newfoundland mail boats."

"And do you know the Hagerforse Guest House?" my mother said.

"On Robie Street, as you know."

"And how to get there?"

"Up Barrington to Spring Garden, past the park, right on Robie. A big white house with a porch and gables, oak trees all up and down. In direct view of the Citadel stockade. That's your most prominent landmark. I'll get you a carriage."

"Can we walk?"

"I'll get you a cheap carriage."

He called out, "Zasy!" A boy of about twelve left a game of dice with three other boys, all dressed in blood-splotched aprons.

"Get the ice wagon, son. Take these people up to the Hagerforse Guest House, on Robie," the peddler said.

In a few minutes the boy drove up a horse-drawn wagon. He handled the reins well. "Get on up, then," he said.

My mother and I sat on planks opposite each other. The wagon reeked of fish. There was a layer of wet, moldy newspapers and the planks were rough. My mother tucked her dress tight to her legs and brought her feet up and sat lengthwise. Zasy drove us past the enormous Lord Nelson Hotel. It had chairs on its porch, a chandelier hanging from the porch ceiling. We crossed the public garden. I saw a hoe lift above the hedges but did not see the gardener. We went up Sackville Street, full of shops and restaurants. Through a window I saw a woman lift a cup to her lips.

"Saturday's a big shopping day," Zasy said. "But seeing as I'm not getting paid to guide . . ."

The horse clomped on cobbles as we turned onto Bell Road, then along the park again, turning right onto Robie. There were four or five wagons moving along in both directions. I counted eight houses, and Zasy pulled up in front of the ninth, the Hagerforse Guest House. "Fare's a dollar," he said.

"I take a week to knit a shawl for two," my mother said. "I'll pay you a quarter of that, young man."

"Canadian," Zasy said.

I leapt down. I placed our suitcases next to the wagon, then helped my mother down. She handed Zasy a coin.

He flipped it into the air and caught it. "It's a quarter more than I had an hour ago," he said. "And it was time away from cleaning fish, is how I see it."

"Don't you carry in the suitcases?" my mother said.

"No, ma'am, I don't. I'm apprenticed to my father at the bins. I'm not a bellhop. Thanks for the coin, Newfies."

175

He swung the wagon around and moved down Robie Street.

"You didn't much come to my chivalrous rescue, Fabian."

"His father said 'Newfies,' and so did he."

"Well, let's hope that Mrs. Hagerforse is civil."

We walked up the stairs onto the porch. I used the brass knocker. Mrs. Hagerforse answered the door. We stepped inside. The hallway led directly to a drawing room; it had red couches, chairs with wooden armrests, a chandelier, and a fireplace. "You've arrived the afternoon of the wedding," Mrs. Hagerforse said. "How—unusual. We thought you'd perhaps be here last night, latest. For the rehearsal. And a lovely dinner as well. Oh, but just listen to me, reprimanding like a schoolmarm to weary travelers. Was there bad weather? And where, pray tell, is Mr. Vas?"

I would say that Mrs. Hagerforse was in her late fifties or early sixties. She had a brisk, restrained way of talking. Her grey hair was up in a tight bun. She tended to push out her lower lip into a child's pout. She waved her right hand around like a choirmaster. Her voice was pleasant enough, though, and while slightly nervous she seemed a sympathetic, attentive sort.

"I'm of course not invited to the wedding," she said. "But I've worn this formal dress simply because there's a wedding in my house."

"I take it that you're Mrs. Hagerforse," my mother said.

"Yes, and what's gotten into me! Yes, I'm Meredith Hagerforse. Welcome, of course. I don't know what's gotten into me, not properly introducing myself, I must seem frazzled as an egg on a skillet."

"I'm Fabian Vas, and this is my mother, Alaric—"

"Alaric Vas," my mother said. "Mr. Vas took sick along the way and went ashore. And where is Mr. Hagerforse?"

"I'm a widow."

"I might be now, too. I haven't gotten any news about Mr. Vas, you see."

"He was that ill, then?"

"I'm afraid so."

"Prayers are in order."

"We'll need to freshen up."

"Of course."

"And we'd like two separate rooms. One for me, one for my son. There's one for the newlyweds, already arranged."

"Well, yes, fine. There *is* an extra room available. Just for tonight, it happens. Mr. and Mrs. Holly, and Cora, the bride-to-be, are all settled in nicely. They slept well, they tell me."

"We're filthy top to bottom," my mother said. "From the long journey, you see. We must really now have some time."

"Let me show you to your rooms, then. My goodness, so little time," Mrs. Hagerforse said, frowning all the way down the hallway.

We stopped in front of room number 6. "This is yours, Mr. Vas."

"We'll pay for last night, too," I said. "The night we weren't here for but were supposed to be. And the extra room, too. My father made a lot of money killing birds on

177

Anticosti Island to earn it. He gave us some, all in Canadian."

"I have no doubt that any of what you tell me is true," Mrs. Hagerforse said. "Mrs. Vas, you'll be in room 8."

The hallway had braided rugs. So did the rooms. I bathed quickly, got out my strop razor, shaved, donned my suit, combed my hair. I knocked on my mother's door. "Fabian, come in," she said. I saw that she was dressed in her most formal church clothes, a black dress with small red flowers at the lacy cuffs, flowers along the neck. She had on white gloves. She looked quite beautiful, though her eyes were bloodshot, her skin windburned. "I didn't bring my creams," she said. She fidgeted, kneading up under her cheekbones with her hands as if trying to get the circulation going, draw up some color. She fussed with her hair, though it was braided as precisely as ever.

Mrs. Hagerforse appeared in the doorway. "I understand that Justice of the Peace Averell Grey will arrive promptly at five of four. The wedding is at four o'clock, of course. It's now—" She looked at the grandfather clock in the hallway. "Oh dear—it's almost that. The newlyweds' room, number 23, is upstairs. It has a private bath, naturally. The Hollys will be there now, I trust. Please excuse me." She hurried out.

"Particularly jittery woman, isn't she?" my mother said. "For an experienced innkeeper, you'd think— Well, I'm going to finish unpacking. They can't begin without us, can they? We'll stay calm."

She took care to smooth out each item of clothing—

sweater, shawl, nightgown, stocking—before placing it in a drawer or hanging it in the closet. "I managed a well-rounded wardrobe in my frantic state," she said. "I'm pleased."

I sat at the desk, looking out through the open door into the hallway, though only the enormous clock was in view. It was 4:16. That precisely was when the sight of a man sent a shiver through me, as though I had just put my feet into a tub of ice. He had stepped into the doorway and folded his arms across his chest. He stared at me. My mother did not see him. She was half inside the closet. I recognized him immediately. It was Mitchell Kelb, the constable from St. John's who had traveled down to investigate the death of Dalton Gillette. These many years later his features were more settled, his sideburns grey, but otherwise he looked as trim and neatly attired as he had in 1900. He turned and checked the time. Then, after quickly surveying the room, he nodded to me and was gone.

"He's here because we are," I said out loud.

"What? What did you mumble just now?"

"Mother, if you traveled overland, then caught the *Doubting Thomas*, you could get from Witless Bay to Halifax in good time."

"Well, we didn't have the proper amount of time to figure out a different travel route, did we?"

"It—I'm sorry, it was just something that got into my head."

Mrs. Hagerforse bustled into the room again. "My, you both look so nice. Groom and mother of the groom."

179

My mother sighed. "Perhaps this is all too rushed," she said. "This is a moment in life to savor, not simply get over with."

Although my mother had not addressed anyone in particular, Mrs. Hagerforse suddenly looked alarmed, all but horrified at the notion of postponement.

"Oh—" she said, then stammered, "There's, as I mentioned, no rooms for tomorrow night. None available. Tonight, by chance, there was the one vacancy."

My mother turned from the closet and looked at Mrs. Hagerforse. "I only meant we might have the ceremony later this evening."

Again Mrs. Hagerforse's composure seemed shattered by such a harmless suggestion. She left the room.

"Peculiar," my mother said.

Keeping to the doorway, I peered down the hall. There I saw Mrs. Hagerforse knocking on a room door. The door opened and Mitchell Kelb beckoned her in. I stepped back and had such an overwhelmingly clear image of when I had first seen Kelb eleven years before that the words "Do you know what happened to Margaret's bicycle?" seemed to rush forward from that very day.

"You *are* talking pure nonsense. Nervous groom, is all. Come with me. I've straightened up in the mirror. It's time."

She took my arm and walked me down the hallway to the staircase. We went upstairs to room 23. My mother knocked.

But Mrs. Hagerforse suddenly appeared, out of breath, and knocked on the door herself, then opened it.

Near the bay window, Pavel and Klara Holly stood holding hands. While Mrs. Hagerforse's voice was full of cheer,
the Hollys' expressions were at best confused. They both
looked to be in their late forties. Mrs. Holly struck me as
an outsized woman; she was not ungainly, mind you, or fat,
but big-boned, as they say. She was a good two inches taller
than Pavel Holly. She wore a broad sloping hat rimmed
with flowers. It actually hid all of her forehead. But I could
see that she had generous features, and, to steal a phrase
from Isaac Sprague, "uncompromised blue" eyes. Her smile
truly broadened her cheeks, though at the moment it took
real effort for her to smile. At 4:30 the planter's clock on
the desk behind Klara set itself in motion; a farmer and his
wife paraded out the hinged door, each holding a pitchfork,
trailed by three goats. The figures completed a half-circle,
then disappeared back into the clock. The sun, moon, and
stars clicked a bit to the right on their copper sky and Klara
suddenly said, "Mrs. Hagerforse, might that clock be for
sale?"

"Klara!" Pavel Holly said. "Now is hardly—"

"Quite so, and I'm—" Klara said.

"We can discuss—" Mrs. Hagerforse said.

Each sentence had been brought up short; immediately,
everyone but Pavel and my mother found a chair and sat
down.

Klara, who wore a formal dark blue gown with a pale
white corsage attached with a long, black-headed pin, used
a polished cane even to shift a step or two to the side. She
seemed to have shinnied down the cane, fixing it into the

rug in front of her chair. I liked her face. Even at a glance, it was not hard to see that her arthritic movements revealed long suffering. I wondered if it had been physically painful for her to have sat for hours, composing letters to my mother. She now leaned forward on her cane.

Pavel had been standing stiffly in his black suit. The way that he held his fists at his sides not only betrayed tenseness but also reminded me that Cora had stood a similar way in the photograph. Whether it was part of his natural countenance or born of the awkwardness of the moment, he had a morose look. When he stepped forward to shake hands with me, he said, "Fabian, Fabian, yes, well," in a low, blustery voice. He had a strong handshake. I realized that I did not know what line of work he was in. "What line of work are you in?" I said. Slightly taken aback, he said, "The exact question a man might ask of his future son-in-law, except I know that you repair boats." He laughed without smiling. "Well," he said, "I'm a hooper. I forge barrel hoops. That's my specialty. And I'm an all-around blacksmith, though hoops are the mainstay, you see." His handshake made more sense to me then. His black sideburns thickened into a beard that accentuated his dark eyes. When he looked at me, he held his lips slightly open, and I saw that he had prominent buck teeth.

"Where is Cora?" my mother said, walking up to Klara first, kissing her cheek, then over to Pavel, and kissing his.

"It has been some years now, hasn't it, Alaric," Klara said. "More than I care to count. Anyway, we had so looked forward to seeing Orkney. His illness—Mrs. Hagerforse told us—sounds grave. It must have been painful to leave him."

"Where is Cora, though?"

"You see," Pavel said, "the bride-to-be is using all the water in Halifax, it seems. She's on her third or fourth bath, I've lost count."

"Why won't she come out?"

"It may just be a case of matrimonial jitters," Klara said. "I'm quite sure, had there been more time, you and I could have gone into a separate room and told stories of our own wedding days. Perhaps later, in a letter."

I had not seen Averell Grey step into the room. "Ahem, excuse me. Welcome," he said.

"Now isn't this nice," Mrs. Hagerforse said. "Justice of the Peace Grey, this is Alaric Vas, Fabian Vas, Klara Holly in the chair, and Pavel Holly."

"Pleased. And where is Cora Holly?"

Grey, a slim man of perhaps sixty, had wispy white hair and age spots on his face, so many it was like a map of islands. "I forgot my Bible," he said. "Of course there's one in this good Christian home."

We heard the sound of splashing behind the door.

"I'll be direct here," Pavel said. "There was a Bible in the room here, and by some ingenious means our Cora has wedged it so that the door is impossible to open from the outside. That, along with the lock, of course."

"I'll need a Bible," Grey said. "For the ceremony."

"I'll see to it," Mrs. Hagerforse said, leaving the room.

183

"Fabian," Pavel said, "as her future husband, you might try and convince—"

"I'd like to look at her," I said. "What I mean is, all I've ever seen of your daughter is the photograph."

"It was an exact likeness," Pavel said. "A few years back likeness."

"There is a practical side to her coming out of the bath," Grey said. "To have the wedding itself. Nothing more practical than that, eh?" He was the only one who laughed.

"We're getting along so well here," Klara said. "Let's all, except for Fabian, go into one of our rooms, or that lovely sitting room downstairs, and continue to."

And in a moment I stood at the bathroom door, waiting for the spigot to be shut off. When I heard more splashing, I said, "Cora, it's me, Fabian Vas."

"I'm actually dressed," she said. "I've been dressed for more than an hour. I did take a bath, but then got dressed. I've been filling and emptying the bathtub. All done through pipes here. Not like at home."

The door opened and I stepped back. Add the years hence, but Cora looked much as she had in her photograph, except now she had on a high-collared white lace wedding dress. "You're shorter than in my imagination," she said. "Do you look like your father?"

"A little."

"I've never seen him or you in a photograph. Why wasn't one sent?"

"I don't know."

"Take a good look. I was an ugly child. Then, at age

thirteen, I was dizzyingly beautiful. That was my father's opinion, my mother's, my neighbors in Richibucto's. I weighed their opinions carefully, then agreed. First I was ugly, though, then quite the opposite. And now I'm aware I contain both. But that doesn't mean I feel average. I've never felt that. No, it's more that I remember being both ugly and beautiful, and hope that one stays and the other doesn't come back. We'll just have to wait and see."

"Sit down, Cora. Please. In that chair, and I'll sit on the other chair."

We sat looking at each other. I stood, walked into the bathroom, poured a glass of water, and handed it to her.

"Thank you." She drank the water, then held the empty glass. "This is the worst moment of my life."

"I don't know anything. I don't know anything, except one thing that's true—"

"One."

"—it's that my mother and father wanted me to get married in the worst way. Not to Margaret Handle, who—"

"I see."

"Did you get to read my mother's letters?"

"I had parts read to me."

"There's a man in the hallway that probably won't allow this wedding."

"Who can you be talking about?"

"I've slept with Margaret Handle, whom you've never heard of, I know, until just now. I've shot a man named Botho August and he died."

"Please stop now. I'm going back into the bath."

185

"No—don't."

I reached over to the table and took up the drawing of the garganey. Handing it to Cora, I said, "Here's something I drew for the occasion."

She unwrapped it from its cloth.

"It's a garganey," I said. "A kind of sea duck."

"A lovely memento. I've room for it in my suitcase, I'm sure."

"I know about birds. One of Newfoundland's specialties is petrels, did you know that?"

"Tell me something not to be frightened of you."

"Petrels, they're rarely found inshore. Though sometimes they come in on a storm and fly overland a day or two. We call them 'Mother Carey's Chickens' in Witless Bay. They get almost tame, some of them. They'll sit right on your hand. We've got Leach's petrels, dovekies, puffins, razorbills, murres, terns, kittiwakes. We get ibis. Crows. Ducks. Many different ducks. Bullbirds. We even see a garganey now and then."

"The worst, worst day."

"You look very nice in the wedding dress. It's not that, Cora. It's that there's a man in the hallway going to arrest me. I know it."

The door opened. "The photographer's here!" Mrs. Hagerforse announced. "Shall we proceed?"

Klara, my mother, and Pavel came in. "All acquainted now?" Klara said, sitting in a chair.

"I need to wash my face," Cora said.

Leaving the bathroom door wide open, Cora washed her face in the sink.

"Privately bathing one minute, a public display of cleanliness the next," Pavel said. "An interesting young lady, wouldn't you say, Fabian?"

"Yes, I would."

A tripod camera, a black box on spindle legs, all but hid the photographer who carried it into the room. He set down the camera, splayed open its legs, steadied it, turned to the room, and bowed. "Alex Quonian," he said.

He was lanky, about forty years old, had long black hair combed to one side of his face. His brown trousers were belted tightly. He had on a collarless white shirt and a white smock coat. He was all matter-of-fact. He began to organize his thoughts by chopping at the air, as though adding angles to the room. He hummed. Cora began to laugh. It was true, Quonian went about things with comic deliberation. He frowned at Cora. As he stepped by me, I noticed that he used moustache bleach. He looked harassed. He plucked a dust mouse from the floor near the sofa and said, "My wife's the better photographer of the two of us. She's working in the darkroom today."

"Oh, I've seen Mr. Quonian's work," Mrs. Hagerforse said. "And I assure you, he's being modest."

"Let's rehearse a pose," Quonian said.

The room contained a dark blue sofa with quilted pillows, four chairs, a table, a night table next to the bed. On the mantel was an ebony swan vase full of violets. There were lace curtains on the windows to either side of the large bay window. A scrimshaw tusk was in a glass case on the center table.

Taking each of us firmly by the shoulders, Quonian

placed me next to Cora. Klara and Pavel stood to Cora's right, my mother to my left.

"Children, please. Rehearse a smile. You look as though I should place black hoods over your heads and call a priest."

"Normally—that is, under different circumstances," Mrs. Hagerforse said, "there would have been less of a rush." She stood near the door.

"Well, after the vows are exchanged," Quonian said, "just turn and look at the camera." He walked to the door and stood next to Mrs. Hagerforse.

Mitchell Kelb now wedged past Quonian.

"Oh yes, sir—please, do come in," Grey said.

"Who's this?" Klara said.

"You see, Mrs. Holly," Grey said, "we need an official witness, other than family. Mrs. Hagerforse preferred not to."

"I see," Klara said.

"Legalities and all that," Grey said. "This is Mr. Mitchell Kelb."

If in fact my mother had ever seen Mitchell Kelb back in 1900, she did not recognize him now, nor did she remember his name.

"Congratulations," Kelb said to me. He lifted my hand and shook it.

"A tourist?" Klara said.

"Of sorts," Kelb said.

"Well, it's kind of you to help out," Pavel said.

"Not at all."

My throat went dry and suddenly I said to Grey, "How much do you charge? I want to get this settled."

"Fabian, please—" my mother said.

"No, no, that's fine," Grey said. "Four dollars. It's understandable. Newlyweds often like to know just what they have. You'll have just four dollars less than you had before, Mr. Vas."

"Mother, give him that amount, will you?"

My mother reached into her snap purse and handed me four Canadian dollar bills. I handed them to Grey.

"That's taken care of," Grey said. Mrs. Hagerforse handed him a Bible. "Please, now, Cora, Fabian, your hands clasped on the Good Book."

Cora put her folded hands on the Bible. I put my hands on top of hers. The ceremony was mercifully brief. At the last moment Cora stepped out of her shoes. I could not possibly know why, except that it was her one personal choice in the matter.

Grey said a few words about life from his own experiences, not mine, not Cora's; then we said the vows. "By the powers invested in me—"

"Fabian, you may kiss the bride."

"No, first the rings," Pavel said.

My mother handed me the rings. She had got them from Romeo Gillette. We exchanged rings. They fit perfectly.

"Fabian—"

My lips—or was it Cora's—were dry as paper.

We posed for Quonian. His head disappeared under the black canopy. The black apparatus connecting the box and lens was ridged like an accordion. Feet wide apart, voice muffled, Quonian called out, "Smile!" He pressed the shutter bulb. The powder gusted. Quonian emerged from under the canopy, slid out the film, looked at us, and said, "Perfect."

Even to this day I feel, as though it is in my blood, the acceleration of events that followed, and the bewilderment that accompanied them.

Mitchell Kelb reached into his trouser pocket, pulled out and shook loose a pair of handcuffs, then clamped them over my wrists. He took a piece of paper from his shirt pocket, unfolded it, and said, "I have a warrant for the arrest of one Orkney Vas—absent. For one Fabian Vas, present. For one Alaric Vas, present. For suspicion of the murder, or conspiracy to murder, one Botho August, citizen of Witless Bay, Newfoundland Territory, on or approximately on October 8, 1911. The execution of this warrant is so witnessed by all gathered here on October 24, 1911. I'll have each witness sign the warrant. It is my sworn duty to return Fabian and Alaric Vas to Witless Bay to stand trial. But I'm willing to wait, out of heartfelt courtesy, for the groom. Fabian, you may sit with your bride for one hour. No more."

Kelb removed one handcuff, led me to a chair, pushed me down into it, fastened the loose handcuff to the table, then looked at my mother.

"Mrs. Vas," Kelb said, "I'll now escort you to the mail boat. Courtesy of Mr. Enoch Handle, whom I've only recently spoken to; we'll leave first thing in the morning. I've already added unlawful flight to Orkney Vas's warrant. Fabian, I'll be back to take you in one hour."

"What the hell is this all about?" Pavel said.

"Didn't you hear what I just said?" Kelb said.

"I'll slip over the side," my mother said.

"Will she try to do that?" Kelb said to me.

I stood up as far as the cuffs allowed.

Pavel Holly all but tore the ring from my finger. Klara threw her arms around Cora. Pavel picked up the wedding certificate and tore it into confetti. "This marriage is no longer!" he said.

"Shut the goddamn hell up and control yourself," Kelb said. He turned to me again. "Would your mother go over the side of the boat?"

"She might."

"Well, as for anyone in my custody going over the side, fine. Mrs. Vas, you go right ahead. Do that. Public opinion will no doubt consider it an admittance of guilt, and what's more, it won't exonerate anyone else. Son or husband. It'd just save England a little time, having to try two instead of three, should we catch Mr. Orkney Vas, that is. Four, if we add Miss Margaret Handle to the mix."

"Why in God's name did you ever allow this wedding to take place?" Klara shouted, swinging her cane at Kelb and falling to the floor. Pavel helped her up. She sat back in her chair. "Why weren't we spared this humiliation? This is our daughter, brought all the way in from Richibucto. This is her wedding day."

Kelb folded the warrant into his pocket again. "Forget the signatures," he said.

"I asked you a question," Klara said.

Mitchell Kelb clipped the handcuff key to his belt. He stared at his shoes. "I don't know for certain," he said. "I could have prevented it. I apologize. I got caught up in a romantic moment."

Pavel Holly stepped forward and slammed his fist into my jaw. I reeled backward, table and all, into the camera. Sprawled on the floor, I looked up to see Quonian dragging the camera from the room. From out in the hallway I heard him say, "There's been damages."

Kelb had drawn his revolver and pointed it at Pavel. "It's over now," he said. "Fabian Vas here may be a witness to a murder. Don't strike him again." He tucked the revolver into his belt.

Looking down at me, Pavel took Cora by the arm and said, "My daughter won't spend a single minute further with you."

And she did not. The Hollys moved to the door. "Mr. Kelb, you are correct," Pavel said. "This is over. We are going home."

"Goodbye, Fabian Vas," Cora said. The Hollys left the room.

Kelb said, "Mrs. Vas, let's go. The boy no doubt can still use an hour to think. He's woke up from a bad dream into a worse one."

Quonian was gone. Mrs. Hagerforse was gone. My mother, Mitchell Kelb, and Grey followed. Grey closed the door.

Dragging the table, I moved to the bay window. My

mouth was bleeding. My jaw felt broken. I pulled myself up and looked out. On three parallel clotheslines stretching across someone's back yard, there was an abacus of sparrows. I don't know the birds in this city, I thought. I did not even know the drab sparrows.

9

T *h e* H *e a r i n g*

In clear weather we returned to Witless Bay in two days. Immediately we were put under house arrest. We could not leave our house, except under Mitchell Kelb's supervision. Romeo brought us groceries. On our fourth day back, sunny, cold, Kelb took my mother out rowing in the harbor. My mother had simply said, "Mr. Kelb, I'm cooped up here. Would you take me rowing," and Kelb had obliged her without a fuss. Except that he did handcuff her to the thwart she sat on. When they returned, my mother said, "It was a perfectly nice morning. Mr. Kelb preferred not to talk, so he was especially good company. He's a bachelor. I think I'll knit him a sweater. I assured him I wouldn't leap into the sea. He said the handcuffs assured him more."

At night my mother kept to her bedroom. I kept to mine. Margaret slept on the sofa and Kelb would lay out a rucksack on the kitchen floor. We would sit together at meals. "This arrangement is hell on earth," Margaret said one evening. No one disagreed.

On our seventh night under house arrest, Romeo brought us a pot of cod stew, two loaves of bread, and a pan full of cod tongues. "Young Marni Corbett made this fruitcake for you," he said, putting the cake on the table. "Wasn't that nice? I don't know all what a child her age can understand about your situation. But she baked this on her own and said it might cheer you up."

"Stay for supper?" my mother said.

"I can't. We're meeting a new lighthouse keeper tonight. Me, Boas, Enoch, some others."

My mother drew up a pained expression, looking away from Romeo.

"What's his name, this new lighthouse keeper?" Margaret said.

"Odeon Sloo."

Despite our somber mood the name made us burst into laughter. "Sloo" was local slang for "get out of the way."

"Well, odd name or no, he seems just right for the job," Romeo said. "He's brought his wife and daughter with him, all willing to move in promptly and get used to things over the winter. The wife is Kira, the daughter Millie—Millicent, I imagine. He's brought his family. He's a family man. And he's had lighthouse experience in two places north of St. John's."

"What drove him from those?" Kelb said.

"I asked him that. He said that he wanted to live south of St. John's."

Even though it was none of his business, Kelb seemed satisfied with the answer.

"Has he been in our lighthouse?" Margaret said.

"He's toured it, yes. He, his wife, and his daughter all did."

"Did he show interest in the gramophone?" Margaret said.

"As a matter of fact, he commented on it. He said he admired it but didn't want it. He said if hired he'd bring in his own possessions."

"What day has been settled on for our hearing to start?" my mother said.

"Ask Mr. Kelb there," Romeo said.

"Tomorrow," Kelb said.

"Romeo," said Margaret, "please ask my father not to forget to bring me what I asked for. He'll understand."

"I'll tell him tonight."

"Thank you."

Late that night, after my mother and Kelb had fallen asleep, Margaret and I sat at the kitchen table. "I notice you gave Kelb your bed tonight," she said to me.

"I told him I wanted to stay up painting. To get my mind off things. But I won't paint. I'll just sit here."

Margaret stood up, stretched, and said, "Groan my bones, a woman my age shouldn't be so tired. But I am." She sat down.

"Margaret, what happened after we left Witless Bay, my father, mother, and me?"

"Mitchell Kelb was sent for right away. He began snooping, a regular detective. All but door-to-door. I knew that sooner or later he'd come to my house. Do you know how I prepared for that?"

"Tell."

"I hoarded away five bottles of Enoch's whiskey, plus three I bought myself. They're all smuggled in and hidden in your pantry, right here."

"Then Kelb arrested you?"

"Yes. But he was polite about it. He knocked on my door. I looked him over. I said I remembered him. He said, 'I remember you, too, Margaret. May I call you that?' I said that he could. 'I'm going to officially place you under house arrest,' he said. 'Suspicion of murder, or being part of a conspiracy to murder Botho August.' Words to that effect. 'Do you want to put up a fuss?' I said I didn't. He took me directly to your house. He assigned a deputy, a man named Llewellyn Boxer, to keep an eye on me while he tracked you and Alaric and Orkney down. Boxer showed up a few hours later. Kelb was right out front about his plans. No secret there. He said he was going overland to the south to try and catch the *Doubting Thomas*. Romeo had told him your wedding date. Kelb said he had to leave right away. He went out on the porch, then came back in. 'I've seen you twice in my life,' he said to me. 'Both times I find that you're in trouble. If coincidence were otherwise merciful, we'd have run into one another, just to nod in passing somewhere in Newfoundland, on a day that you were happy.' "

"Did you have a reply?"

"I said, 'I'm a girl who looks to the future.' "

198

"The future, even for the next day, looks pretty bleak to me. In fact, it scares the hell out of me."

"I sit here. I look at you, Fabian. I think, I'm sitting across from a man who was married for less than five minutes. My father told me that news. He said that Mitchell Kelb was holding forth in Gillette's store one morning. He had everyone enthralled, a regular talking whirligig, for such a composed man."

"I was hoping you wouldn't hear details of the wedding."

"Hear them or not, they'd still be the truth. You're the village idiot, Fabian. You deserve what you get. An arranged marriage can't mean you can arrange how the marriage will go. I laugh. Our time in the marriage bed alone would've been hours. Not five minutes, that's for sure. What was the room number you got married in?"

"Twenty-three."

"I've jotted that down in my mind."

Margaret went to the pantry. She opened a bottle of whiskey, poured a glass for herself, then came back and sat at the table.

"The night Botho was shot," she said. "Do you remember it raining cats and dogs? Well, inside the lighthouse the rain was drumming in my ears. Botho had come down from the housing and he got me right into his bed. When we were done, he went up to the foghorn again."

"I asked about after we left, not that night."

"I'm starting my little tale earlier. Don't interrupt a guest in your house, Fabian."

I poured a glass for myself.

"Back down from the housing later," Margaret said, "Botho got it into his head to show me his hobby. Hobby other than the gramophone, that is. This was a man who didn't just stare at the walls between foggy nights. No. He invented a whole menagerie, hours' worth of animals, and he had all of these ways of clenching and bending his fingers to make shadows. It was child's play, but he took it deadly seriously. And he was showing me his skills when you shot out the window."

"I saw your hand helping his out. I was in the yard looking up. I saw your hand."

"I'd had a good bit to drink."

"Had I gone to your house earlier that night, it might have kept a murder from occurring."

"I don't know."

"You might not have gone to the lighthouse. I might not have shot Botho August."

"He still would have died, is my bet. You just got there first."

"Maybe so. Maybe my father—"

"You know, I didn't actually see you shoot Botho. But I know that you did, Fabian. I know it. I heard the shots. But at first I didn't dare go to the window."

"I heard that goddamned gramophone."

"God, he was stingy with those records. Would not let me touch a one, or even make a selection. That night I was reeling around. I laid a hand on a record, tore a rut. A terrible sound, really. Louder than a gull close-up."

"Why, Margaret? Why did you go there that night?"

"To punish you for being a moron. I had half thought out a plan. First, I would go see Botho. Second, I'd tell you about it. And third, I'd tell Romeo, so everyone else would know. Then I was going to go up and live with my aunt for a week or so, and let you think me over. I hoped that jealousy might shake a clear notion into your head, or shake the arranged marriage out, one and the same. Every plan's really half thought out, isn't it, because you can't know the consequences. But any plan was better than none, and it was getting close to your wedding."

"They might ask you intimate things at the hearing, you know."

"Of course they will. What's a hearing for? They'll cross-shackle me, make me tell my part in it. What I was doing in the lighthouse, as if they don't already know. They'll want to hear me say it, though. It's only natural."

"I suppose so. What did you do once you heard the shots?"

"I walked down the stairs. Botho was coughing up blood, all down his shirt. You'd left him for dead, maybe because he looked dead. But he wasn't. Not yet. I looked close, too. I saw the revolver. I started for it, but then—how could this happen?—Botho went for it, too. It was like the first moment of his being a ghost; he mustered up enough strength. He tore off his nightshirt. He went for the gun. I got to it first. I looked at him. It went off. Bang! Fabian, I don't remember pulling the trigger. I swear. I don't know what happened. I hated him, true. I had just lain with him. But did I want to kill him? That I don't know. Maybe I just wanted to finish what you'd started, then hope you'd get blamed, I was that angry at you. I did shoot him, though. Then I heard someone slapping through the mud."

"That must have been my father."

"It was. It was Orkney. I went back up into the lighthouse. I stood at the window. He took Botho's pulse. He picked up the revolver, then dropped it and ran off. I went back down the stairs. I took the revolver and went home. Enoch was asleep. I sat on my bed, drinking. Then—I don't even know what time—Alaric and Orkney were in my house. I heard their voices. They woke up my father. They were talking, then they were gone."

I finished my drink. Margaret poured herself another. "Your father didn't fire a shot," she said.

We sat awhile in silence.

"Was there a funeral?" I said.

"The morning after the murder, a lot of people actually saw Botho lying in the mud. It was like a procession. And guess what? I got right in line. When that old buzzard Sillet got wind of what had happened, he took over. He got to Botho's body and he was just fuming. He waved everyone off. He got some men; it was Giles, Peter Kieley, and Romeo. They carried the body to the funeral parlor. Peter Kieley dispatched himself to St. John's to report the murder. Two days later Mitchell Kelb showed up. He moved into Spivey's. The rest went as I told you."

"But, Margaret, was there a funeral?"

"Yes, but the strange thing was, who could people offer condolences to, really? August had no family. And people over the years hadn't exactly come to feel family feelings toward him, or vice versa. In the very next Sunday's sermon, Sillet took a moment to remember Botho."

"You were in church?"

"I sat front and center. Me and my paramour, Llewellyn Boxer."

"And what did Sillet say?"

"Not much of anything. But he called on Patrick Flood. And Patrick stood right up. He recounted close scrapes he'd had out in his boat, how Botho threaded the needle with his lighthouse beam, and how he—Patrick—appreciated being alive. 'When a sudden gale catches you—' and, 'I have other thoughts about Mr. August, but that's the one I think is most fit, seeing as he's deceased.' Patrick was evenhanded and calm throughout."

"Where is Botho buried?"

"Tucked to the northeast corner of the cemetery. A flat stone."

"And who buried him?"

"If you're wondering, Fabian, was there a nice, respectful ceremony graveside, no, there wasn't. No SACRED TO THE MEMORY on the marker. But at the same time, it was a clear, beautiful day, and people did turn out. Not many, but some. I was escorted by Llewellyn Boxer. If it was all a lark to him, he was still a gentleman about it. Just a young man of eighteen, I'd guess. Early to the law enforcement profession. Maybe ten others were there. Counting Sillet, naturally. Counting the gravedigger, Darwin McKinney. Counting Isabel Kinsella, the seasoned griefmonger; she was there. No tears were shed as far as I could see. But there were a few people who looked to be barely holding back tears. Any funeral will cause that."

"I'm surprised you attended."

"It got me out of the house. I simply dressed in black. I walked with Llewellyn Boxer, not arm in arm, to the cemetery. Amen. Amen. And how do you suppose I spent the hour or two after?"

"I don't want to guess."

"All right, I'll tell you. The only men I'd ever known intimately were either dead or in Halifax getting married. I couldn't freely go out and shoot ducks. Most ducks were gone from the harbor, anyway. I couldn't leave this house. House arrest. And Llewellyn Boxer saw that my poor brain was on the loose. We sat at the table and I just started to talk. Talked and talked and talked. I fixed us each a sandwich. The poor boy. He got an earful, but don't ask me of what. I can't remember what I said at all. It was just talk. And when I was done, I wanted to take a nap and told Llewellyn Boxer. He just said, 'Fine,' as if I'd used up every other word in the dictionary, with all my talking. And I slept the rest of the day and night. And as you well know, that's not a traditional habit with me."

Margaret walked to the window and looked out. "Hey, look!" she said. She opened the door and dragged in her childhood bicycle. "My father must have brought it. He didn't knock to say hello, though."

"He might have been afraid of violating house arrest."

"He might have."

She propped the bicycle against the wall. She stooped and checked the spokes, the tires, the handlebars. "My pop's got this in top shape," she said.

"I'm going over to the sofa now," I said. "I'll stay to one side of it, if you want the other. I'm more tired than I thought."

"No, help yourself. I'll sit awhile."

I fell off quickly. The next morning, I found Margaret asleep at the table. The bottle was empty.

My mother was making tea. Mitchell Kelb was smoking a cigar on the porch.

"Margaret was talking in her sleep," my mother said. "It woke me. I came out to listen, but for the life of me, and I leaned close, I couldn't make out a word she said."

The hearing was held in Gillette's store.

Romeo sat on a barrel of nails, in the front row of barrels. To his immediate left sat Boas LaCotte. To his right, Enoch Handle. Margaret, my mother, and I sat at the defendant's table, to the direct right of the judge's table at the front of the store. The hearing was popular. There was want of room. People even sat on the porch, dressed in coats and sweaters.

As a formality, Mitchell Kelb stood up from his seat at the judge's table and announced, "November two, nineteen and eleven, ten o'clock in the morning."

"Duly noted," Mekeel Dollard said. She was taking down the proceedings in shorthand.

"Now, this is just a preliminary hearing," Kelb said. "To

determine whether to transfer it up to St. John's, where the worst crimes end up. I'd sent, as some of you know, Enoch Handle up to St. John's to fetch a presiding judge. Honorable Judge H. L. Fain. But Enoch Handle returned to say that Judge Fain is bedridden, and he's appointed me representative of His Majesty. Representative magistrate. So that's what I am to you. I didn't expect this, but now it's official."

He fell silent. He closed his eyes a moment. Then he looked at the gathering. "I'll tell you a thimbleful about myself," he said. "Then we'll get on with it. I was born in Cupids, Newfoundland, in 1864, but by the time I was three I was in England. That's private family circumstances. I grew up there, and when I came back I was trained in law enforcement in St. John's, paid for by the crown. I had a year of law books to boot. I've presided over one previous hearing, but that was merely for theft."

Kelb paused. "Now," he said, "who examined the body?"

"I did," Romeo said.

"Stand up."

Romeo stood.

"Why you?"

"I'm half a doctor," Romeo said.

"And what did you discover in your examination?"

"Three bullets hit Botho August."

"And that makes up the physical evidence, three bullets?"

"Yes. Plus the revolver." He pointed to the revolver on the table.

"Thank you, Mr. Gillette. Mrs. Dollard, did you get all that?"

"Yes," Mekeel Dollard said.

"Good."

Romeo sat down.

"We'll talk about the revolver now," Kelb said.

But there was a commotion in the back of the store. Along the middle aisle people stepped back. I saw Bevel Cabot, Miriam Auster, Giles LaCotte, Ruth Henley, Olive Perrault. Toward the back were Elmer Wyatt, Peter Kieley, Patrick Flood holding his son Colin, Seamus Doyle. Carrying a Bible, Reverend Sillet made his way to the front. He stood sideways to Kelb, facing me and Margaret. "If one be found slain," he said, reciting by heart. But now he opened the Bible. "—in the land which the Lord thy God giveth thee to possess it, lying in the field, and it be not known who hath slain him: Then thy elders and thy judges shall come forth, and they shall measure unto the cities which are round about him that is slain: And it shall be, that the city which is next unto the slain man, even the elders of that city shall take an heifer—"

"Reverend Sillet, sit down," Kelb said.

Sillet ignored him and went on: "—heifer which hath not been wrought with, and which hath not drawn in the yoke; And the elders of that city shall bring down the heifer unto a rough valley, which is neither eared nor sown, and shall strike off the heifer's neck there—"

"Mrs. Dollard," Kelb said, "this is not testimony. Don't bother."

"—in the valley: And the priests the sons of Levi shall come near; for them the Lord thy God hath chosen to minister unto him, and to bless in the name of the Lord; and by their word shall every controversy and every stroke be tried: And all the elders of that city, that are next unto the slain man, shall wash their hands over the heifer that is beheaded in the valley: And they shall answer and say, Our hands have not shed this blood, neither have our eyes seen it. Be merciful, O Lord, unto thy people Israel, whom thou hast redeemed, and lay not innocent blood unto thy people of Israel's charge. And the blood shall be forgiven them."

Sillett glowered at Kelb. "Deuteronomy 21:1–8," he said. He then all but pulled a barrel out from under Boas LaCotte and maneuvered it next to the judge's table as Boas stepped to the wall. He sat down on the barrel, staring fixedly toward the back of the store. He slapped the closed Bible once against his open hand.

John Rut, a man who had fished off Newfoundland for forty years, called out, "There's no Levis who live here, so there's no goddamned sons of Levi."

"Mr. Rut, it is, I believe," Kelb said. "I didn't ask your opinion."

"I'll offer it, anyway, free of charge. My opinion is this: Somebody *did* shed some blood, and whoever did probably watched themselves do it. Their eyes *did* see it done. Why not ask, Mr. Kelb, straight out. Ask one question straight out: 'Is there anyone here in this room murdered the light-house keeper Botho August?' It might get direct results."

"That's maybe more effective than English proceedings," Kelb said, "but it's not my protocol here. The truth doesn't usually come that quick in such cases, anyway."

"It came quick to Botho August," Rut said. "It came quick three times."

"Let's stay calm and clear-headed and respectful here," Kelb said. "This is not an easy task. Here are three people whom you've known many years: Margaret Handle, Fabian Vas, Alaric Vas. Plus Orkney Vas, not here today, but still, you've known him and he is on trial. Calm and respectful, please. I don't want to have to clear the store. Now I want to continue. I want to follow the revolver. Mr. Gillette, do you keep transactions written down?"

Sillet slapped the Bible. Kelb glared at him and Sillet stayed quiet.

"Yes," said Romeo. "For the past eight years, I've jotted things down and Margaret Handle tallies them up. She keeps the ledgers. She keeps them in her attic."

"Previous to today, did I ask you to look up the particular revolver in question?"

"Yes, you did. You said to look it up and see if Orkney Vas, Alaric Vas, Fabian Vas, or Margaret Handle ever bought it from me."

"What did the ledgers say?"

"Margaret Handle bought it from me on September 5, 1908. She put it in the ledger herself. In her own writing."

Kelb looked at Mekeel Dollard and spoke slowly: "Now, I've had three men, pretty much bullet and gun experts in Witless Bay, match up the murder bullets to this revolver. Two were in Botho August. The one in the neck and the gut shot. At first the one that went through the high ribs was missing. But later we found it on the ground."

Sillet was overwhelmed and stood up. He pointed at Margaret. "I hope you're not carrying Botho August's child!" he said. "Because if you are, you only need to turn to chapter

and verse, you'll see there are things a person can do that'll
put a curse on a family, legitimate or not, for a hundred
generations."

"Reverend Sillet!" Kelb said, slamming his fist on the
table. "We're establishing the nature of the actual shooting
itself, slow as the truth comes. We're conducting a hearing,
not a Sunday-school class. If need be, we'll hear about relations between Mr. August and Miss Handle later on. I
won't tolerate your interruptions."

"God held the first trial. He has to be present at every
one."

"All right, He's here. Are you satisfied, Reverend? You
seem to want a drama of your own making."

"Why not go upstairs to the lighthouse," Margaret said
to Sillet, "put on one of Botho's gramophone records, sing
at the top of your voice, 'Almighty Vast and Blessed Is
Thine Heart That Confer Baptism Upon the Very Creatures of Thy Wondrous Sea,' window open, citizens of this
fine village paying a price for a ticket?"

"A murder shouldn't draw out her sense of humor, should
it, now, Mr. Kelb?"

"I adjourn," Kelb said. "I'm a magistrate highly annoyed
just now."

"It's been just over an hour, though," Mekeel Dollard
said.

"Well, note that down, then."

Sitting at my father's place at our table, Kelb unpacked
his lunch. He set out a cold baked potato, then poured a
glass of water from the pitcher. He took out a jackknife,

then a small whetstone. He sharpened the knife. He cut the potato into four equal parts. He stuck the knife into a piece and put it into his mouth. He wiped the knife across his trouser knee, then set it on the table. My mother sat down with a cup of tea across from Kelb. Margaret and I sat in the other two chairs.

"Mr. Kelb," my mother said, "would you care for some potato-leek soup, like the rest of us?"

"I prefer my potatoes out of soup."

"Mr. Kelb, do you think that our hearing will last until Guy Fawkes?"

One of the traditional festivals was Guy Fawkes Night, held on November 5. Huge bonfires were lit in memory of the attempt to blow up the Parliament buildings in the time of King James I. People stacked up green boughs, and tar barrels were used to make a thick smoke, and people danced in and out of the smoke, colliding, laughing, shouting. This went on in most Newfoundland villages. It was Romeo Gillette's favorite holiday, more than Canadian Thanksgiving or Christmas.

"It might well," Kelb said. "It's hard to predict how long a hearing will last."

"Because if it does," my mother said, "you should really see it here in Witless Bay. The festivities, I mean. People do have great fun."

"It'd be awkward, me being a representative of the crown."

"Do you mean to say that you've never attended one single Guy Fawkes?"

"If I went this year I'd be a novice."

211

He took up another piece of potato with his knife, ate it, and again cleaned the blade on his knee. He took a sip of water.

"A novice gets smeared with ashes, isn't that right?" Kelb said.

"But once that's over, you can have a wonderful time," my mother said.

"I just might go. If the hearing lasts till then, naturally. I'm sure there's somebody who'd take my guard duties for an hour or two, which is all I'd attend for."

"There's a feast, too. Better than this prison food you eat," my mother said.

"I'll finish my meal now," Kelb said. "Then I'll escort you all back to the store."

Margaret and I each finished our soup. I had two cups of coffee. My mother sat and watched Kelb eat.

"Is there any pepper?" Kelb asked.

"Sorry, no," my mother said.

Kelb sprinkled salt on the two remaining pieces, ate one with quick dispatch, washing it down with water. The other piece he wrapped in a cloth handkerchief and put in his suitcoat pocket. He stood up.

"Let's go, then," he said.

"May I ride my bicycle to the hearing?" Margaret said.

"Miss Handle, you can walk there on your hands, for all I care."

Kelb tapped a gavel on the table. The room hushed down. "Getting back to the revolver," he said. "Mr. Gillette,

would you say that Margaret Handle—let's start with her
—that she could shoot a gun?"

"Everybody knows Margaret could," Romeo said. "She
took one out in the harbor now and again. To shoot ducks,
mostly."

"From some distance, I imagine."

"Depends on the duck. Some are quite stupid. You might
say too trusting. Some don't use their natural skittishness
to their best advantage around people."

"But ducks don't come right up to a boat."

"No, sir. To shoot one at twenty yards, say, takes a steady
hand and a good eye. Especially in the rain."

"I didn't ask you about rain."

Kelb turned to Margaret. "I've kept too long on ducks
here," Kelb said. "We aren't really concerned with them.
We're talking about killing a lighthouse keeper. From close
up. Because at least one bullet went straight on through.
Miss Handle, was the revolver you purchased in your possession on the night of October eight, nineteen and eleven?
The night that Botho August was shot dead. You don't
have to stand up to answer."

"If what you mean by possession—"

"Did you carry it to the lighthouse yourself?"

"We haven't established that she was in the lighthouse,"
Romeo said.

"Well, I *was*. You know it, Romeo. Everyone does. I was.
But I didn't have the revolver with me," Margaret said.

"Do you know, Miss Handle, whose possession it was
in?" Kelb said.

"The only person I saw with my own eyes, who had the gun—the revolver *in hand*—was Orkney Vas."

"His wife committing adultery almost every night while he was on Anticosti Island!" Sillet shouted.

Most people turned to the back of the store where Sillet stood.

"To my mind, that very thing could argue *against* Orkney Vas, true," Kelb said. "But it's not your place to prosecute here, Reverend. Please shut up. Orkney Vas's knowledge about his wife must have been a hard fact to swallow. But Mrs. Vas is not on trial here for adultery. Come to think of it just now, I want you to leave the room."

Looking cowed but tightening his fists, Sillet turned to the door. He put on his wool cap. Still facing away from Kelb, he called out, "I'd be a hypocrite not to provide a voice of reason." He left the store.

"Mr. Fabian Vas," Kelb said, looking at me. He checked a piece of paper with his own writing on it. "Margaret Handle told me that on the night of September 28, the dance in Boas LaCotte's barn, she gave you the revolver. Is that correct?"

"Did you tell him that?" I asked Margaret.

"Yes," she said.

"It's true," I said to Kelb.

"And that you hid it in the woodshed behind your house."

"Under a plank," I said.

"Margaret, did you see Fabian Vas outside the lighthouse on the night of October 8?"

"No."

"At any time that night did you see Fabian Vas in actual possession of the revolver? I know you told me you didn't, but here's a second chance to remember."

"No, I didn't."

"Well, just what did you see that night? Tell us."

"A bullet shatter the window in the room where Botho August and I—"

"Did he say anything at that time?"

" 'That has to be Orkney Vas,' he said."

"Then what?"

"He stomped downstairs. Botho did. Mad as a hatter."

"What did you do then?"

"I pulled the sheets up to my chin."

"Were you—imbibing? Did you have your customary whiskey with you?"

"I had a bottle there and had drunk a good bit of it."

"Did you hear more gunfire?"

"Yes."

"How many shots?"

"Two more shots."

"Did you go to the window then?"

"No, between the shots I stumbled to the gramophone. I fell against it."

"But you hadn't yet looked outside."

"No. But except for the rain it was godawful quiet."

"At any time after the shots did you look out the window?"

"Yes. Finally, I did."

"What did you see?"

"I saw Orkney Vas."

"Doing what? Orkney Vas doing what?"

"He had a revolver in his hand. He had a lantern in the other hand. He ran off."

"How much time—just guess. How much time had passed between when you heard the last shot and when you saw Orkney Vas?"

"I don't know. When you're drinking like that, a long time can pass quickly, and a minute can stretch."

"Did you eventually go down the stairs?"

"Yes, I did. I did go down the stairs. Because I heard shots, didn't I? And because Botho August hadn't come back up."

"What did you find in the yard?"

"Botho August lying there."

"Was he dead?"

"No—no. Well, at first I thought he was. He was bleeding all over. Rain was hitting his face. Blood, and he was coughing. More, then, it was a wheeze. I thought, He is not dead. He was trying to say something."

"Did he succeed?"

"He said, 'Cirala.' "

"I didn't hear that clearly. Would you repeat it?"

"*Cirala.* I'll spell it out. C-i-r-a-l-a."

You could have heard a pin drop.

"It's my name spelled backwards," my mother said.

"Mrs. Vas," Kelb said, "can you say that again, for the record?"

My mother shifted in her chair, rubbed her face with her hands, then laid her hands flat on the table.

"Alaric," she said. "If you spell my name backwards, it comes out just as Margaret pronounced it."

"Cirala," Kelb said. Then he all but whispered the word. "Whatever in God's green acres could that word have meant, spoken as his life was fading?"

"I can tell you," Margaret said.

"Go on, then."

"Me and Botho August— I hadn't carried on intimately with him for many years. Yet now and then I'd visit him in his lighthouse. We—Botho and me. We did entertain ourselves. What I'd bring to his lighthouse was a deck of Old Maid cards. He called it 'Old Hag.' Old Hag. As we say around here, 'Old Hag' means to have a nightmare. You see, Mr. Kelb, in our village you call a nightmare 'Old Hag.' And if you want to *cure* a nightmare, you try and figure out who's really causing the nightmare. If you can figure it out, then you say that person's name backwards. That's the cure."

There was about thirty or so seconds of utter silence. Then Mitchell Kelb reached into his pocket and took out the last piece of potato, chewed and swallowed it, all fidgety as a squirrel. He rubbed his hands against his trouser leg a moment. He cleared his throat. "Am I being made a visiting fool of?" he said. He perused the faces in the row of barrels. "This hearing is not going in pristine order. And now we have superstitions involved. I need to organize my thoughts. Mrs. Dollard, please write: Mitchell Kelb adjourned to organize his thoughts, one after the other. We'll take a full day's recess. Everybody leaves the store now. Just get out."

10

The Guy Fawkes Tragedy

"News of Orkney Vas might interest you," Mitchell Kelb said. Revolver holstered on his right hip, he ate pancakes doused in butter, shredded cabbage, and brewis, which was a boiled biscuit with pork fat. It was the evening of November 3. Margaret, my mother, and I sat with Kelb. Kelb ate his last bite, stood, stretched in an exaggerated way. "My sources keep me informed. Mr. Llewellyn Boxer travels back and forth, here to St. John's. Well, Orkney was seen in Lamaline, of course, where neither you, Alaric, nor you, Fabian, nor Enoch Handle, for that matter, saw fit to stop him from going ashore. Not that you could have stopped him. After Lamaline, there were sightings in Garnish, Terrenceville, and Bay du Nord. We have a professional tracker out after him. A part-Micmac named Poomuk, first name of Albert. He's done good work for us in the past. He found an escapee in a cave once."

"Mr. Kelb, did you ever escort a man who was criminally insane," I said, "down the coast to a sanatorium?"

"As a matter of fact, I did. Ten or so years back. Enoch Handle took us down."

"I'd heard that rumor," I said. "I was just asking."

"Getting back to Orkney Vas. We figure that he has headed into Canada, possibly overland, because the skipper of the *Doubting Thomas*, Mr. Arvin Flint, has been notified. I notified him through Llewellyn Boxer, who sent his brother Perry to Flint. Now, Mr. Flint is a former constable himself. He retired because of how his character is made up—he wasn't cut out for the job, really. The job got him too close to lowlife sorts who weren't well met with his more cheerful notions of humanity. Whereas, for me, it's all a perfect fit. Anyway, Arvin Flint still carries a sidearm and knows how to use it. Orkney Vas, I believe, knows all of this and will keep to dry ground."

"Well, thank you for telling us," my mother said. "I think personally I'll skip dessert. I'm quite tired. But we have duff; we make that pudding with flour, fat, and molasses, Mr. Kelb. And you can see there's syrup. Good night, then."

"Good night, *Cirala*," Kelb said, then snickered.

"Old Maid?" Margaret said to Kelb, holding up the deck. My mother left the kitchen.

"No thanks," Kelb said. "I'm turning in. I've got your room again tonight, eh, Fabian?"

"Help yourself."

Mitchell Kelb washed his face in the kitchen sink, then went into my bedroom.

"Cuts up a potato and then doesn't use a fork," Margaret said. She looked out the window. "It's duckish."

Helen Twombly liked that word; it meant the time between sunset and dark.

"Want some coffee?" I said.

"There's bottles and bottles left, and I'm taking one with me to the sofa. I'm bottomed out, Fabian, just empty. I have no one to talk with."

She went to the pantry, took up a bottle, went into the living room, and lay down. "Fabian," she said. I stood in the hallway. "Seeing that Botho's left no will and testament, does that mean his gramophone's up for grabs?" I doubted that she expected an answer. She turned her face to the back of the sofa. "Goddamned Mitchell Kelb will probably get it."

I went out and sat on the porch. House arrest included the porch, I thought. There was a saw-whet owl on a lightning-struck tree nearby, a harbinger of nothing. Seeing a Boreal owl was supposed to mean "Don't go to sea." Sighting a snowy owl meant that "bones would ache," but without further consequence; they would simply ache for a while, then stop. Gulls seen more than a mile or so inland were supposed to be wandering ghosts, or meant that ghosts would soon force themselves into your dreams, possibly your daytime imagination as well. The saw-whet owl called a few times, then with a slight gust of its wings flew past the porch, off toward Giles LaCotte's orchard.

"Fabian—"

Hearing my own name startled me. I stood up and saw a figure step from the side of the house.

"Fabian, it's me, Sebastian."

"Jesus—Uncle Bassie."

I had not seen my uncle since I was seven years old. He had last visited for Christmas dinner, 1898. I remember that he had been out of prison then for less than a week. Actually, it was because of Christmas that the warden had cut a week from his sentence. After supper my father and Bassie had gone into the living room and talked much of the night. Bassie had brought me a clipping from a newspaper in St. John's, where his most recent bank robbery had been reported. It included an artist's rendition of my uncle, not a good one. I kept it in a drawer for years. When he had given it to me, he had said, "From that drawing, who could recognize me? I should thank the man who did it for some extra weeks of freedom, no doubt."

Now Bassie looked so much older, his features somehow more angular. He had a small, pointed beard. He was an inch or so taller than my father, yet all the other family resemblances were strong. He had on a black greatcoat, under which was a sweater. The sweater was frayed. But it still had all the evidence of my mother's handiwork. In fact, I suddenly recalled her having knit it that same Christmastime, day after day. Bassie had stayed for two weeks. I remember him sitting at the fireplace, watching her knit it. I remember him putting it on and looking at himself in the mirror. I remember him saying, "Thank you for the sweater, Alaric," but not saying goodbye.

He got me in a bear hug, then let go and stepped back. "Orkney said I wouldn't believe how you'd grown."

"It's been a few years, Uncle Bassie."

"It has indeed."

"You talked to my father, of course. You said, 'Orkney said—' which meant you were coming to see me. He must know the law is after him."

"It's almost laughable, isn't it? Here, for the first time in a long time I'm not on the lam, and Orkney is."

"How did you find him? Or he find you?"

"Let's step away from the house, all right? I don't want to wake up Mr. Mitchell Kelb. He's got a reputation. I know that he's in the house. I was over to see Romeo Gillette, who remembered me. I don't want to wake up Alaric, either. She wouldn't be all that pleased to see me, I'm afraid."

We walked past the charred tree and sat down.

"I'll fill you in," Bassie said.

I could not see him all that clearly; in the starlit dark, his voice so closely resembled my father's that it was difficult to tell the difference. Perhaps Bassie's was a bit raspier, but that was all.

"Orkney stayed in Lamaline for one night," he said. "I know that's where you watched him come ashore. He said he slept in the cemetery, having taken a blanket from somebody's wash out on the line. Said he neatly folded the blanket and returned it before daylight. Now, that does sound like Orkney, doesn't it?"

"Neatly folding it. Yes, it does."

"He traveled mostly by dark, though. He made his way to Burgeo. He found a mail boat there."

"The *Doubting Thomas*."

"By chance and by luck. He persuaded the skipper, man named Arvin Flint, to carry him to Halifax. And what do you suppose he did then? He wrote me, his brother, a letter. Care of Buchans, because he knew I'd been a free man awhile this time around, and always after prison I go home. Which in fact I'd done.

"The letter said he was staying under an alias in the Hagerforse Guest House. He asked that I come see you, and that if I got to see you, to mention the Hagerforse Guest House in particular and wait for a confused smile to cross your face."

He leaned close, peering into my face, contorting his mouth the way he had when I was a boy and he was trying to make me laugh. I smelled sweat, snuff tobacco, and hair grease on him. "I'm not a kid," I said. "I'm not going to laugh at that." And then I did laugh.

"Orkney's gone from Halifax now," he said. "He's somewhere else. I know where, but I can't tell you. Because then you'd have that knowledge. If you don't have it, you can't be responsible."

"I bet he's hightailed it into Canada. Somewhere into Canada."

"Let me put it this way. Basically, there's Canada and there's the United States of America, and Orkney, since he was a boy, never had one spark of interest in going to the latter."

"Will you go see him? Will you join him, or will he be alone?"

"I'm a free man now, Fabian, for the eighth or ninth time, I forget. So if I want to go and visit my brother, I can, and most likely I will. Hell, if he and I reminisced about everything that's happened even since we last saw one another, we'd walk out of the room old men!"

"Uncle Bassie—"

"Now, who's this Margaret?"

"My father mentioned her?"

"Yes, he did. He said he was out of his mind trying to persuade you to marry the girl from Richibucto, New Brunswick, whose name I've misplaced. He said he was trying to force a life outside of Witless Bay on you. But he realized—too late—you were striving for an outside life on your own. He thought this Margaret Handle might have kept you here, locked into sameness. Orkney used to like sameness—until he didn't. I guess he found out the hard way how Alaric dealt with sameness, didn't he. Between men and women, it's complicated and simple at the same time, eh? Anyway, I don't know all the man-and-wife details. So far I have only the one letter from Orkney, though it was a long letter. He says he was wrong. He is ashamed. He wants to be forgiven for his mistake."

"Maybe he just now wants to disagree with my mother about Margaret. About everything."

"Could be. I don't know. But to my mind, it's just a straight-out request for forgiveness."

"Why did you come here, Uncle Bassie? I know, to tell

me that my father was all right. But he would have been all right whether you came all this way or not."

"I broke his jaw. I owe him."

"I'm happy to see you, don't get me wrong. I could use you here, too. Believe me, I could. Just to know you're here, during the hearing. Just to have you sitting in the store, so that later, if they don't hang me, I can say, 'Did this really happen?' and you can say, 'Yes, it did.' "

"I know you can use me here. I'm a free man. I'll stay through Guy Fawkes, at least."

"Thank you."

"I have to stay away from the house, though. Mr. Kelb is not my friend."

"I understand."

"Now listen carefully, Fabian. There's one last thing that Orkney insisted I tell you. Listen carefully to it. He said, 'Tell Fabian it's fine to blame me for the murder. They won't catch me. I'm far out of jurisdiction, or at least the means of the magistrate. If it can guarantee your freedom' —he didn't mention anyone else's—'then go ahead. Go ahead, twist the story around to blame me.' Blame him for the lighthouse keeper's murder. Even to the point of being an eyewitness to Orkney having shot the bastard."

"I could just as easily say it was my mother who did it."

"You'd have to look her in the eye, though. And a son sending his own mother to Mr. Ellis—"

"Either way is sickening."

"More if someone hangs. Now, did you hear clearly what Orkney wanted me to tell you?"

"Yes."

"Good. I'm going to leave now and get some sleep somewhere."

We embraced for a long time. When Bassie was out of sight, I realized that I was shaking. I do not believe I have ever wanted someone to stay near me as much as Bassie over the next few days. I realized, too, that I had given Bassie no return message for my father. Now it was too late to shout one out or catch up with my uncle.

I fell asleep on the kitchen floor. What startled me awake the next morning was the sound of Margaret crashing into furniture on her bicycle. I got up and saw her sprawled on the floor, spokes spinning. She was bleeding at one knee. She looked up at me. "I'm riding my bicycle under house arrest," she said.

Kelb appeared in the doorway. "How can you drink that poison so early in the morning," he said, picking up a bottle from the floor. He looked in a foul mood. "Goddamn it, Miss Handle. You woke me up. And I've got to keep a clear head today."

We had a breakfast of eggs and fried potatoes, prepared by my mother. Then Margaret wheeled her bicycle outside and rode it to Gillette's store.

In the store, Kelb shut the windows against the cold. He announced, "It's November four, nineteen and eleven." Mekeel Dollard wrote that down.

The store was as crowded as ever, less Reverend Sillet.

"I'm back to the gun," Kelb said. "Mr. Gillette, how did the revolver get into your hands after the murder?"

"Margaret Handle gave it to me."

"In your opinion, why?"

"I don't know. I only know what she said when she gave it to me. She said, 'This gun was used to kill Botho August.' Then she walked right out the door."

"At what time of day did this take place?"

"I'd say around 7 a.m."

"How did Miss Handle seem?"

"*Seem?* I don't know that either. But she suddenly came back into my store and said, 'If you walk to the lighthouse, you'll find Botho lying in his yard. He's dead and I've covered him up."

"Is that all she said?"

"Yes."

"What did you do then?"

"I placed the revolver inside an oilcloth. I put on my coat and walked to the lighthouse. You can imagine how high my curiosity might have been."

"And found what? At the lighthouse."

"Just as Margaret said. Botho August, dead as a doornail. His nightshirt torn away, right next to him on the ground. He was covered with a wet blanket. I went to the wharf, told some men. They went back with me. I went to get Reverend Sillet, but he wasn't at home. I looked for him. I found him at the Harbisons' house having a late breakfast. By the time he and I got back to the body, people were gawking."

"You can sit down."

"All right." Romeo sat down.

Mitchell Kelb looked at John Rut. He sighed, then

turned toward Margaret. "Miss Handle," Kelb said, "is what Mr. Gillette just reported how you remember it—the parts about you giving him the revolver and so forth?"

"Yes. Except I forgot I'd covered Botho August with a blanket," Margaret said. "Do you want to hear about that?"

"Not necessarily—"

"I took the blanket off his bed, brought it down the stairs. It was raining hard still. I covered him with it."

"Did you participate directly in the murder?"

"I saw Orkney Vas run off from the body. I came downstairs. As I said. As I said, I found the revolver."

"Did you put a bullet in Botho August is what I'm asking?"

"We're not wasting the crown's time now!" John Rut said.

"Miss Handle?" Kelb said.

"Yes, I did."

"Even after he'd been shot twice already. How—"

"It all happened very fast. Fast in the rain. That Botho seemed to fly awake and reach for the revolver. I grabbed it first. I thought he'd kill me. I don't know what I thought. I shot him."

Margaret did not break down; she in fact stiffened her posture.

"So you lied before. Perjured yourself before, when I asked if you at any time that night had possession of the gun."

"Yes. I'm sorry."

"Did you at any time that night see Fabian Vas?"

"No. That's the truth. No."

"A lie will come back around at you some way or another. You know that. That's all of my questions for you just now, Miss Handle. Mr. Vas, stand up, will you?"

I stood up.

"Fabian Vas," Kelb said, "that night, did you participate in the murder?"

"Be sure to speak up, Fabian, so we can hear you!" a voice said from the back of the store. It was my Uncle Bassie; it was my father's messenger.

His presence, and my cowardice, emboldened me to lie. I knew then and there I would lie. I lied. "My father and mother had been quarreling all night. It was awful," I said. "My mother kept crying out, 'Do you want me to drown myself in the sink?' Other things. Other things out of shame at the adultery. It went on for a long time. Hours. I'm their son and I heard it all. I heard my father say, 'I'll kill him!' "

"Kill whom?"

"Botho August."

"Orkney Vas actually said he was going to kill Botho August?"

I looked at my uncle. "Yes, he did. I heard him."

"On the night of October 8, did you *see* Orkney Vas in possession of the revolver?"

"This is my father—"

"I'm asking."

I took a deep breath. Bassie stepped out onto the porch.

"Yes, I saw him go to the woodshed. I kept out of sight, following my own father that way. Out of sight in the rain, on to the lighthouse. He shot out a window. That happened right away. Then Botho stepped out of the door. They had words. I heard words but couldn't hear what they were exactly. My father—"

"Fabian?"

"Shot Botho August. He shot him twice. He dropped the revolver and ran."

"Orkney had a lantern, as Miss Handle testified. Did you see the murder by lantern light, then?"

"What I saw of it, yes. Then my father doused the wick."

"Did you see Miss Handle fire the third shot?"

"No, I did not. I was very confused. I was afraid for my father. I hated Botho August. It was as if I'd shot him myself. I was afraid for my father, for what he'd done. I went to my childhood hiding place, though I'm twenty years old."

"Where was that?"

"Boas LaCotte's barn."

"And before dawn, there was a family reunion, you might say—"

"I wouldn't call it that."

"—wherein, you, Alaric Vas, and Orkney fled Witless Bay. On the *Aunt Ivy Barnacle*."

"For Halifax. Yes."

Kelb picked up the revolver, spun the empty cartridge, then said, "Mr. Gillette said he emptied this cartridge. Mrs. Dollard, be sure to note that." He inspected the revolver for a moment, for all the world like a man browsing in a store. Holding it by the barrel, he tapped the table with the handle. "I've got some thinking to do," he said. "Adjourned."

Margaret rode her bicycle back to the house.

Though I did not attend that year's Guy Fawkes activities until the very last moment, I can describe them in general, because I had been to them since I was four years old. During the day, wood is stacked: warped doors, driftwood, fireplace logs, sticks thrown in by children, and mostly green boughs and tar barrels, as they produce the thickest smoke. I remember when I was eight a house burned down in September; in late October, the charred roof beams, windowsills, porch railings, steps, and scraps of furniture were hauled by wagon to the Guy Fawkes bonfire heap.

Potluck supper is served at the church around six o'clock. The bonfire has blazed since dark, and by its light a mocking rendition of the original Guy Fawkes Day is performed. Traditionally, in Witless Bay, Romeo Gillette dressed up as King James I. He might wear a white wig with exaggerated curls; one year curls fell to his waist. Another year he wore a miniature weathervane on top of a hat. He might wear a vast, flowing court robe hemmed with cork net floats that drag along, all festooned with fishbones. Cotton stuffing protrudes from the robe in fistfuls at the sleeves. His king's throne is ten feet high, making him look like a dwarf. When I was fifteen, Romeo asked me to paint a flock of gulls on a bedsheet, and to have the gulls raining down gull shit. The sheet was stretched between poles and held above Romeo during the procession. The sheet took me three whole days to complete.

Near the bonfire, novices would have tar pitch applied to their faces, smeared on arms and legs. Then they were led through the smoke, and the wild dancing and reveling began, all to the accompaniment of drums, accordions, even a bagpipe, if the only bagpipe player in the region, Peter Reid, accepted Witless Bay's invitation. He was in popular demand, though. Most every year, too, a few people succumbed to smoke and had to be dragged away and revived. The dancers all had smoke tears streaming down their faces.

The failed ambush on the throne was at once laughable and serious: the king had to go, if not this time, then soon! One year Romeo stood up and said, "I declare a free Newfoundland!" His declaration was his way for history to service his own hopes, and he drew applause and drunken cheers.

Anyway, around dusk on that November 5, Mitchell Kelb walked into our kitchen, took up an iron pot, and clanged it with a ladle. We all came in, obedient as schoolchildren. "I've decided, out of curiosity, mind you, to attend the Guy Fawkes bonfire," he said. "Llewellyn Boxer seems to be a day late getting back here. Much to my chagrin, I can't find a guard for you, so you'll be on your own, which I've advised myself against. Nonetheless, I'm going. I can't allow you to attend, naturally. I can't allow you to leave this house, so don't. House arrest is serious business. Each of you will be accountable. I'll be gone no more than two hours, maybe three, according to my timepiece."

He took out his watch, gold-rimmed, on a chain. He looked at the watch and said, "Exactly 4:18." He returned the watch to his pocket. "Difficult and lonely as it might be, try and have a pleasant dinner without me."

He set out down the road. We all stepped out onto the porch. There was a clear sky, night falling. We could see smoke from the bonfire. They had begun it a bit early this year, I thought. It looked to be where it always was, though, a few hundred yards south of the lighthouse, in a field back from the cliff.

I turned from the porch and saw Margaret go into the pantry. I went into the kitchen. My mother joined us there. Margaret threw back three shots in a row.

"Oh yes, to be sure, Margaret Handle," my mother said. "That's your way in times of trouble, isn't it?"

"Not just at those times," Margaret said, pouring another shot.

My mother began to cook furiously. She sliced and fried some onions. Scraping the onions from the cutting board into a bowl, she then filleted a sea trout that Romeo had brought us. "There's leftover codfish stew, but I don't want any more of that," she said. "Three days in a row it's been in the house." She rolled the trout in butter and fried it on a skillet. When this was ready, she all but slammed a loaf of bread onto the table.

"My God," she said, holding on to the table edge. "Why don't we simply call ourselves by our true names here! Adulteress, murderer, and murderer!"

My mother opened a window. She leaned out and

breathed the night air. When the smell of onions died down a little, she served supper.

"The harbor's been smooth as a mirror all day, I bet, since there's been so little wind," my mother said. "And I'm so cooped up inside. Have you noticed that since our one time rowing, Mr. Kelb has refused to take me out again? He's outright refused. I call it mostly his fault I'm so cooped up. Therefore, I'm going to act directly against his orders. I'm going to ignore his warning. I have to. I'm going to row out. I want to see the bonfire from a harbor view. I've always wanted to."

Margaret made a hollow clucking. "Alaric," she said, "Helen once warned me never to row in one direction if seabirds are towarding in the other. A sea hag will capsize you. So, Alaric, if you see gulls or the late-staying bullbirds flying toward shore, don't, don't, don't row out to sea. Just float in on the tide. Or wait till the birds are out of sight, then do what you please."

"I'd gladly ponder advice from Helen. But coming from you, Margaret, in your condition just now, I think I'll row in any direction I choose, thank you."

"Helen wasn't drunk when she gave me that advice, so what's it matter to the truth if I am?"

"This conversation is over," my mother said. "Besides, who can see birds in the dark, bonfire or no?"

I watched as she put on a sweater, then a coat. She took a rain slicker from its peg, tucked it under her arm, then put on a stocking cap.

"And how will you two spend this Guy Fawkes evening,

once I'm out of sight?" she said. "Having some sort of close reunion?"

"For us to know and you to find out," Margaret said.

"Mother, you never asked me if I spoke to Bassie. You must've seen him during the hearing," I said.

"Bassie is a convict, whether in jail or out. And we never got along. Not really. Though I admired, at least, the fact that robbing a bank was a clear, stalwart decision on his part. He could make a true decision in his life. Though again and again a wrong one. Bassie. Yes, well, whenever he sat at our table, he never said, 'Now, should I pick up the fork or knife first?' He'd just pick one up and let the other follow."

"This is *your* decision, then? To row out in the harbor."

"Yes. It's something I want to do. Just consider it an evening stroll, except on the water."

And she left the house.

Margaret was quite drunk by now. She had eaten only a few bites of supper and had worked through half a bottle of whiskey. She slid back in her chair. "I lied," she said. "I lied, there, in that goddamned hearing, just by not telling what I really know, about who shot whom. I lied, but I can't bear that I did. In my life I've done about everything that's not good for the soul, except for lying. Now I can notch that one up, too.

"If Orkney—if your very own father, whom I admired from a distance and so wanted to like me—if your father had been in the store, I swear I could not have lied. I could not have blamed him. And I wouldn't have, anyway, Fabian, if I didn't think that you loved me. That there was some future for us, difficult as it might be. I tried to lie my way out of no future with you."

"My Uncle Sebastian told me that my father said to blame him."

"And you took the first convenient advice that came along, didn't you? You took that advice as easy as you'd filch a piece of candy from Gillette's store."

I had nothing to say.

"You know what's always been some people's problem?" Margaret said, taking a swig. "They look at something and right away they start thinking how to improve it. Not me. I look at you, for instance, and I think: Fabian's painting of birds maybe can be improved, but Fabian himself can't, not much at least. Yet I still love him. And now he's murdered a lighthouse keeper. And every day of his life is anchored to that fact. Mine, too. I look in the mirror and say, 'Now we're the same.' "

I took up the bottle and poured a glass of whiskey, drank it right down. Margaret poured me another. "I propose a toast," she said. "To Botho August, who brought us closer together!"

"I won't drink to that."

"I'm pleased with myself for thinking it up."

I fell asleep on the sofa. When I woke, groggy and with a sharp pain in my head, I sat up and cleared the dizziness, then saw flickers of light on the windowpane. The Guy Fawkes bonfire was blazing at its peak, I thought. I half stumbled out to the porch. "Margaret! Come look at this!"

I called back into the house. "Mother, come look!" There were no answers.

Then the lighthouse beam came on. Mr. Sloo must've been hired, I thought. Such a clear, simple thought. The stars were out, no fog, though—the beam slanting out— then I was overtaken by panic, as if the source of it was the beam itself. I ran toward the lighthouse.

At the cliffs, the first person I made out clearly was Oliver Parmelee, who stood holding his accordion. Panting, I tapped him on the shoulder and he turned with a start. "Fabian, what's got into your mother, rowing out there? Jesus!"

"Why's everyone at this cliff?" I said. And then a rough sleeve had me in a choke. At my ear I heard, "I'm Mitchell Kelb. What in hell are you doing out of your house?" But I could not answer. I could not manage a single word.

I looked around me. All along the cliffs people were holding lanterns, standing with their families, dozens of silhouettes facing the sea. "There she is!" Oliver said. He pointed. The lighthouse beam had caught the *Aunt Ivy Barnacle*, swathing it in white-yellow light, as it slowly moved across the harbor.

I do not remember how long we stood there. Perhaps it was only minutes. It was a perfectly clear night out, smoke drifting off to the west behind us. There was not a moon, but the sea always gave off some light.

The foghorn sounded once, twice—a third blast.

Then I heard a cry: "Margaret!" I turned to my left; down the row of my neighbors, Enoch was clawing at his face.

We saw the *Aunt Ivy Barnacle* collide with the dinghy a few seconds before the sound carried to the cliff. There was a hollow thud, like a tree hitting the ground, splintered wood echoing across the harbor. The lighthouse beam slid away, and for the first time I noticed that Margaret was not running with lanterns. None was lit on rail or bow. Mr. Sloo caught the mail boat again as it drifted and bobbed on a gentle swell, engine shut off, an oar bobbing in the wake.

Already men were scrambling down to the wharf.

11

Birds of

Witless Bay

I was legally acquitted. Yet a village has an intuition of its own, plus which everyone knows that the truth is larger than the law. Whatever it did not prove, the hearing taught my neighbors that I had murdered Botho August. They had studied my face when I lied. They came to their own conclusions. In fact, a few weeks after the hearing Boas LaCotte cornered me and said, "Orkney didn't pull the trigger. You should be ashamed." I was ashamed. I am now. I am sorry. Sorry that I followed my father's advice and betrayed him.

Once in a while I hear *Slieveen*—a deceitful person—whispered as I pass by, as though it was my epitaph even before I have a gravestone. I heard Mekeel Dollard say it once. Martha Wheelock said it. I was hurt, though I do not deserve to be. If you lie, you become the lie. Everyone knows that, too.

The murder of Botho August continues to haunt my village, simply because, young children aside, it persists in everyone's memory.

At the hearing, Margaret had at least admitted that she pulled the trigger. She told more of the truth than I had. What is more, she had spirits-in-a-bottle, as Helen called whiskey, as a punishment. I had only, as Reverend Sillet put it, the fatal consequences of my weakness to offer up to people for forgiveness. Sunday after Sunday, my family was a topic for his sermons. I came to sit in the front pew. I would even linger on the steps or lawn after church. It was as though I had become two people: Fabian Vas, and Fabian Vas the murderer.

"Fabian Vas has acquired for our village a second name," Sillet said from the pulpit. "A stranger might ask, 'Where are you from?' You might answer, 'Witless Bay, Newfoundland,' and immediately a small voice of conscience adds, *A place of a murder.*"

On yet another Sunday, he said, "God forgive me, but sometimes in contemplating human nature, I think that the Ten Commandments are in the wrong order. That *Thou Shalt Not Kill* should follow *Thou Shalt Not Commit Adultery*, the one so often born of the other."

I said, "Amen," as loud as anyone. Margaret heard that I had. She was disgusted. She told me that.

Mitchell Kelb admitted that he felt partly responsible for my mother's death. To his way of thinking, he had been tempted by the Guy Fawkes festivities, seduced from his obligations. "I shirked my duties," he said. "I shouldn't have ever left the house. It's that simple."

I never did learn, in any exact detail, how Kelb's report to Her Majesty's Court in St. John's read, though, as I have mentioned, I was found guilty of no crime. Before he made his report, however, Kelb said to me, "I'm going to fight to get your mother's name erased from the printed indictment. A document concerning murder shouldn't be the last place her name appears in this world." He surprised me further by purchasing a stone and having *Alaric Banville* engraved on it. He helped me situate the stone atop the cliff where most of the village had watched her die. Kelb had his own turmoils with the incident. He had his guilts. It seemed that the death of Botho August and the death of my mother drew out a particularly strong sympathy for Margaret. "I'm going to officially interpret Margaret's testimony about October 8 as drunken hearsay, though it wasn't that, not entirely at least. And as for you, Fabian, a son's testimony against his father, who by all accounts loved him, well, I won't soil my hands with that. I'm taking it all personally. I consider it inadmissible because it is so disgusting. Besides, at this point, it's useless—we won't find Orkney Vas, because we'll stop looking for him, unless he gets influenced by that crazy brother of his and robs a bank in Newfoundland. Albert Poomuk figures that Orkney is off in the deeps of Canada by now, maybe even a city. There it is, then."

It was Mitchell Kelb, too, who set another example of forgiveness in Witless Bay. He took it upon himself to take

Margaret to a sanatorium in Garnish. In the collision she had received broken ribs, a concussion, and a gash on her forehead that needed fifty-one stitches. She had been quite battered up. Altogether, she was a resident of the Garnish sanatorium for six months. I did not visit her there. However, Mitchell Kelb, who may have been a little in love with her (Margaret thought so), found it in his heart to make a separate visit to me, in order to explain the whys and wherefores of her condition. On the freezing night of January 19, 1912, he knocked on my door.

He took off his coat, set his boots by the fireplace, and came back into the kitchen. "Home sweet home," he said. "I know where the tea is." He made a cup of tea for himself. I had coffee, five or six cups, as we spoke.

"Fabian," he said somberly, "Margaret is in a sanatorium hospital down in Garnish. I took her there with Enoch's permission. I'd suggested it to the court in St. John's, who agreed to it. In fact, insisted. They said since I'd already gone ahead and done it, well, fine. Enoch Handle is with his daughter now. He moved down to Garnish. Found a room there for the winter.

"I'm sorry as hell we all had to see Alaric meet her maker. That *you* had to see that. Terrible, terrible luck to have been drawn to the cliff at such a moment. Yet I admit the tragedy got me thinking about the past. Back to when I first met Margaret Handle. Circumstances I'm sure you remember, since you were in the store that day, just after she'd run her bicycle into old Dalton Gillette. Collisions seem part of her fate on earth, eh?

"Anyway, Margaret is in Garnish. It's not a lock-up place. It's not a prison. It's got nurses. More, it's for people— who—on whom life bears down hard, is the best I can say it. Bears down hard and won't let up. You know how Margaret's brain is fairly buoyed up by alcohol some days? Well, the doctors have fancy names for her troubles. Sprinkle their explanations with Latin. Now, the broken ribs, that was easy. The gashes and bruises and the like, healing nicely. Dizziness from the concussion they say will wear off in due time. She has some mysterious internal malady—the doctors say it won't kill her but they can't figure it out, except to say it doubles her over now and then. She's not sleeping. Maybe an hour a night she sleeps. They'll try a pharmaceutical for that. Still, given the collision, it's a miracle she's alive. Alive, yet in a generally harassed mental condition.

"What the doctors do say plain and simple is that she probably is too stubborn to stop her drinking. It's what might eventually kill her, rot her from the inside out, to put it bluntly. She's not allowed to drink in hospital, naturally. But doctors aren't truant officers. They suspect that once out, she'll want to line up every last whiskey bottle in Newfoundland and invite just herself to the party.

"I've talked for hours with Enoch Handle. I've even slept on his floor in Garnish. He says that you and Margaret have both bad and good influences on each other. One of those, I guess, has got to win out, maybe the good.

"Look—to hell with my advice. It's not even real advice. I'm not your father, and I'm not Reverend Sillet.

"As for what happened on Guy Fawkes being an *accident*, well, that's the official version. Leave well enough alone is my motto here. On paper up in St. John's it says accident. But for the life of me, I couldn't tell from the cliff that night if Alaric rowed toward the mail boat or if Margaret zigzagged and aimed, or just what happened."

We sat and talked late into the night. Finally, he stood and said, "I'm at Spivey's tonight." He offered his hand and I shook it. He put on his coat, hat, and scarf, opened the door, and set out.

I have not seen or heard from Mitchell Kelb since.

I had lost all contact with the journals. When the *Aunt Ivy Barnacle* was again repaired (I was hired to help in this) and went out on its first spring run, I posted a letter to Isaac Sprague. Even as I wrote the letter I had no real expectation that he would reply. He did not. Twice again in April I sent him sketches. No reply. Then, at the lowest point in my finances and spirits, something occurred which proved to me it was indeed a mercilessly low point. Reverend Sillet came to see me.

I was sitting on my porch. It was May 2, and I remember the moment so clearly that I recall what I was wearing. It was one of Lambert's checked shirts that my father had obviously borrowed on Anticosti and by some oversight had left at Spivey's. It was sizes too large. I had the sleeves rolled up to my elbows. I also had on dark brown trousers and boots. One heel was badly nicked. It was near dusk. I recall seeing a sharp-shinned hawk glide out of Giles LaCotte's orchard behind Sillet as he walked up the road.

The hawk had a mouse dangling from its beak. On the porch, I had propped up an easel and was working on a sketch of a shearwater from memory, as it was too early to see one. Shearwaters did not nest in Witless Bay, but sometimes, I don't know why, a dense fog brought one or more in during the summer.

"Good evening, Fabian," Sillet said, placing one foot on the bottom step.

"Reverend."

"Fabian—" I had the feeling that if I had gone inside my house, he would have followed me, so I stayed on the porch. "Fabian, I understand, perhaps better than you, your, shall we say *dislike* of me. A grisly, vigilant dislike, perhaps influenced by Margaret, perhaps original. But you should realize that my Sunday sermons are on everyone's behalf, not against you in particular. Or against your family. I merely organize God's words to judgement, Fabian. It's simply that in my professional domain, I let those words serve me from the pulpit.

"Be that as it may, all God's children are equal in His sight, even though you won't accept forgiveness from Him through me. I'll be direct: though you attend church, you scowl. You have no use for me. Yet I might have a use for you.

"You're a painter—an artist, though with very few people, I imagine, who see your art. A few magazine subscribers and the like. People whom you may never meet. In addition, you're a person who of late hasn't had much employment at the dry dock. Those are facts. Now, let me wed facts together. Let me make an offer.

"I want to put you in the service of my church. I've approached the church elders with an idea for your redemption, as it were. I suggested a mural. And the elders listened. They are patient, good men. I broached the idea of a mural on the north wall of the church. A mural that might serve to lighten the congregation's spirits, especially through our long winters.

"For the most part the idea was graciously received.

"And while the name Fabian Vas soured the elders a bit, I argued that we really could not afford to hire an outside artist. And who else in Witless Bay, truth be told, has the required talent?

"Now, what is the bribe behind my generosity?

"If you paint a mural, I won't mention Alaric Vas, Orkney Vas, or Fabian Vas ever again from my pulpit. Or Margaret Handle."

"Well," I said, "you've already mentioned us enough for a lifetime."

"Not for ten lifetimes, as far as I'm concerned. That's my own private opinion, however. But some good people in Witless Bay have taken me aside and suggested leniency."

We just looked at each other a hard moment.

"You know," I finally said, "you're just like me."

"In what respect?"

"You found your true subject. Mine is birds. I paint birds now, no matter if anyone sees them or not. It's my heart's logic. As for your true subject, I believe it's my family. Me, my father, my mother—we're your subject, all right. So,

Reverend, why not continue being loyal to your calling and keep your sermons aimed at us?"

"Don't flatter yourself, Fabian. If you think I'm beholden to you in any regard for murdering Botho August, which I know you did, you have gone mad."

"To use your kind of language, Reverend, God gave me a small gift to help me clarify my world." (In fact, Isaac Sprague had written this to me.) "Maybe in turn He gave you me and my parents, plus Botho. We've gone and made your reputation, is how I see it."

"Your misguided opinions don't interest me, Fabian. A mural does."

"No, no. No, go ahead, talk about us every Sunday till hell freezes over. I'm your best customer now. In the front pew as soon as you open your doors. I'm sure you've noticed."

"Fabian, do you feel anything in your heart toward the man you murdered? Toward Botho August, these months later."

"I feel I did myself a favor."

Sillet ran his hand through his hair, sat heavily on the porch step, and stared at the ground.

"Well, think over my proposition, if you would."

"And what would the subject of this mural be?"

Sillet stood up. "Along the lines of a Peaceable Kingdom, I'd think. Newfoundland—Witless Bay in particular. Your own artistic interpretation, naturally. Though I'd be concerned in a close-up way."

"What would my wages be?"

"We'll call a meeting about it."

He walked down the path through the orchard.

I had thought almost constantly about Margaret.

Though we had not seen each other since the hearing, Enoch Handle, up from Garnish, stopped by the same night, May 2, to say that he was going to bring Margaret home. "Thank you for telling me."

"I thought you'd want to know."

Three days later, Giles LaCotte called from his orchard as I walked by, "Mail boat's in!" I hurried to the wharf. The *Aunt Ivy Barnacle* had just tied up. Enoch set the plank, went down to the bunkroom to get Margaret. When she saw me on deck, she disappeared back below. Enoch spoke with her for a few moments, then came up and walked over to me. "She'll see you later, Fabian," he said. "Let's meet at Spivey's on Sunday night. How's that?"

"I'll be there."

"Good."

I walked up from the dock and sat on Spivey's porch. I took my binoculars out of my satchel and watched as Enoch escorted Margaret down the plank, then along the path toward their house. Enoch carried her bag; it was brown with a Victorian tapestry-of-roses pattern, a hummingbird suspended above the roses. I had once tried to paint a hummingbird, using the one on Margaret's bag as a model, but hummingbirds, I suppose, were not part of my native intelligence, and the painting failed. The way that Enoch held her arm, it appeared that Margaret needed to walk terribly slowly. But then she hugged Enoch, placed his hands on her ribs, and laughed, then took up her travel bag and carried it the rest of the way.

On Sunday evening I dressed in my church suit and got to Spivey's at six o'clock. A short time later Margaret came in with Enoch. They sat four tables away near the window. All evening the restaurant was crowded, and I could not always see Margaret across the room. She looked lovely, however. Her hair had a long braid down the back. She wore the same dress she had worn to the barn dance, though with a black sweater over it. It was her first night out in public since Guy Fawkes. She and Enoch were celebrating. No one came over to their table, but plenty of people looked and said hello. It would be my guess that Bridget and Lemuel did not ask them to pay for the meal.

They stayed after all the other customers left, except for me. They had talked and talked, tea to dessert, and half an hour after their dishes were cleared. I was not so much as glanced at or nodded to, or acknowledged at all. In a way I was grateful, because for once my expectations were perfectly well met by what in fact took place. When Margaret and Enoch rose from their table and walked to the door, Margaret looked at me and said, "Meeting me at the dock was necessary for you, but not for me."

"Good evening, Fabian," Enoch said.

On May 9, Sillet came to report the results of the elders' meeting.

"It's been decided to go ahead with the mural," he said,

"and pay you what you'd otherwise earn at the dry dock. Fifty cents Canadian a day, if you work all day, that is."

"Once I make preliminary sketches, I call that working on the mural already."

"Fair enough."

"Then I accept."

Beginning the very next morning, I worked from dawn until dusk, seven days a week, though on Sundays I had to wait until the last of the congregation left. I worked through ten sketchbooks in three weeks. I outlined the wharf, lighthouse, cliffs, jetty, various birds. Some days I sat in the pews, imagining it all on the wall. I actually took up charcoal on June 1. My plan was to outline the entire mural in charcoal, then work on each section, then step back and see what I had accomplished.

Throughout June and July, the wharf, jetty, and old docks to the south came fully into view. I charcoaled in the lighthouse, sawmill, the peninsula houses, stilt houses, fishing shacks, Helen's cold-storage shack. I drew Giles's orchard. I drew the saw-whet owl careening between its trees.

Each evening after I was done working, I covered the wall with bedsheets. I had worked entirely without an audience, until quite early on the morning of August 8 Reverend Sillet walked into the church and sat at the end of a pew near the mural. At first he said nothing. I was putting the final touches on a glossy ibis. I had seen three ibis foraging in the shallows south of Witless Bay at Tinker Point one summer, but in the mural I placed a single ibis in a tidal inlet at the southernmost point of Witless Bay Harbour.

It was warm in the church and Sillet fanned himself with a Bible he had taken from a wooden pocket on the back of a pew. The ribbon bookmark flapped up and down. He had rolled up his cuffs to near his knees, snapped open his suspenders, and was rubbing ointment on a patch of heat rash on his neck.

"Progress is being made," he said. "Now, that bird, the one you've just finished. What is it?"

"An ibis."

"It looks Egyptian."

"I wouldn't know. I haven't seen birds in Egypt."

"Take my word for it."

"Is that my wages in the envelope you brought in? Because I need to buy some supplies at Gillette's store."

"It is your wages."

"You can leave it there on the pew. I'll work straight through lunchtime today."

"You're no slacker when it comes to this mural, Fabian. I've let the elders know that. I said, 'He's no slacker.' "

"Supplies are costing me a little more than I'd expected. I could use a two-dollar advance."

"You can't be spending everything you're earning, now, can you?"

"I'm saving half, because after this mural, what work might there be?"

"I don't know."

"There sure isn't going to be need for another mural."

"I suggest that you give yourself the advance out of your own savings."

"You're not all that welcome to watch me paint."

"In my own church I'll make myself welcome, thank you. Anyway, I have a suggestion."

"I'm sure you do."

"Seeing as how the ability to paint is a gift from God and therefore a very, very personal thing. Seeing as how inspiration is a mystery, I won't interfere by trying to comment on a beak or feather or the way you see the natural world. I won't do that. I wonder, however, about just what this mural might contain as a higher calling. What the mural might call to in yourself, Fabian. How it can become a redemption. Redemption for you by fixing the truth to the church wall in a way you didn't with your testimony at the murder hearing."

"You used my mother in a sermon last week. You said you wouldn't."

"You aren't finished with the mural yet."

"Getting in your last licks, eh?"

"Fabian—I've been thinking that your mural might want to have more human nature in it. Not just birds. Not just portraits of birds."

"You mean what? You want me to show the murder?"

"I don't want the mural as a confession. No. That's for Catholics. I simply want there to be some higher purpose involved."

"God's wild creatures are perfect. You've said so yourself, even in their savage grace. You used those very words. What's a higher purpose than that? Birds are enough. The birds of Witless Bay are enough."

"I'm afraid I'm put in charge of your wages, Fabian. Birds are not enough. I'm your patron. And as your patron, I have a liability. I have an obligation to strongly suggest the best ways for you to put your patronage money to use. Consider it a kind of inspiration."

"I don't consider it that, though. I think I'll quit here and now. I'll whitewash the wall. All you'd have is a freshly painted wall, no mural. Now, that wouldn't be much of a redemption, would it? So what would be in it for you if I quit?"

"Before you put your brushes down and make a rash decision, try and understand the opportunity I'm offering. Let me spice up the bargain. You paint in the murder, I'll personally add ten dollars Canadian. Five in advance."

"The Bible is full of murders. And you've made direct mention of Botho's in your sermons. You've brought murder into the church left and right. So I'd just be falling into tradition, eh? Is that how you'd care to see it?"

"Think of me thinking of it any way you want."

"I will."

"I won't take public credit for the idea, Fabian. It'll be part of our secret collaboration."

"That is kind of you."

"Perhaps you'd include other citizens of Witless Bay as well, who did not murder Botho August. You were a friend of Helen Twombly's, for instance. Why not put Helen in? Helen was an odd soul, now, wasn't she?"

"She hated you, oddly enough."

"Yes, I'm certain she did. Someone can't go through such a long, long life without hatred toward somebody. It wouldn't be natural."

I stepped back from the ibis. It was finished.

"All right," I said. "I'll put Helen Twombly in here somewhere."

"You know, Helen took up with Reverend Weebe less than two years after her dear husband, Emile, passed. You didn't know that, did you? And why should you? You weren't born yet. It's the truth. And it was why Reverend Weebe finally left this village. It was one sad incident. Weebe's invalid wife—name was Elizabeth—lived up in St. John's, looked after by a nurse. She never once visited Witless Bay. And Weebe seldom got up to see her. When she finally got news of Weebe's infidelity, she put a gun to her head. But she fell asleep, a kind of reverie, they say. Isn't that the grandest scrinshank? Oh yes, maybe that's a word from before your time as well. It means a hesitation so as to avoid an issue, scrinshank does. Elizabeth Weebe hesitated and dozed off, right in her chair! The nurse found her. Said the pistol was on her lap. The nurse figured old Elizabeth had put the gun to her head because she'd seen her do it before. One big opera, that house. And do you know what the nurse said? It's famous gossip from that time and place. She said, 'Tis not every day that Morris kills a cow.'"

"I don't know that saying either."

"It means, a favorable opportunity comes but seldom."

"It sounded like she only had to stay awake long enough to do herself in."

"The favorable opportunity, in this case, was to leave Reverend Weebe an inheritance of guilt. To cause him torment for the rest of his days."

"What happened? I mean, after that."

"Well, Elizabeth Weebe and the nurse had a good laugh over it all later on. And Reverend Weebe did in fact outlive his wife by ten years. He thought he'd inherit her considerable wealth. But he was wrong. Because Elizabeth left every last penny to—"

"Helen."

"That's correct, to Helen Twombly."

"Talk about the last laugh."

"Indeed. Helen accepted her money, too. Later still, Reverend Weebe came to Helen to beg for some of it, and she refused him. Tail between his legs, he left the village."

"Well, live and learn. But I don't love or miss Helen any the less for knowing."

"So be it."

"I'll paint in Helen. You come back in a few days, Helen will be here."

"That's a good beginning. I'll leave your wages on the pew, the way you asked."

Sillet dusted along the pew with his open palm, then left the church.

After lunch the next day, I took a walk to the wharf, and when I got back to the church, I saw a group of boys playing jackstones out front, and off to the side some girls played the ring game Little Sally Saucer. Millie Sloo crouched in the center, while the others held hands and danced around her, singing:

> *Little Sally Saucer, sitting in the water,*
> *Weeping and crying for her young man.*

Rise up, Sally, wipe away your tears,
Point to the east, point to the west,
and choose the one that you love best.

Inside the church I found a dozen or so children gathered in front of the mural. Three were clustered near the ibis: Andrew Kieley, Lucas Wyatt, and Sophie Auster. Carson Synge, Emma Shore, Petrus Dollard, Sally Barrens, Marni Corbett, Arden Corbett, Philomene Slater, Chester Parmelee, and some others I cannot remember just now, were looking at other parts of the mural. When I walked up the aisle, they all scattered, a few making wild crow caws, flapping their wings, racing down the pews. Seeing them I suddenly heard, as if it were yesterday, Helen saying, "I could have educated the village children." And then and there I decided to paint Helen as a mermaid. I set to work. Since in one sense the mural was a map of the coastline, I placed Helen where I had discovered her body, in Caroline Cove. I detailed the gather of rocks, then drew a mermaid. I painted in eyes, nose, mouth, fish scales in rows on a wedged tail. It was a child's version, mostly based on mermaids I had seen in several of Mrs. Bath's collections of fairy tales. Stepping back in an hour to appraise it, I thought, This might have actually pleased Helen. I touched up the mermaid. There, in the mural, she would remain a basking presence two harbors away from the murder, which I began to sketch out late on the same afternoon.

I worked well into that night. I worked late for four nights in a row. Just before supper on the fifth, Margaret showed up in the church. She walked to the mural and immediately said, "That mermaid looks a bit like Helen Twombly. Only you've made Caroline Cove heaven for her. She looks happy. According to what you told me, Fabian, she was all mangled up, head to foot, when you found her. So, as I see it, in a painting you get to change bad luck to good, eh?"

"It's nice to see you, Margaret."

"Thank you."

"About Helen—yes, it's her. I thought that the children would like it."

"Makes a death at sea hold out some hope for the future, is that it?"

"No, Margaret, I didn't think it through. Helen liked to talk about mermaids, is all."

"I knew her better than you did, and I don't think she'd approve."

"You made a pretty quick judgement."

"No, I've been here a few times already. In the middle of the night, with my lantern. I hardly sleep. Anyway, *ha!* Helen's finally allowed in Sillet's church! That's a lark on him."

"I guess it is."

She lay down on a pew, propping her head on her folded hands.

"I'm back to keeping books for Spivey's, Gillette's, and my father," she said. "I was thinking how odd it is, you learn a little arithmetic and it makes you a living. I could take my work with me almost anywhere, I suppose. If I moved to Halifax or Montreal, I could bring my arithmetic and all my bookkeeping experience with me and find a job in one of those cities. It'd be like opening the same suitcase over and over, just in a new place."

"I was in Halifax, as you know. I can't highly recommend it."

"You weren't a tourist, though. Not a relaxed, sightseeing sort, at least. It might be nice just to be a tourist somewhere someday."

She closed her eyes and appeared to sleep a moment. "Fabian, when I was in hospital, I tried to put a name on everything that's happened to us. Everything that's happened in Witless Bay. All the funerals over so short a time. I don't know. I just don't know. But can I tell you something?"

"Yes."

"You can go for a stroll with me this evening after supper. I don't want to sit down to supper with you. Not yet. Just a stroll after."

"That's being out in public together, wouldn't you say?"

"Yes, even if nobody sees us, we'll know we risked that."

"All right. Where should we meet?"

"Along the path, between your house and the orchard."

"Fine, then."

She left the church. I painted gulls near the lighthouse wind sock. I put away my charcoal and paints, washed out my brushes and placed them in a jar of water. At home, I fried up a potato and ate it with bread and coffee and codfish cheeks. I had two more cups of coffee, then set out along the path. I pissed against an apple tree. Stepping away from the tree, I saw Margaret in the distance. She hallooed and waved. I waved back and saw that she had a blanket tucked under her other arm. She was wearing a blue cotton dress and was barefoot.

"Balmy out," she said. She kissed me on the cheek. "There's a place I want to walk to."

"What's in the blanket?"

"Oh, rudiments of life."

"I thought the doctors warned you."

"Oh, they did, Fabian, they did, for whatever business it is of yours. I heed their warning some of the time. For instance, I haven't had so much as a drop yet this evening."

"Where do you want to go?"

"You might first politely say, Lucky, lucky me, out loud. Lucky that this beautiful woman has even seen fit to stroll with me, so soon after my divorce."

"Margaret, it wasn't a real marriage. It wasn't a divorce."

"It was both of those things, only not done on the straight and narrow."

"Margaret, I *am* happy that you came to see me in the church. Happier yet you wanted this stroll. And you do look beautiful."

"Thank you for repeating my opinion so nicely."

"All right, then."

She took my hand in hers and led me toward the light-house. We said very little. It was near dusk and a few lingering boats could be seen out in the harbor. As we walked past the lighthouse yard, we saw how cheerful things looked. There were some wooden children's toys near the door. The door was open. There were lace curtains.

We walked from the lighthouse south along the path that ran along the cliff. "Over there," Margaret said, pointing to a grassy place just back from the edge, next to a scrag spruce. She reached into the folds of the blanket and took out a bottle. She put the bottle on the ground, then spread out the blanket. She opened the bottle and took a drink, but then secured the cork. Gazing out at the horizon, her eyes teared up. "Stars know just the proper distance to keep from one another," she said. "That's what my mother used to tell me. She's the only one in the world I'd want to come back, if a séance could work."

Not looking at me, she slid her dress up over her head and folded it neatly near the blanket. "I lost a little weight in hospital," she said, "but it's the same old me, except for all the new thoughts I've been having."

I thought this: For all my painting of rapturous shorebirds, long-necked herons, ibis in dusky light, I did not have the means to describe how passionate I felt toward Margaret just then, without having yet touched her. Her very skin seemed to hold twilight, delay it, and I retreated to the edge of the blanket. She slid over to me and began to unbutton my shirt. She put my hand on her breast. Looking at my face she said, "Fabian, this is where I collided with Dalton Gillette, when I was thirteen years old. I thought that this very spot was a good place to start courting again. I'm sure you agree."

12

Isaac Sprague

Late in September 1912, I had supper with Margaret and Enoch at Spivey's. We met at seven o'clock and sat at the same table. That morning Enoch had returned from ten days along the northern coast, and would leave in a week for Halifax. When our meal was served, Enoch said, "Here's something," taking a bite of codfish stew. "Back in December 1901, when that Italian fellow Marconi—" He took a few more bites by way of backing up to where he had originally intended to begin. "Do you remember, Margaret, me telling you that in 1866 I saw the *Great Eastern*, wonder ship of her day, at Heart's Content, towing up the first Atlantic cable?"

"Yes, Pop, I do."

"And that in December 1901 that Italian fellow Marconi got the first wireless signal across the ocean? Well, of course

I've mentioned this so many times we could almost dance to it. But what I haven't yet told you is they've just completed a statue of Marconi in St. John's. I want to take you to see it. It overlooks their harbor. Very prominent. A big piece of granite, Marconi carved leaning over his wireless, granite table, granite people huddled around, listening in. A moment for posterity. I never thought a statue could bring tears to my eyes. But this one did."

"I'd like to ask Fabian along."

"Fine by me."

I began my meal then. "There's an engraving of an auk —an extinct bird that couldn't fly. In a museum there. I saw it a number of years ago. I've lost count. But I'd like to see it again."

"The person whose auk it is, what's his name?" Enoch said.

"Ole Worm."

"Not a local name."

"No, he's a Dane."

"A lowly curse of a name." Enoch chuckled alone at his own turn of phrase. "Worm."

"Maybe not a peculiar name in Denmark, though, Pop," Margaret said. "I don't know. I haven't been there."

"Well, as I see it, you wouldn't have to go to Denmark to think of Worm as a peculiar name."

"Let's spend two whole days in St. John's, Pop. A real outing. We can stay in a hotel. A big city like that would specialize in hotels, I imagine."

"There's a number of them there."

Bridget brought three helpings of pudding to our table. "None of you has ever turned down dessert," she said.

"Thank you," Enoch said.

Bridget went back into the kitchen.

"Fabian here has been working on a letter to Mr. Isaac Sprague," Margaret said.

"I'd rather not talk about it."

"He worked on it every night for a couple of weeks, Pop. You know the red-throated loon Fabian's got tacked up?"

"For years above his desk."

"That's the one. Well, he worships it, but in the letter he berates it to Mr. Sprague, his teacher. Fabian's hurt as a child that Mr. Sprague hasn't written back to him."

"A person writes a letter," Enoch said, "a person expects a reply."

"He's a busy man," I said.

"I don't think you ever should *send* a nasty, angry letter." Margaret looked right at me. "I think you should write it but not send it."

"I'm not expecting he'll teach me again. I just wanted him to—"

"To what?"

"I don't know, exactly. To write me back."

"What's that you told Sprague about his loon, the one you worship? I read the letter carefully, Fabian, but I can't remember."

"The wing looks a bit too high on the shoulder."

"Yes, that's it."

"Boy, you and this Sprague do get down to details, don't you," Enoch said.

"We used to."

"I'd tear up the angry letter and write another," Margaret said.

"And what would you write, then?"

"Just what my pop said: Dear Mr. Sprague, A man sends a letter, a man expects a reply."

"All right, I'll try that."

"Fine, then. It's settled. You write it, I'll deliver it."

"Fine," I said.

"Good pudding," Margaret said.

"Fabian, speaking of letters—" Enoch reached into his back pocket and produced an envelope. "It's postmarked Canada, no return address, you'll notice. I got it from Arvin Flint, up in Cook's Harbour."

He set the letter in front of me on the table.

I cleaned a butter knife with my napkin, then slid the knife along the envelope. I took out the letter and unfolded it. For some reason, before I read a word I counted the pages: sixteen. All the words were printed in capital letters and the sentences were wide apart. In a rush of memory, I saw my father hammering a nail, oiling a door, scaling fish, but I could not for the life of me conjure up an image of him reading or writing. It certainly was possible that he could not write longhand. He never read to me when I was a boy; my mother had taken on that task and had, I thought, enjoyed it. My father had liked sitting in the same room as she turned the pages, reading in an animated, even boisterous fashion, if the story called for it. Later, my father might refer to the story, though. He liked *Blackbeard the Pirate*, for instance. He once said, "There were cold-water pirates in Newfoundland. But old-fashioned saber and yardarm pirates seldom got this far north. They preferred the tropics. Tropical islands where they could revel and plunder. I got those words from books, 'revel,' and 'plunder.' I tried using the word 'plunder' once when talking to Romeo Gillette, and he just said, 'What?' All we ever got from history up here in Newfoundland was thieves like Bassie. Well, I suppose to somebody reading a book down in the tropics, a bank robber like my brother would fall into a colorful tradition of sorts."

"Who's the letter from?" Margaret said.

I had just read, on the final page, without having read anything else: TRY AND NOT FORGET ME. YOUR LOVING FATHER, ORKNEY VAS. I slid it over to Margaret.

Margaret read it. "I'll be damned," she said. She handed the page back to me. "Should we leave you alone here to read it, Fabian?"

"No, I'll read it later. I'm going to finish my pudding. I'll read it later."

I put the letter in my shirt pocket and said nothing for the rest of the meal. Margaret had tea. I had coffee. We paid for supper, each exactly a third. Enoch and Margaret walked home. I went to my house and sat on the porch steps. I did not open the letter just then. I went into the kitchen, percolated coffee, poured five cups and lined them

up on the porch step. I lit a lantern. I sat staring at the
envelope. The words FABIAN VAS, WITLESS BAY,
NEWFOUNDLAND were perfectly centered. I took out the
letter.

DEAR FABIAN,

THE NIGHT I RETURNED FROM ANTICOSTI, I ALREADY
KNEW. ENOCH HAD TOLD ME. WHEN WE ENTERED THE
HARBOR I ASKED HIM TO ANCHOR OUT A WAYS AND HE
DID. I STOOD ON DECK LOOKING AT THE VILLAGE LIGHTS.
I LOOKED AT THE LIGHTHOUSE. I LOOKED AT WITLESS BAY
A LONG TIME AND THOUGHT, SUDDENLY I'M A STRANGER
TO MY LIFE. ENOCH CAME UP BESIDE ME AND SAID, IT'S
TIME WE EITHER TAKE YOU SOMEWHERE ELSE OR WE TIE
UP. I COULD HAVE GONE SOMEWHERE ELSE. I BELIEVE
THAT ENOCH WOULD HAVE TAKEN ME RIGHT BACK TO
HALIFAX HAD I ASKED. I COULD HAVE THEN SENT A
LETTER, FOUND OUT THE EXACT DATE OF YOUR WEDDING,
EVEN MET YOU AND ALARIC AT THE HAGERFORSE GUEST
HOUSE! I COULD HAVE STOOD UP AT YOUR WEDDING AND
BOTHO AUGUST WOULD HAVE BEEN ALIVE. BUT THINGS
DID NOT GO THAT WAY, DID THEY?

FABIAN, SON. AS BASSIE TOLD YOU, I REALIZED I WAS
WRONG, VERY WRONG ABOUT CORA HOLLY. IT WAS ALL
MORE A NEED FOR ME TO SEE YOU OUT IN THE WORLD
MARRIED THAN ANYTHING. IT WAS WRONG. I'M SORRY.
ALARIC BANVILLE MIGHT HAVE BEEN CORRECT IN SAYING
THERE'S ALL SORTS OF WAYS FOR A MARRIAGE TO BEGIN,
BUT THERE ARE WRONG WAYS AMONGST THOSE, AND

WHAT HAPPENED TO YOU IN HALIFAX HAD TO BE ABOUT
AS WRONG AS COULD BE. ROMEO TOLD BASSIE THE WHOLE
STORY AND BASSIE IN TURN TOLD ME. I AM TRULY SORRY.

AT THE HAGERFORSE GUEST HOUSE I SLEPT IN ROOM
NUMBER 5. WHEN I ARRIVED THERE, HAVING FLED THE
AUNT IVY BARNACLE IN LAMALINE, HAVING HELD THE
LANTERN TO MY FACE BECAUSE I KNEW YOU'D BE WATCH-
ING, I SMELLED LIKE LARD IN A BUCKET, WHEREAS THERE
WAS THE SWEET SMELL OF TOILET SOAP IN THE BATH-
ROOM. NEVER HAD A BODY EARNED A HOT BATH SO WELL,
ABOUT THE ONLY THING I DID DESERVE, I SUPPOSE. THE
FRESH CLEAN SHEETS WERE A HEAVEN. AS A MATTER OF
COURSE, I COULD NOT TELL MRS. HAGERFORSE MY RE-
LATION TO YOU, NOR LAUGH WITH HER, PARTICULARLY
NERVOUS BUT JOVIAL WOMAN THAT SHE IS, IN THE DRAW-
ING ROOM ABOUT THE TURNS A LIFE CAN TAKE. NOR
COULD I CRY OVER WHAT HAPPENS BETWEEN A FATHER
AND SON IN FRONT OF HER. NOT THAT I HAVE A GOOD
WORKING PHILOSOPHY ABOUT ALL OF THAT ANYWAY. I
JUST DON'T.

IT MAY BE OF INTEREST OR ENTERTAINMENT TO YOU TO
KNOW HOW IT WENT WITH ARVIN FLINT. HE WAS NOT DIF-
FICULT TO PERSUADE. I MET UP WITH HIM IN BURGEO.
ARVIN USED TO BE IN THE CONSTABLE PROFESSION. HE
STILL CARRIES A SIDEARM. I SAID TO HIM, I'M LEAVING MY
FAMILY, CAN YOU TAKE ME TO HALIFAX, NOVA SCOTIA,
I'LL MAKE IT WORTH YOUR WHILE. I SHOWED HIM SOME
OF THE MONEY I EARNED FROM SHOOTING BIRDS. I SAID
I'D MAKE MY WAY INTO A NEW LIFE FROM HALIFAX.

BASSIE, YOUR LONG-LOST UNCLE, FOLLOWED A LETTER I HAD SENT TO HIM AND CAUGHT UP WITH ME HERE IN CANADA. OF COURSE THAT WAS AFTER HE'D COME TO SEE YOU AND THE HEARING, WHICH HE REPORTED TO ME IN DETAIL. NATURALLY HE TOLD ME ABOUT ALARIC BANVILLE'S DEATH ON GUY FAWKES DAY. AS YOU CAN IMAGINE THAT TOOK ME ABACK. I'M RELIEVED, AS CONCERNS THE HEARING, THAT YOU GOT MY MESSAGE FROM BASSIE AND ACTED ON IT. AND WHAT IS TRUE IS THAT BY YOUR ACTING ON IT, I FEEL A KIND OF REDEMPTION. I FEEL REDEEMED BY YOUR GOING FREE. I KNOW THAT YOU WENT FREE BECAUSE BASSIE TRAVELED ALL THE WAY TO ST. JOHN'S TO FIND OUT AND BROUGHT THAT NEWS BACK TO ME. YOU SEE, FABIAN, LOOKING BACK ON THINGS I ONLY WISH THAT I'D HAD A STRONGER DOSE OF WRONGHEADED CONVICTION THAT RAINY NIGHT TO WALK UP THE ROAD AND MURDER BOTHO AUGUST MYSELF. INSTEAD, I LEFT YOU TO MAKE THAT VERY CONVICTION UP ON MY BEHALF IN THE HEARING. THAT IS MY CROSS TO BEAR. THAT, AND SHOOTING SO MANY BIRDS ON ANTICOSTI ISLAND, ALL FOR MONEY AND FOR A MISGUIDED WEDDING.

HAD I STAYED HOME AND NOT GONE TO ANTICOSTI, IT IS TRUE THAT ALARIC BANVILLE MIGHT HAVE DRIFTED PERMANENTLY TO THE OPPOSITE SIDE OF THE HOUSE FROM ME, BUT NOT TO THE LIGHTHOUSE. NOT THERE.

WELL, I'M JUMPING AROUND A BIT HERE. BUT LET ME SAY THAT I SLIPPED OFF THE AUNT IVY BARNACLE IN LAMALINE BECAUSE I COULD NOT BEAR THE HUMILIATION THAT I'D BEEN HANDED, AND BECAUSE I WAS AFRAID FOR MY LIFE. PAIN I COULDN'T SHAKE OFF FROM THE ADUL-

TERY, ADDED TO COWARDICE, IS ONE NASTY RECIPE, AND
I CONCOCTED IT MYSELF AND SWALLOWED IT. AND ITS EF-
FECTS MADE ME SLIP OFF THE MAIL BOAT AND FLEE INTO
CANADA.

AS FOR YOUR MOTHER, I ALLOW MYSELF TO GRIEVE FOR
HER BY THINKING OF OUR EARLY YEARS TOGETHER. I TRY
AND STOP MY THINKING THERE, AND OFTEN I AM SUC-
CESSFUL.

DURING THE LAST FIVE MONTHS BASSIE AND I HAVE
ENGAGED IN THREE ROBBERIES AND ARE MOVING INTO THE
HEART OF CANADA. THERE WAS A BANK, ANOTHER BANK,
AND A MINING CAMP PAYROLL WHICH WE TOOK EN ROUTE
FROM A TRAIN. I AM CERTAINLY FIELDING TROUBLE IN MY
LIFE NOW. TROUBLE GALORE, NOW THAT I AM RUNNING
WITH BASSIE. WHEN WE WERE CHILDREN WE BROKE INTO
OUR OWN FATHER'S SHED WHERE HE MADE GOOSE AND
DUCK DECOYS AND STOLE TWO OF THEM. WE THEN WENT
TO A DIFFERENT TOWN AND SOLD THEM THERE. AS THE
STORE OWNER REACHED INTO HIS TILL TO PAY US WE SAW
MONEY. THAT SAME NIGHT WE ROBBED THE TILL OF IT. I
NEVER TOLD ANYBODY OF THIS PERSONAL HISTORY AND
THAT INCLUDES YOUR MOTHER. I TELL YOU NOW, BECAUSE
I HAVE, GOD HELP ME, RETURNED TO A FORMER WAY OF
LIFE, A WAY OF LIFE I HAD LONG BEFORE I EVER MET
ALARIC. I NEVER INTENDED TO RETURN TO THIS. I NEVER
WANTED TO, NOR THOUGHT IN MY WORST DREAMS THAT I
WOULD. YET NOW I HAVE. IT IS PATHETIC AND WILL SUS-
TAIN ME FINANCIALLY UNTIL IT ENDS, AND A LIFE SUCH
AS THIS ONE CANNOT END WELL.

I SEE THAT I AM STILL JUMPING AROUND HERE. IT HAS

BEEN SO LONG SINCE I WROTE OUT WORDS LIKE THIS. I
NOTICE THAT IT TAKES PRACTICE, NO MATTER HOW CLEAR
YOUR THOUGHTS ARE. PLUS WHICH THIS IS A LETTER I'D
NATURALLY HOPED NEVER TO WRITE.

FABIAN, CONSIDERING THAT WE MAY NOT ACTUALLY SEE
EACH OTHER AGAIN, HERE IS SOME ADVICE. I WOULD AD-
VISE THAT IF YOU START ACTING MORE MARRIED TO MAR-
GARET, SHE'LL NOTICE AND IT COULD LEAD TO MARRIAGE.

SON, IF YOU COULD JUST ONCE CLOSE YOUR EYES AND
THINK OF ME IN ONE OF MY STRONGER AND FINER MO-
MENTS, SAY TALKING AMONGST FRIENDS IN GILLETTE'S
STORE AFTER A DAY'S WORK AT THE DRY DOCK SIDE BY
SIDE TOGETHER, A LITTLE MONEY JANGLING IN OUR
POCKETS, THEN I WOULD BE HAPPY.

TRY AND NOT FORGET ME. YOUR LOVING FATHER,

ORKNEY VAS

Through the rest of September and October 1912, I
worked steadily on the mural. I charcoaled and painted. I
would arrive at the church at six o'clock, work until noon,
eat lunch, then continue at least until supper, sometimes
late into the night. I sketched thick-billed and common
murres on Green Island, Leach's petrels, herring gulls,
black-legged kittiwakes, shearwaters. Puffins on Witless
Bay Island and at Bay Bulls. Much of October I completed
sandpipers and moved inland. I finished the general store,
sawmill, Helen's garden. I detailed the inlet where Enoch
and Margaret's house was situated. In that inlet, I crowded
a buff-breasted sandpiper, little blue heron, ring-necked
duck, blue-winged teal, and hooded merganser. I then

added a small cove that did not really exist in Newfoundland and painted a garganey there. The last two days of October, I painted Lambert's trout camp; I put osprey and kingfisher in the air directly over Lambert as he gutted a trout. Off to the side, his crippled owl tore at a trout head on the ground.

November. The first of this month I reserved for the murder.

I did not depict anyone actually shooting Botho August, only my painter's rendition of the aftermath. In the mural —now—Botho stands in the topmost window of the lighthouse, black wings spreading from his back, three splotches of blood on his nightshirt. He is the presiding angel of Witless Bay. I stepped back to look. I left him that way. I painted the gramophone in on the roof.

In the mural, Odeon Sloo and his family are unloading a horse-drawn wagon in the lighthouse yard. The door is open.

Out in Witless Bay Harbour, my mother is peacefully rowing a dinghy. She has an umbrella fixed to a thwart, shading her from the sun. On a nearby swell, there are black ducks. On a buoy off to her left is a cormorant.

Reverend Sillet is standing above the weathervane atop his church. Except for this act of levitation, I think that his portrait is an admirable likeness, right down to his ever-present handkerchief in his black suit jacket pocket, button-down shoes.

On the rotted dock at the southernmost point of the harbor, Margaret is a grown woman riding her bicycle.

Village life, plain village life, is what the rest of the mural contains. People drying cod, milling about in front of the church, children fishing from docks, the *Aunt Ivy Barnacle* just leaving the wharf; though I did add a bevy of gulls marauding off from its bow, one of Klara Holly's letters in each beak. Water, clouds, sky, birds, and no murder taking place—my perfect day.

In my estimation, I completed the mural on November 4.

I had much apprehension about showing it to Sillet. It was not that I truly believed I had attained any sort of redemption by having painted it; nor would there be any lack of redemption if he did not approve. More, it was the act of being judged by him at all, and my knowing that the next Sunday the sheets would be taken down and the congregation would see where their money had gone.

Jittery or not, I wanted to celebrate. I got dressed up, called on Margaret at her house, asked her to come and see the mural, then out to Spivey's for supper.

"I'll act as if I was in a real hurry," she said, "and that not to waste time, I have to change clothes in front of you."

In the church, she studied the mural for quite a while. She tilted her head, stepped up close, stepped back, sat in a pew, and shifted expressions. "You're not included in it," she finally said. "Is that the artist's modesty, or cowardice?"

"I was waiting to ask where you thought I should be."

"Well, it's *your* masterpiece, Fabian. Though considering what liberties you've taken with certain people, Sillet in particular, up there rusting with his weathervane, I'd guess he won't call it a masterpiece."

"I thought I'd paint me lying facedown in the mud. In the lighthouse yard."

"That word 'redemption' has really got to you, hasn't it? Fabian, if you believe that just by painting it you can become the man you murdered—go ahead, think that. Paint yourself in Botho's place. I for one wouldn't be persuaded. I wouldn't take it to heart. Though I'd bet bottom dollar that Sillet would praise you to the rafters."

"Margaret, I told you the arrangement. I just want him to leave you and my family out of his sermons."

"Whitewash the whole thing, Fabian. Now. Before it's too late. Before you lose your soul."

"I can't."

"In the least, then, don't consider me part of this arrangement. Don't you dare. I'd rather stay in sermons as a murderous harlot. It doesn't bother me. Not one bit."

I hung up the sheets on their nails. We went to Spivey's.

At our table, before we had supper, Margaret said, "Tomorrow's Guy Fawkes Day. A year's gone by, Fabian. A person can pack a lot into a year, can't a person. It's Guy Fawkes, plus it's a Thursday. I'd agree to sleep at your house if we pass up the festivities."

"I wasn't planning to attend."

That Thursday night—the bonfire blazing near the lighthouse—Margaret and I met in my kitchen just after dark.

"I want to get into bed right away," she said.

Before we took off our clothes, Margaret did not have a

drink of whiskey as she customarily did. She just began kissing me, tenderly one moment, the opposite the next. She kissed every part of my face, then moved down my shoulder to my chest. I was so taken by her dreamy expression—eyes half closed, glancing at my face now and then, arms holding on for dear life more than in an embrace—that at first I did not fathom the words she whispered between kisses. Words having nothing yet everything to do with the moment. "You have to build a new bed." She kissed my neck now. "I want every last thing of Alaric's out of the house." She wrapped her leg around mine and held my hands above my head. "I'll have supper once a week alone with my father." Now she gently rocked on top of me, eyes closed. "I wouldn't be a bride in front of that mural. Never." She lay across my chest, breathing into my ear, and continued with the rules of our marriage. "Halifax is out, for a honeymoon place. I'd rather not go anywhere." Now, lost in her motion, she grasped the headboard, her words deepening to moans, and suddenly she kissed me hard, bit her lip, moaned again, closed her eyes, and said, as though forcing out the first part of a song, "This child . . ." She pressed her forehead to mine, collapsing against me.

"I never left you, Margaret, not really. Yet at the same time it's strange, I feel that I've come back around to you."

"Get me a glass of water, will you, darling."

I got up from the bed and poured each of us a glass of water. I sat on the edge of the bed. Margaret pulled the sheets up to her chin.

"Did you just propose to me?" I said.

She drank the water to the bottom of the glass.

"Only if you say yes."

Here is how we planned our wedding. Margaret said, "How about November 10? It's soon enough to stay excited about till it happens, and to not wait too long to get over with." I agreed.

We asked Enoch to officiate. "I've been volunteering for years, haven't I?" he said.

On my wedding day I went early to find Sillet and, when I found him in the store, asked him to finally come and see the mural. I met him in the church at three o'clock.

"You have your church suit on," he said. "Do you consider this a pious occasion?"

"Showing you the mural? No. I'm just going to show it to you, after which I'm getting married."

"Sander Muggah isn't going to officiate, is he?"

"Enoch Handle."

"Ah, a marriage at sea."

"Well, anchored in the harbor. Or tied up at the dock. A plain and simple location."

"Legally, I know he can. But has Enoch ever performed a marriage?"

"He hasn't performed his daughter's, which is all that counts to me."

"Well enough and good."

"Take a look now."

"Indeed."

I took down the sheets. As I sat in a pew, Reverend Sillet walked the length of the mural, inspecting it close up, bird by bird, person by person, house by house. "Oh, Lord" is all he said at first. He stepped to the other side of the church for a long view.

"Interesting enough, through and through," he said, somber-voiced. He walked over and stood next to me. "Yet in the main, in my humble opinion, your imagination went a bit—awry. I admit to recognizing certain things. I recognize certain people and the things they do. I recognize our village in general. But as for the unfortunate event—"

"The murder."

"—You don't really— Your rendering of Botho August. Of myself. There's a certain folly. But, alas, I privileged you that, didn't I? I paid you to paint this mural as you saw fit for the most part, didn't I? However, I would have thought the process of redemption—"

"That's me lying facedown in the mud."

A gunshot exploded in the air and set the church to ringing, louder than the bells ever had. A second shot—a third. I felt Reverend Sillet throw himself in fear, protection, or sheer clumsiness over me, and we toppled to the floor. Looking up from under his body, I saw that the cluster of ducks near where my mother rowed on the mural had been pulverized.

Sillet gathered himself back up to his feet. "Margaret!" he said, with seething restraint. He brushed himself off.

Margaret shrugged. She had on her mother's wedding

dress. She held the revolver by her thumb. "Mitchell Kelb sold this back to Romeo Gillette," she said, holding forth the gun. "The damning evidence revolver here. Did either of you know that? Well, you just don't keep up on things, now, do you? My father in turn bought it from Romeo to take along on his mail route. He says that times are changing for the worse where human nature is concerned. He says there's a rougher sort in Halifax than there used to be. Even mail—just everyday letters and packages—is fair game to galoots, he says. I just borrowed the pistol for the purpose you just witnessed. There now, I've added the right touch of spice to the mural, don't you think?"

Sillet moved toward Margaret, holding his fist in his hand. He stopped a few steps in front of her. "You'll never, *never* set foot in my church again," he said. "Margaret Handle, I could easily have you arrested for damaging church property."

"If I wanted to damage church property, I'd start with you," she said.

"Very well, then, Margaret. You are who you are. I'll simply have the holes puttied and sanded, and there'll be no trace of your wrongdoing. Fabian, I'm sure, will paint in new birds. Now kindly leave."

I looked at Margaret. Her expression of nonchalance. The revolver held now against the wedding dress. Her hair done up in coiled braids.

"Fabian," she said, "I'll need an escort."

Sillet turned back to the mural.

As we walked along the cliff path to the wharf, Margaret

slipped a coat over her shoulders. I took the revolver from her hand and tossed it into the sea. "I'll get Enoch a new one if he wants," I said. "Margaret, what got into you back there?"

"Believe me, husband-to-be. I changed a lot in hospital and have changed some since. But not entirely."

When we reached the *Aunt Ivy Barnacle*, Enoch was waiting on deck. It was a cold afternoon, with a biting, wet chill off the water. The sea was calm, though, and waves lapped evenly against the hull.

"Were those shots I heard echo down?" Enoch said.

"Yes, Pop, they were."

Enoch waited a moment, then decided to ask nothing. "Well, you and Fabian look healthy enough."

"Let's all go to Spivey's after," Margaret said. "I'll sit there in my wedding dress."

"I'm sure Bridget and Lemuel will compliment it," Enoch said. "I'm ready when you are. I've brushed up on the vows. You two will be your own witnesses. We'll call that legal. Let's go into the steerage, out of the wind."

In the cabin we held hands and Enoch conducted the ceremony. Bible, rings, vows, all in as few words as possible. It pleased us.

"You may kiss the bride," Margaret said.

We kissed a moment, then we heard Enoch say, "My God, some courtships are more difficult than others, aren't they?" He pointed to his eyes, which had teared up. "This is from giving the bride away and your mother not here to see it, Margaret."

"Cry all you want, Pop. As long as it's in the knowing that I'm happy."

She kissed her father's cheek and wiped his tears with her fingers.

Enoch left for the south on the last mail run of the year, and Margaret and I set up house. I built a new bed, putting the other in storage. We slept in my parents' old room. I began to use my former bedroom as a place to paint and draw. I set up my easel. I set out my paints. Enoch had given us fifty dollars as a wedding present, a lot of money, which handsomely tided us over. When asked, I worked at the dry dock. I was not shunned. Margaret kept her employment as a bookkeeper, working in Enoch's attic. Things were all set up in perfect order there, so why change it?

By November 23 Enoch had not returned. That evening Margaret had no appetite. "Why not just go to Spivey's and have supper?" she said. "I really don't mind. I know you'll come back. I'm going to sleep. Besides, we're out of coffee, so you might want to get some at Gillette's. I'm sleeping so well these days, and at odd hours, too. The bottles all out of the house. And look at me, drinking tea. Just look at me. I really just want to sleep now. Have a nice supper."

I went to Spivey's, but as it turned out, the only available place was at a two-chair table where Reverend Sillet was already seated. Seeing me hesitate at the door, Bridget whistled and pulled out the empty chair, then went into the kitchen. I sat down. We ate mostly in silence. When our dishes were cleared, I said, "You were a fair employer, and you paid me on time."

He wiped his mouth with his napkin, paid up, and left Spivey's.

"Any mail for me?" I asked Romeo the next afternoon in his store. The *Aunt Ivy Barnacle* had tied up that morning. Enoch was over to visit Margaret.

"No," said Romeo. "But Enoch brought a visitor, come all the way from Halifax to see you."

"I can't imagine."

"He's gone to Spivey's to freshen up, then was going to look for you. That's what he said. A gentleman from the city."

I walked to Spivey's and asked Bridget about my visitor, and she said he was resting up in the spare room, where he would spend the night.

"Can I knock?" I said.

"I don't see why not."

But before I could, the man appeared in the restaurant. "Fabian Vas?" he said.

"That's me."

He was, I would guess, in his early sixties and wore a black overcoat partly open at the collar. He was neatly dressed. Though this was my first glimpse of him, his face looked ravaged by poor health. He had thick white hair combed to one side. He had dark pouches of skin beneath his eyes. It struck me as a very tired, proud, dignified face.

"I am Isaac Sprague," he said.

"I don't understand."

"I'll say it slowly. Isaac Sprague. From Halifax. You wrote me of late. I'm here in person to answer."

"Do you want me to go upstairs?" Bridget said.

"No, we'll step outside," I said.

On the porch I said to Isaac Sprague, "My letter, I— Nothing much in it was true. The wing was not too high on the shoulder." I hesitated, then looked at Sprague. "You can't imagine how much I relied on your—correspondence." It wasn't easy for me to say.

He looked at the harbor. I looked to see what bird he might have seen, but the harbor was empty of birds. He buttoned his coat at the collar.

"The most recent kingfisher you sent," he said. "The one above the pond. It was adequate. But the bird's reflection itself too closely resembled the actual bird's face. It was not even slightly distorted on the surface, so the texture of the water wasn't at all represented. There's no such thing as a perfectly still watery surface. I once saw a kingfisher dive right into its own face on the water—it was on a branch as low as the one you drew. Though usually a kingfisher prefers a higher branch."

"I'll draw that over again, then."

"Yes, well. Let's sit down, shall we?"

We sat on the porch step.

"Why am I here, you asked. You see, Mr. Vas—look closely at my face. When there's little time left, one perhaps tends to say things even more bluntly. I am dying. It's not important from what cause, but is important to me how I spend my remaining days. My painting is completed, my teaching almost. In perhaps a moment of delirium and weakness, I decided to visit certain of my students. I agonized over the names. I didn't want to visit the utterly hopeless ones, simply because they are hopeless. So many of those over the years, it makes me shudder to think of it. And I didn't want to visit my one or two geniuses, who really didn't need me to begin with.

"Let me put it this way: where you are concerned, Mr. Vas"—he began coughing, then righted himself, slouching only slightly—"I don't exclude potential. I've come to see your work. May I?"

"There isn't much of it of late."

"On the contrary. Enoch Handle told me about an extensive mural."

"Well, there are birds in it."

"Let's have a look."

The church was empty. I sat in the rearmost pew. Sprague walked slowly to the mural. Much as Sillet had, he inspected it closely, though he used a monocle as well. He sat down in a pew and continued to study the mural.

"I've never been a sentimentalist, Mr. Vas, as you know from my letters. Especially when it comes to bird art. And I won't start to be one now," he said.

He stood, thought better of it, and sat down. He spoke while looking at the mural.

"Overall, I'd say there's been improvement.

"Now, I realize that a wall is not as useful to bird art as a canvas or a white piece of paper, except to certain geniuses throughout history, particularly in Europe and the Orient. But, yes, I'd say there definitely has been an improvement. Especially with the petrels, kittiwakes, and most of all the sandpipers. The teals and mergansers—excellent, within your limitations.

"The cormorant, while perhaps your best thus far, is pitiful. That species is simply too much for you, Mr. Vas. I once had a student for whom owls were an insurmountable torment, more to him than to me, I imagine. Mr. Vas, do them a favor and leave cormorants alone.

"I won't bother to remark upon the people you've represented here. I don't know this village, obviously. And I don't care. For the purposes of my visit, I'll simply block out certain scenery. I don't much care for people anyway, in painting or in life, truth be told. That's my failing and I've relied on it for much of my happiness. I'm sixty-seven.

"The ibis is splendid. The owl working over the trout with its talons has a proper ferocity, and I'd recommend that you put birds into action more often—have them *doing* something.

"Now, over there, that teal—blue-winged—though the hazy blue is slightly off. The veins on its webbed feet can be seen from too far away, which is inaccurate. And yet, at the same time, you've managed to reveal the pattern of its feathers as one would see it from the same distance, and a more detailed feather-pattern close up. That's highly commendable. A difficult accomplishment.

"That lagoon, or inlet, with all its birds in close proximity! We're in Eden, are we? Ridiculous.

285

"In this mural the ibis, sandpipers, and ring-necked ducks are your very best. Clearly your strength is shorebirds and ducks.

"My best guess is that you'll continue to contribute. You'll place your ducks, sandpipers, crows perhaps, and a few others in journals. For practicality's sake, you might specialize in those.

"You've got a knack. And while you may never wholly earn a living from bird art—difficult for anyone—your mergansers, teals, all of your ducks, and if you work at it, a garganey or two, may secure you some small reputation outside of Witless Bay. I'm sure, anyway, you're highly valued at home."

He stopped talking and we sat for perhaps half an hour in silence. I thought that he was working more ideas and comments around in his mind, yet when I stood and approached, I saw that he was asleep. I sat in front of him and said, "Mr. Sprague," in a loud whisper.

Blinking, coughing a few times, he said, "Yes, well—"

"Mr. Sprague, how long do you expect to stay?"

"I've arranged with Mr. Handle to go on to student number—I think it's seven on my list. In a Canadian city. I'll leave tomorrow afternoon."

I walked arm in arm with Isaac Sprague out of the church, then to Spivey's, where he took a nap.

The next afternoon I found him at the wharf. "I studied your harbor here, on my way in," he said. "I was surprised to see even one duck this far north so late in the season."

"Each year is slightly different. One year, I forget which, a few teal were here till mid-December."

Isaac Sprague nodded. He looked as if he had not slept all night. "We had a Siberian plover in the harbor in Halifax this summer," he said. "How remarkable, to be carried so far off course, and where could it have thought it was going? And how did it manage to cross the Atlantic? Let alone the mass of Russia. No one but God can answer this. Just my luck. So, the plover in the harbor where I've spent my entire life is the mystery I'll take to my grave, to puzzle over in eternity. Do you think that's a foolish notion? I don't. No matter. It *was* a Siberian plover, of that I'm certain. I sat hours and matched my sketches of the plover to paintings from Siberia, which I found in books. And it was indeed the same bird. I lived to see it visit my harbor. And seeing it, I was suddenly inspired to travel, to die en route. I think that will happen."

He coughed deeply.

"I was so certain I wouldn't see my harbor again," he said, "that I closed up my house in Halifax. My sister will look after it."

Enoch walked up and said, "Mr. Sprague, your bag is on board."

Enoch continued on down the dock and climbed onto the *Aunt Ivy Barnacle*.

Isaac Sprague and I shook hands.

I stayed on the dock until the mail boat was out of sight.

The next year's spring issue of *Bird Lore* contained a photograph of Isaac Sprague, and his obituary. He had died of tuberculosis in Yarmouth, Nova Scotia, on March 4, 1913.

I tell all of this in summer 1923, twelve years after I murdered the lighthouse keeper Botho August. Since his retirement last year, Enoch has been to St. John's twice, but Margaret and I still have not been at all. In fact we have not left Witless Bay. Our daughter, Claire Helen Vas, was born on July 17, 1913. Typical, I suppose, but we keep saying, "She looks like Alaric," or Orkney, or me, or Margaret or Enoch, though this year, Claire has looked more like Margaret than ever, I think. She knows one grandfather, Enoch, and that is some consolation. But there are no photographs of Alaric, Orkney, or Margaret's mother, Claire, whom our daughter is named after. Someday I will try sketching those faces. As far as I know, Mekeel Dollard has the only photograph album in Witless Bay to speak of, but none of the Vas or Handle family is in it. I think that I should have a family portrait taken. Who can take it? Perhaps Romeo Gillette. I think he learned how to take photographs in London. Mekeel Dollard just might lend him her camera.

There has been steady work at the dry dock. As for painting, it has not been poor fare; I have already sold drawings of an ibis and a merganser this year, and it is only July. I am hardly in demand, though, and last year there were no requests at all, and only one the year before that, a kittiwake for a private patron in Halifax. I imagine life will go on like this, when it comes to birds. On his last run,

Enoch brought home a new journal, *Canadian Naturalist.* I intend to try it unsolicited with murres, red knot, and teal.

We have become friends with Odeon and Kira Sloo. Their daughter Millie looks after Claire now and then. We have eaten at Spivey's together, and at each other's houses.

I am a bird artist.

Just yesterday Isabel Kinsella hissed, "Slieveen!" near the orchard. Yet I have to say this was a rare occurrence. Isabel was just out for a walk, I imagine, lost in thought, when she saw me and was overcome.